A SECOND-RATE WOMAN

The Sahib Edition of
Rudyard Kipling

UNDER THE DEODARS
AMERICAN NOTES

Illustrated by
SIR E. BURNE-JONES
REGINALD BOLLES
W. KIRKPATRICK

P. F. COLLIER & SON COMPANY
Publishers New York

MANUFACTURED IN U. S. A.

UNDER THE DEODARS

CONTENTS

LIST OF ILLUSTRATIONS

THE EDUCATION OF OTIS YEERE

I

In the pleasant orchard-closes
"God bless all our gains," say we;
But "May God bless all our losses,"
  Better suits with our degree.
—*The Lost Bower.*

THIS is the history of a failure; but the woman who failed said that it might be an instructive tale to put into print for the benefit of the younger generation. The younger generation does not want instruction, being perfectly willing to instruct if any one will listen to it. None the less, here begins the story where every right-minded story should begin, that is to say at Simla, where all things begin and many come to an evil end.

The mistake was due to a very clever woman making a blunder and not retrieving it. Men are licensed to stumble, but a clever woman's mistake is outside the regular course of Nature and Providence; since all good people know that a woman is the only infallible thing in this world, except Government Paper of the '79 issue, bearing interest at four and a half per cent. Yet, we have to remember that six consecutive days of rehearsing the leading part of *The Fallen Angel,* at the New Gaiety Theatre where the plaster is not yet properly dry, might have brought about an unhingement of spirits which, again, might have led to eccentricities.

Mrs. Hauksbee came to "The Foundry" to tiffin with Mrs. Mallowe, her one bosom friend, for she was in no sense "a woman's woman." And it was a woman's tiffin, the door shut to all the world; and they both talked *chiffons,* which is French for Mysteries.

"I've enjoyed an interval of sanity," Mrs. Hauksbee announced, after tiffin was over and the two were comfortably settled in the little writing-room that opened out of Mrs. Mallowe's bedroom.

"My dear girl, what has *he* done?" said Mrs. Mallowe, sweetly. It is noticeable that ladies of a certain age call each "dear girl," just as commissioners of twenty-eight years' standing address their equals in the Civil List as "my boy."

"There's no *he* in the case. Who am I that an imaginary man should be always credited to me? Am I an Apache?"

"No, dear, but somebody's scalp is generally drying at your wigwam-door. Soaking, rather."

This was an allusion to the Hawley Boy, who was in the habit of riding all across Simla in the Rains, to call on Mrs. Hauksbee. That lady laughed.

"For my sins, the Aide at Tyrconnel last night told me off to The Mussuck. Hsh! Don't laugh. One of my most devoted admirers. When the duff came—some one really ought to teach them to make puddings at Tyrconnel—The Mussuck was at liberty to attend to me."

"Sweet soul! I know his appetite," said Mrs. Mallowe. "Did he, oh *did* he, begin his wooing?"

"By a special mercy of Providence, *no*. He explained his importance as a Pillar of the Empire. I didn't laugh."

"Lucy, I don't believe you."

"Ask Captain Sangar; he was on the other side. Well, as I was saying, The Mussuck dilated."

"I think I can see him doing it," said Mrs. Mallowe, pensively, scratching her fox-terrier's ears.

"I was properly impressed. Most properly.

I yawned openly. 'Strict supervision, and play them off one against the other,' said The Mussuck, shoveling down his ice by *tureenfuls,* I assure you. '*That,* Mrs. Hauksbee, is the secret of our Government.' "

Mrs. Mallowe laughed long and merrily. "And what did you say?"

"Did you ever know me at loss for an answer yet? I said: 'So I have observed in my dealings with you.' The Mussuck swelled with pride. He is coming to call on me to-morrow. The Hawley Boy is coming too."

" 'Strict supervision and play them off one against the other. *That,* Mrs. Hauksbee, is the secret of *our* Government.' And I dare say if we could get to The Mussuck's heart, we should find that he considers himself a man of the world."

"As he is of the other two things. I like The Mussuck, and I won't have you call him names. He amuses me."

"He has reformed you, too, by what appears. Explain the interval of sanity, and hit *Tim* on the nose with the paper-cutter, please. That dog is too fond of sugar. Do you take milk in yours?"

"No, thanks. Polly, I'm wearied of this life. It's hollow."

"Turn religious, then. I always said that Rome would be your fate."

"Only exchanging half a dozen *attachés* in red for one in black, and if I fasted, the wrinkles would come, and never, *never* go. Has it ever struck you, dear, that I'm getting old?"

"Thanks for your courtesy. I'll return it. Ye-es, we are both not exactly—how shall I put it?"

"What we have been. 'I feel it in my bones,' as Mrs. Crossley says. Polly, I've wasted my life."

"As how?"

"Never mind how. I feel it. I want to be a Power before I die."

"Be a Power then. You've wits enough for anything—and beauty?"

Mrs. Hauksbee pointed a teaspoon straight at her hostess. "Polly, if you heap compliments on me like this, I shall cease to believe that you're a woman. Tell me how I am to be a Power."

"Inform The Mussuck that he is the most fascinating and slimmest man in Asia, and he'll tell you anything and everything you please."

"Bother The Mussuck! I mean an intellectual Power—not a gas-power. Polly, I'm going to start a *salon*."

Mrs. Mallowe turned lazily on the sofa and rested her head on her hand. "Hear the words of the Preacher, the son of Baruch," she said.

"*Will* you talk sensibly?"

"I will, dear, for I see that you are going to make a mistake."

"I never made a mistake in my life—at least, never one that I couldn't explain away afterward."

"Going to make a mistake" went on Mrs. Mallowe, composedly. "It is impossible to start a *salon* in Simla. A bar would be much more to the point."

"Perhaps, but why? It seems so easy."

"Just what makes it so difficult. How many clever women are there in Simla?"

"Myself and yourself," said Mrs. Hauksbee, without a moment's hesitation.

"Modest woman! Mrs. Feardon would thank you for that. And how many clever men?"

"Oh—er—hundreds," said Mrs. Hauksbee, vaguely.

"What a fatal blunder! Not one. They are all bespoke by the Government. Take my husband, for instance. Jack *was* a clever man, though I say so who shouldn't. Government has eaten him up. All his ideas and powers of conversation—he really used to be a good talker, even to his wife, in the old days—are taken from him by this—this kitchen-sink of a Government. That's the case with every man up here who is at work. I don't suppose a Russian convict under the knout is able to amuse the rest of his gang; and all our men-folk here are gilded convicts."

"But there are scores"—

"I know what you're going to say. Scores of idle men up on leave. I admit it, but they are all of two objectionable sets. The Civilian who'd be delightful if he had the military man's knowledge of the world and style, and the military man who'd be adorable if he had the Civilian's culture."

"Detestable word! *Have* Civilians culchaw? I never studied the breed deeply."

"Don't make fun of Jack's service. Yes. They're like the teapoys in the Lakka Bazar—good material but not polished. They can't help themselves, poor dears. A Civilian only begins to be tolerable after he has knocked about the world for fifteen years."

"And a military man?"

"When he has had the same amount of service. The young of both species are horrible. You would have scores of them in your *salon*."

"I would *not!*" said Mrs. Hauksbee, fiercely. "I would tell the bearer to *darwaza band* them. I'd put their own colonels and commissioners at the door to turn them away. I'd give them to the Topsham girl to play with."

"The Topsham girl would be grateful for the gift. But to go back to the *salon*. Allowing that you had gathered all your men and women together, what would you do with them? Make them talk? They would all with one accord begin to flirt. Your *salon* would become a glorified Peliti's—a 'Scandal Point' by lamp-light."

"There's a certain amount of wisdom in that view."

"There's all the wisdom in the world in it. Surely, twelve Simla seasons ought to have taught you that you can't focus anything in India; and a *salon*, to be any good at all, must be permanent. In two seasons your roomful would be scattered all over Asia. We are only little bits of dirt on the hillsides—here one day and blown down the *khud* the next. We have lost the art of talking—at least our men have. We have no cohesion"—

"George Eliot in the flesh," interpolated Mrs. Hauksbee, wickedly.

"And collectively, my dear scoffer, we, men and women alike, have *no* influence. Come into the veranda and look at the Mall!"

The two looked down on the now rapidly filling road, for all Simla was abroad to steal a stroll between a shower and a fog.

"How do you propose to fix that river? Look! There's The Mussuck—head of goodness knows what. He is a power in the land, though he *does* eat like a costermonger. There's Colonel Blone, and General Grucher, and Sir Dugald Delane, and Sir Henry Haughton, and Mr. Jellalatty. All Heads of Departments, and all powerful."

"And all my fervent admirers," said Mrs. Hauksbee, piously. "Sir Henry Haughton raves about me. But go on."

"One by one, these men are worth something. Collectively, they're just a mob of Anglo-Indians. Who cares for what Anglo-Indians say? Your *salon* won't weld the Departments together and make you mistress of India, dear. And these creatures won't talk administrative 'shop' in a crowd—your *salon*—because they are so afraid of the men in the lower ranks overhearing it. They have forgotten what of Literature and Art they ever knew, and the women"—

"Can't talk about anything except the last Gymkhana, or the sins of their last nurse. I was calling on Mrs. Derwills this morning."

"You admit that? They can talk to the subalterns though, and the subalterns can talk to them. Your *salon* would suit their views admirably, if you respected the religious prejudices of the country and provided plenty of *kala juggahs.*"

"Plenty of *kala juggahs.* Oh my poor little idea! *Kala juggahs* in a *salon!* But who made you so awfully clever?"

"Perhaps I've tried myself; or perhaps I know a woman who has. I have preached and expounded the whole matter and the conclusion thereof"—

"You needn't go on. 'Is Vanity.' Polly, I thank you. These vermin"—Mrs. Hauksbee waved her hand from the veranda to two men in the crowd below who had raised their hats to her—"these vermin shall not rejoice in a new Scandal Point or an extra Peliti's. I will abandon the notion of a *salon.* It did seem so tempting, though. But what shall I do? I must do something."

"Why? Are not Abana and Pharphar"—

"Jack has made you nearly as bad as himself! I want to, of course. I'm tired of everything and everybody, from a moonlight picnic at Seepee to the blandishments of The Mussuck."

"Yes—that comes, too, sooner or later. Have you nerve enough to make your bow yet?"

Mrs. Hauksbee's mouth shut grimly. Then she laughed. "I think I see myself doing it. Big pink placards on the Mall: 'Mrs. Hauksbee! Positively her last appearance on *any* stage! This is to give notice!' No more dances; no more rides; no more luncheons; no more theatricals with supper to follow; no more sparring with one's dearest, dearest friend; no more fencing with an inconvenient man who hasn't wit enough to clothe what he's pleased to call his sentiments in passable speech; no more parading of The Mussuck while Mrs. Tarkass calls all round Simla, spreading horrible stories about me! No more of anything that is thoroughly wearying, abominable and detestable, but, all the same, makes life worth the having. Yes! I see it all! Don't interrupt, Polly, I'm inspired. A mauve and white striped 'cloud' round my excellent shoulders, a seat in the fifth row of the Gaiety, and *both* horses sold. Delightful vision! A comfortable armchair, situated in three different draughts, at every ballroom; and nice, large, sensible shoes for all the couples to stumble over as they go into the veranda! Then at supper. Can't you imagine the scene? The greedy mob gone away. Reluctant subaltern, pink all over like a newly-powdered baby,—they really ought to *tan* subalterns before they are exported, Polly —sent back by the hostess to do his duty. Slouches up to me across the room, tugging at a glove two sizes too large for him—I *hate* a man who wears gloves like overcoats—and trying to look as if he'd thought of it from the first. 'May I ah-have the pleasure 'f takin' you 'nt' supper?' Then I get up with a hungry smile. Just like this."

"Lucy, how *can* you be so absurd?"

"And sweep out on his arm. So! After supper I shall go away early, you know, because I shall be afraid of catching cold. No one will look for my *'rickshaw. Mine,* so please you! I shall stand, always with that mauve and white 'cloud' over my head, while the wet soaks into my dear, old, venerable feet and Tom swears and shouts for the *mem-sahib's gharri.* Then home to bed at half-past eleven! Truly excellent life—helped out by the visits of the *Padri,* just fresh from burying somebody down below there." She pointed through the pines, toward the Cemetery, and continued with vigorous dramatic gesture—

"Listen! I see it all—down, down even to

the stays! *Such* stays! Six-eight a pair, Polly, with red flannel—or list is it?—that they put into the tops of those fearful things. I can draw you a picture of them."

"Lucy, for Heaven's sake, don't go waving your arms about in that idiotic manner! Recollect, every one can see you from the Mall."

"Let them see! They'll think I am rehearsing for *The Fallen Angel*. Look! There's The Mussuck. How badly he rides. There!"

She blew a kiss to the venerable Indian administrator with infinite grace.

"Now," she continued, "he'll be chaffed about that at the Club in the delicate manner those brutes of men affect, and the Hawley Boy will tell me all about it—softening the details for fear of shocking me. That boy is too good to live, Polly. I've serious thoughts of recommending him to throw up his Commission and go into the Church. In his present frame of mind he would obey me. Happy, happy child!"

"Never again," said Mrs. Mallowe, with an affectation of indignation, "shall you tiffin here! 'Lucindy, your behavior is scand'lus.' "

"All your fault," retorted Mrs. Hauksbee, "for suggesting such a thing as my abdication. No! *Jamais*-nevaire! I will act, ride, frivol, talk scandal, dine out, and appropriate the legitimate captives of any woman I choose, untill I d-r-r-rop, or a better woman than I puts me to shame before all Simla,—and it's dust and ashes in my mouth while I'm doing it!"

She swept into the drawing-room. Mrs. Mallowe followed and put an arm round her waist.

"I'm *not!*" said Mrs. Hauksbee, defiantly, rummaging for her handkerchief. "I've been dining out the last ten nights, and rehearsing in the afternoon. You'd be tired yourself. It's only because I'm tired."

Mrs. Mallowe did not offer Mrs. Hauksbee any pity or ask her to lie down, but gave her another cup of tea, and went on with the talk.

"I've been through that too, dear," she said.

"I remember," said Mrs. Hauksbee, a gleam of fun on her face. "In '84, wasn't it? You went out a great deal less next season."

Mrs. Mallowe smiled in a superior and Sphinx-like fashion.

"I became an Influence," said she.

"Good gracious, child, you didn't join the Theosophists and kiss Buddha's big toe, did you? I tried to get into their set once, but they cast me out for a sceptic—without a chance of improving my poor little mind, too."

"No, I didn't Theosophilander. Jack says"—

"Never mind Jack. What a husband says is known before. What did you do?"

"I made a lasting impression."

"So have I—for four months. But that didn't console me in the least. I hated the man. *Will* you stop smiling in that inscrutable way and tell me what you mean?"

Mrs. Mallowe told.

* * * * * *

"And—you—mean—to—say that it is absolutely Platonic on both sides?"

"Absolutely, or I should never have taken it up."

"And his last promotion was due to you?"

Mrs. Mallowe nodded.

"And you warned him against the Topsham girl?"

Another nod.

"And told him of Sir Dugald Delane's private memo about him?"

A third nod.

"Why?"

"What a question to ask a woman! Because it amused me at first. I am proud of my property now. If I live, he shall continue to be successful. Yes, I will put him upon the straight road to Knighthood, and everything else that a man values. The rest depends upon himself."

"Polly, you are a most extraordinary woman."

"Not in the least. I'm concentrated, that's all. You diffuse yourself, dear; and though all Simla knows your skill in managing a team"—

"Can't you choose a prettier word?"

"*Team,* of half a dozen, from The Mussuck to the Hawley Boy, you gain nothing by it. Not even amusement."

"And you?"

"Try my recipe. Take a man, not a boy, mind, but an almost mature, unattached man, and be his guide, philosopher, and friend. You'll find it *the* most interesting occupation that you ever embarked on. It can be done—you needn't look like that—because I've done it."

"There's an element of risk about it that makes the notion attractive. I'll get such a man and say to him, 'Now, understand that there must be no flirtation. Do exactly what I tell you, profit by my instruction and counsels, and all will yet be well.' Is that the idea?"

"More or less," said Mrs. Mallowe, with an unfathomable smile. "But be sure he understands."

II

Dribble-dribble—trickle-trickle—
What a lot of raw dust!
My dollie's had an accident
And out came all the sawdust!
Nursery Rhyme.

So Mrs. Hauksbee, in "The Foundry" which overlooks Simla Mall, sat at the feet of Mrs. Mallowe and gathered wisdom. The end of the Conference was the Great Idea upon which Mrs. Hauksbee so plumed herself.

"I warn you," said Mrs. Mallowe, beginning to repent of her suggestion, "that the matter is not half so easy as it looks. Any woman—even the Topsham girl—can catch a man, but very, *very* few know how to manage him when caught."

"My child," was the answer, "I've been a female St. Simon Stylites looking down upon men for these—these years past. Ask The Mussuck whether I can manage them."

Mrs. Hauksbee departed humming, *"I'll go to him and say to him in manner most ironical."* Mrs. Mallowe laughed to herself. Then she grew suddenly sober. "I wonder whether I've done well in advising that amusement? Lucy's a clever woman, but a thought too careless."

A week later, the two met at a Monday Pop. "Well?" said Mrs. Mallowe.

"I've caught him!" said Mrs. Hauksbee; her eyes were dancing with merriment.

"Who is it, mad woman? I'm sorry I ever spoke to you about it."

"Look between the pillars. In the third row; fourth from the end. You can see his face now. Look!"

"Otis Yeere! Of *all* the improbable and impossible people! I don't believe you."

"Hsh! Wait till Mrs. Tarkass begins murdering Milton Wellings; and I'll tell you all about it. *S-s-ss!* That woman's voice always reminds me of an Underground train coming into Earl's Court with the breaks on. Now listen. It is *really* Otis Yeere."

"So I see, but does it follow that he is your property!"

"He *is!* By right of trove. I found him, lonely and unbefriended, the very next night after our talk, at the Dugald Delane's *burra-khana*. I liked his eyes, and I talked to him. Next day he called. Next day we went for a ride together, and to-day he's tied to my *'rick-shaw*-wheels hand and foot. You'll see when the concert's over. He doesn't know I'm here yet."

"Thank goodness you haven't chosen a boy. What are you going to do with him, assuming that you've got him?"

"Assuming, indeed! Does a woman—do *I* —ever make a mistake in that sort of thing? First"—Mrs. Hauksbee ticked off the items ostentatiously on her little gloved fingers—"First, my dear, I shall dress him properly. At present his raiment is a disgrace, and he wears a dress-shirt like a crumpled sheet of the *Pioneer*. Secondly, after I have made him presentable, I shall form his manners—his morals are above reproach."

"You seem to have discovered a great deal about him considering the shortness of your acquaintance."

"Surely *you* ought to know that the first proof a man gives of his interest in a woman is by talking to her about his own sweet self. If the woman listens without yawning, he begins to like her. If she flatters the animal's vanity, he ends by adoring her."

"In some cases."

"Never mind the exceptions. I know which one you are thinking of. Thirdly, and lastly, after he is polished and made pretty, I shall, as you said, be his guide, philosopher, and friend, and he shall become a success—as great a success as your friend. I always wondered how that man got on. *Did* The Mussuck come to you with the Civil List and, dropping on one knee—no, two knees, *a la Gibbon*—hand it to you and say, 'Adorable angel, choose your friend's appointment'?"

"Lucy, your long experiences of the Military Department have demoralized you. One doesn't do that sort of thing on the Civil Side."

"No disrespect meant to Jack's Service, my dear. I only asked for information. Give me three months, and see what changes I shall work in my prey."

"Go your own way, since you must. But I'm sorry that I was weak enough to suggest the amusement."

" 'I am all discretion, and may be trusted to an in-fin-ite extent,' " quoted Mrs. Hauksbee from *The Fallen Angel;* and the conversation ceased with Mrs. Tarkass's last, long-drawn war-whoop.

Her bitterest enemies—and she had many—could hardly accuse Mrs. Hauksbee of wasting her time. Otis Yeere was one of those wandering "dumb" characters, foredoomed through life to be nobody's property. Ten years in Her Majesty's Bengal Civil Service, spent, for the most part, in undesirable Districts, had given him little to be proud of, and nothing to bring confidence. Old enough to have lost the first fine careless rapture that showers on the immature 'Stunt imaginary Commissionerships and Stars, and sends him into the collar with coltish earnestness and abandon; too young to be yet able to look back upon the progress he had made, and thank Providence that under the conditions of the day he had come even so far, he stood upon the dead-centre of his career. And when a man stands still, he feels the slightest impulse from without. Fortune had ruled that Otis Yeere should be, for the first part of his service, one of the rank and file who are ground up in the wheels of the Administration; losing heart and soul, and mind and strength, in the process. Until steam replaces manual power in the working of the Empire, there must always be this percentage—must always be the men who are used up, expended, in the mere mechanical routine. For these promotion is far off and the mill-grind of every day very instant. The Secretariats know them only by name; they are not the picked men of the Districts with Divisions and Collectorates awaiting them. They are simply the rank and file—the food for fever—sharing with the *ryot* and the plough-bullock the honor of being the plinth on which the State rests. The older ones have lost their aspirations; the younger are putting theirs aside with a sigh. Both learn to endure patiently until the end of the day. Twelve years in the rank and file, men say, will sap the hearts of the bravest and dull the wits of the most keen.

Out of this life Otis Yeere had fled for a few months; drifting, in the hope of a little masculine society, into Simla. When his leave was over he would return to his swampy, sour-green, under-manned Bengal district; to the native Assistant, the native Doctor, the native Magistrate, the steaming, sweltering Station, the ill-kempt City, and the undisguised insolence of the Municipality that babbled away the lives of men. Life was cheap, however. The soil spawned humanity, as it bred frogs in the Rains, and the gap of the sickness of one season was filled to overflowing by the fecundity of the next. Otis was unfeignedly thankful to lay down his work for a little while and escape from the seething, whining, weakly hive, impotent to help itself, but strong in its power to cripple, thwart, and annoy the sunken-eyed man, who, by official irony, was said to be "in charge" of it.

* * * * * *

"I knew there were women-dowdies in Bengal. They come up here sometimes. But I didn't know that there were men-dowds, too."

Then, for the first time, it occurred to Otis Yeere that his clothes wore the mark of the ages. It will be seen that his friendship with Mrs. Hauksbee had made great strides.

As that lady truthfully says, a man is never so happy as when he is talking about himself. From Otis Yeere's lips Mrs. Hauksbee, before long, learned everything that she wished to know about the subject of her experiment: learned what manner of life he had led in what she vaguely called "those awful cholera districts"; learned, too, but this knowledge came later, what manner of life he had purposed to lead and what dreams he had dreamed in the year of grace '77, before the reality had knocked the heart out of him. Very pleasant are the shady bridle-paths round Prospect Hill for the telling of such confidences.

"Not yet," said Mrs. Hauksbee to Mrs. Mallowe. "Not yet. I must wait until the man is properly dressed, at least. Great Heavens, is it possible that he doesn't know what an honor it is to be taken up by *Me!*"

Mrs. Hauksbee did not reckon false modesty as one of her failings.

"Always with Mrs. Hauksbee!" murmured Mrs. Mallowe, with her sweetest smile, to Otis. "Oh you men, you men! Here are our Punjabis growling because you've monopolized the nicest woman in Simla. They'll tear you to pieces on the Mall, some day, Mr. Yeere."

Mrs. Mallowe rattled down-hill, having satisfied herself, by a glance through the fringe of her sunshade, of the effect of her words.

The shot went home. Of a surety Otis Yeere was somebody in this bewildering whirl of Simla—had monopolized the nicest woman in it and the Punjabis were growling. The notion justified a mild glow of vanity. He had never looked upon his acquaintance with Mrs. Hauksbee as a matter for general interest.

The knowledge of envy was a pleasant feeling to the man of no account. It was intensified later in the day when a luncher at the Club said, spitefully, "Well, for a debilitated Ditcher, Yeere, you *are* going it. Hasn't any kind friend told you that she's the most dangerous woman in Simla?"

Yeere chuckled and passed out. When, oh

when, would his new clothes be ready? He descended into the Mall to inquire; and Mrs. Hauksbee, coming over the Church Ridge in her *'rickshaw,* looked down upon him approvingly. "He's learning to carry himself as if he were a man, instead of a piece of furniture, —and," she screwed up her eyes to see the better through the sunlight—"he *is* a man when he holds himself like that. Oh blessed Conceit, what should we be without you?"

With the new clothes came a new stock of self-confidence. Otis Yeere discovered that he could enter a room without breaking into a gentle perspiration—could cross one, even to talk to Mrs. Hauksbee, as though rooms were meant to be crossed. He was for the first time in nine years proud of himself, and contented with his life, satisfied with his new clothes, and rejoicing in the friendship of Mrs. Hauksbee.

"Conceit is what the poor fellow wants," she said in confidence to Mrs. Mallowe. "I believe they must use Civilians to plough the fields with in Lower Bengal. You see I have to begin from the very beginning—haven't I? But you'll admit, won't you, dear, that he is immensely improved since I took him in hand. Only give me a little more time and he won't know himself."

Indeed, Yeere was rapidly beginning to forget what he had been. One of his own rank and file put the matter brutally when he asked Yeere, in reference to nothing, "And who has been making *you* a Member of Council, lately? You carry the side of half a dozen of 'em."

"I—I'm awf-ly sorry. I didn't mean it, you know," said Yeere, apologetically.

"There'll be no holding you," continued the old stager, grimly. "Climb down, Otis—climb down, and get all that beastly affectation knocked out of you with fever! Three thousand a month wouldn't support it."

Yeere repeated the incident to Mrs. Hauksbee. He had come to look upon her as his Mother Confessor.

"And you apologized!" she said. "Oh, shame! I *hate* a man who apologizes. Never apologize for what your friend called 'side.' *Never!* It's a man's business to be insolent and overbearing until he meets with a stronger. Now, you bad boy, listen to me."

Simply and straightforwardly, as the *'rickshaw* loitered round Jakko, Mrs. Hauksbee preached to Otis Yeere the Great Gospel of Conceit, illustrating it with living pictures encountered during their Sunday afternoon stroll.

"Good gracious!" she ended, with the personal argument, "you'll apologize next for being my *attaché?*"

"Never!" said Otis Yeere. "That's another thing altogether. I shall always be"—

"What's coming?" thought Mrs. Hauksbee.

"Proud of that," said Otis.

"Safe for the present," she said to herself.

"But I'm afraid I have grown conceited. Like Jeshurun, you know. When he waxed fat, then he kicked. It's the having no worry on one's mind and the Hill air, I suppose."

"Hill air, indeed!" said Mrs. Hauksbee to herself. "He'd have been hiding in the Club till the last day of his leave, if I hadn't discovered him." And aloud—

"Why shouldn't you be? You have every right to."

"I! Why?"

"Oh, hundreds of things. I'm not going to waste this lovely afternoon by explaining; but I know you have. What was that heap of manuscript you showed me about the grammar of the aboriginal—what's their names?"

"*Gullals.* A piece of nonsense. I've far too much work to do to bother over *Gullals* now. You should see my District. Come down with your husband some day and I'll show you round. Such a lovely place in the Rains! A sheet of water with the railway-embankment and the snakes sticking out, and in the summer, green flies and green squash. The people would die of fear if you shook a dogwhip at 'em. But they know you're forbidden to do that, so they conspire to make your life a burden to you. My District's worked by some man at Darjiling, on the strength of a native pleader's false reports. Oh it's a heavenly place!"

Otis Yeere laughed bitterly.

"There's not the least necessity that you should stay in it. Why do you?"

"Because I must. How'm I to get out of it?"

"How! In a hundred and fifty ways. If there weren't so many people on the road, I'd like to box your ears. Ask, my dear boy, *ask!* Look! There is young Hexarly with six years' service and half you talents. He asked for what he wanted, and he got it. See, down by the Convent! There's McArthurson who has come to his present position by asking—sheer, downright asking—after he had pushed himself out of the rank and file. One man is as good as another in your service—believe me. I've seen Simla for more seasons than I care to think about. Do you suppose men are chosen for appointments because of their special fitness *beforehand?* You have all passed a high test—what do you call it?—in the beginning, and, except for the few who have gone altogether to the bad, you can all work hard. Asking does the rest. Call it cheek, call it insolence, call it anything you like, but *ask!* Men argue—yes, I know what men say—that a man, by the mere audacity of his request, *must* have some good in him. A weak man doesn't say: 'Give me this and that.' He whines: 'Why haven't I been given this and that?' If you were in the Army, I should say learn to spin plates or play a tambourine with your toes. As it is—*ask!* You belong to a Service that ought to be able to command the Channel Fleet, or set a leg at twenty minutes' notice, and *yet* you hesitate over asking to escape from a squashy green district where you *admit* you are not master. Drop the Bengal Government altogether. Even Darjiling is a little out-of-the-way hole. I was there once, and the rents were extortionate. Assert yourself. Get the Government of India to take you over. Try to get on the Frontier, where *every* man has a grand chance if he can trust himself. *Go* somewhere! *Do* something! You have twice the wits and three times the presence of the men up here, and, and"—Mrs. Hauksbee paused for breath; then continued—"and in *any* way you look at it, you *ought* to. *You* who could go so far!"

"I don't know," said Yeere, rather taken aback by the unexpected eloquence. "I haven't such a good opinion of myself."

It was not strictly Platonic, but it was Policy. Mrs. Hauksbee laid her hand lightly upon the ungloved paw that rested on the turned-back *'rickshaw* hood, and, looking the man full in the face, said tenderly, almost too tenderly, "*I* believe in you if you mistrust yourself. Is that enough, my friend?"

"It is enough," answered Otis, very solemnly.

He was silent for a long time, redreaming the dreams that he had dreamed eight years ago, but through them all ran, as sheet-lightning through golden cloud, the light of Mrs. Hauksbee's violet eyes.

Curious and impenetrable are the mazes of Simla life—the only existence in this desolate land worth the living. Gradually it went abroad among men and women, in the pauses between dance, play and Gymkhana, that Otis Yeere, the man with the newly-lit light of self-confidence in his eyes, had "done something decent" in the wilds whence he came. He had brought an erring Municipality to reason, appropriated the funds on his own responsibility, and saved the lives of hundreds. He knew more about the *Gullals* than any living man. Had a vast knowledge of the aboriginal tribes; was, in spite of his juniority, the greatest authority on the aboriginal *Gullals*. No one quite knew who or what the *Gullals* were till The Mussuck, who had been calling on Mrs. Hauksbee, and prided himself upon picking people's brains, explained they were a tribe of ferocious hillmen, somewhere near Sikkim, whose friendship even the Great Indian Empire would find it worth her while to secure. Now we know that Otis Yeere had showed Mrs. Hauksbee his MS. notes of six years' standing on these same *Gullals*. He had told her, too, how, sick and shaken with the fever their negligence had bred, crippled by the loss of his pet clerk, and savagely angry at the desolation in his charge, he had once damned the collective eyes of his "intelligent local board" for a set of *haramzadas*. Which act of "brutal and tyrannous oppression" won him a Reprimand Royal from the Bengal Government; but in the anecdote as amended for Northern consumption we find no record of this. Hence we are forced to conclude that Mrs. Hauksbee edited his reminiscences before sowing them in idle ears, ready, as she well knew, to exaggerate good or evil. And Otis Yeere bore himself as befitted the hero of many tales.

"You can talk to *me* when you don't fall into a brown study. Talk now, and talk your brightest and best," said Mrs. Hauksbee.

Otis needed no spur. Look to a man who has the counsel of a woman of or above the world to back him. So long as he keeps his head, he can meet both sexes on equal ground—an advantage never intended by Providence, who fashioned Man on one day and Woman on another, in sign that neither should know more than a very little of the other's life. Such a man goes far, or, the counsel being withdrawn, collapses suddenly while his world seeks the reason.

Generalled by Mrs. Hauksbee, who, again, had all Mrs. Mallowe's wisdom at her disposal, proud of himself and, in the end, believing in himself because he was believed in, Otis Yeere stood ready for any fortune that might befall, certain that it would be good. He would fight for his own hand, and intended that this second struggle should lead to better issue than the first helpless surrender of the bewildered 'Stunt.

What might have happened, it is impossible to say. This lamentable thing befell, bred directly by a statement of Mrs. Hauksbee that she would spend the next season in Darjiling.

"Are you certain of that?" said Otis Yeere.

"Quite. We're writing about a house now."

Otis Yeere "stopped dead," as Mrs. Hauksbee put it in discussing the relapse with Mrs. Mallowe.

"He has behaved," she said, angrily, "just like Captain Kerrington's pony—only Otis is a donkey—at the last Gymkhana. Planted his forefeet and refused to go on another step. Polly, my man's going to disappoint me. What shall I do?"

As a rule, Mrs. Mallowe does not approve of staring, but on this occasion she opened her eyes to the utmost.

"You have managed cleverly so far," she said. "Speak to him, and ask him what he means."

"I will—at to-night's dance."

"No—o, not at a dance," said Mrs. Mallowe, cautiously. "Men are never themselves quite at dances. Better wait till to-morrow morning."

"Nonsense. If he's going to 'vert in this insane way, there isn't a day to lose. Are you going? No? Then sit up for me, there's a dear. I shan't stay longer than supper under any circumstances."

Mrs. Mallowe waited through the evening, looking long and earnestly into the fire, and sometimes smiling to herself.

* * * * * *

"Oh! oh! oh! That man's an idiot! A raving, positive idiot! I'm sorry I ever saw him!"

Mrs. Hauksbee burst into Mrs. Mallowe's house, at midnight, almost in tears.

"What in the world has happened?" said Mrs. Mallowe, but her eyes showed that she had guessed an answer.

"Happened! Everything has happened! He was there. I went to him and said, 'Now, what does this nonsense mean?' Don't laugh, dear, I can't bear it. But you know what I mean I said. Then it was a square, and I sat it out with him and wanted an explanation, and *he* said— Oh! I haven't patience with such idiots! You know what I said about going to Darjiling next year? It doesn't matter to me *where* I go. I'd have changed the Station and lost the rent to have saved this. He said, in so many words, that he wasn't going to try to work up any more, because—because he would be shifted into a province away from Darjiling, and his own District, where these creatures are, is within a day's journey"—

"Ah-hh!" said Mrs. Mallowe, in a tone of one who has successfully tracked an obscure word through a large dictionary.

"Did you ever *hear* of anything so mad—so absurd? And he had the ball at his feet. He had only to kick it! I would have made him *anything!* Anything in the wide world. He could have gone to the world's end. I would have helped him. I made him, didn't I, Polly? Didn't I *create* that man? Doesn't he owe everything to me? And to reward me, just when everything was nicely arranged, by this lunacy that spoiled everything!"

"Very few men understand your devotion thoroughly."

"Oh, Polly, *don't* laugh at me! I give men up from this hour. I could have killed him then and there. What *right* had this man—this *Thing* I had picked out of his filthy paddy-fields—to make love to me?"

"He did that, did he?"

"He did. I don't remember half he said, I was so angry. Oh, but such a funny thing happened! I can't help laughing at it now, though I felt nearly ready to cry with rage. He raved and I stormed—I'm afraid we must have made an awful noise in our *kala juggah*. Protect my character, dear, if it's all over Simla to-morrow—and then he bobbed forward in the middle of this insanity—I *firmly* believe the man's demented—and kissed me!"

"Morals above reproach," purred Mrs. Mallowe.

"So they were—so they were! It was the most absurd kiss. I don't believe he'd ever kissed a woman in his life before. I threw my head back, and it was a sort of slidy, pecking dab, just on the end of the chin—here." Mrs. Hauksbee tapped her masculine little chin with her fan. "Then, of course, I was *furiously* angry, and told him that he was no gentleman, and I was sorry I'd ever met him, and so on. He was crushed so easily that I couldn't be *very* angry. Then I came away straight to you."

"Was this before or after supper?"

"Oh! before—oceans before. Isn't it perfectly disgusting?"

"Let me think. I withhold judgment till to-morrow. Morning brings counsel."

But morning brought only a servant with a

dainty bouquet of Annandale roses for Mrs. Hauksbee to wear at the dance at Viceregal Lodge that night."

"He doesn't seem to be very penitent," said Mrs. Mallowe. "What's the *billet-doux* in the centre?"

Mrs. Hauksbee opened the neatly folded note,—another accomplishment that she had taught Otis,—read it, and groaned tragically.

"Last wreck of a feeble intellect! Poetry! Is it his own, do you think? Oh, that I ever built my hopes on such a maudlin idiot!"

"No. It's a quotation from Mrs. Browning, and, in view of the facts of the case, as Jack says, uncommonly well chosen. Listen—

"'Sweet thou hast trod on a heart,
Pass! There's a world full of men;
And women as fair as thou art,
Must do such things now and then.

"'Thou only hast stepped unaware—
Malice not one can impute;
And why should a heart have been there,
In the way of a fair woman's foot?'"

"I didn't—I didn't—I didn't!" said Mrs. Hauksbee, angrily, her eyes filling with tears; "there was no malice at all. Oh, it's *too* vexatious!"

"You've misunderstood the compliment,"

said Mrs. Mallowe. "He clears you completely and—ahem—I should think by this, that *he* has cleared completely too. My experience of men is that when they begin to quote poetry, they are going to flit. Like swans singing before they die, you know."

"Polly, you take my sorrows in a most unfeeling way."

"Do I? Is it so terrible? If he's hurt your vanity, I should say that you've done a certain amount of damage to his heart."

"Oh, you never can tell about a man!" said Mrs. Hauksbee.

AT THE PIT'S MOUTH

AT THE PIT'S MOUTH

Men say it was a stolen tide—
  The Lord that sent it he knows all,
But in mine ear will aye abide
  The message that the bells let fall,
And awesome bells they were to me,
That in the dark rang, "Enderby."
—*Jean Ingelow.*

ONCE upon a time there was a Man and his Wife and a Tertium Quid.

All three were unwise, but the Wife was the unwisest. The Man should have looked after his Wife, who should have avoided the Tertium Quid, who, again, should have married a wife of his own, after clean and open flirtations, to which nobody can possibly object, round Jakko or Observatory Hill. When you see a young man with his pony in a white lather, and his hat on the back of his head flying down-hill at fifteen miles an hour to meet a girl who will be properly surprised to meet him, you naturally approve of that young man, and wish him Staff appointments, and take an interest in his welfare, and, as the proper time comes, give them sugar-tongs or side-saddles according to your means and generosity.

The Tertium Quid flew down-hill on horseback, but it was to meet the Man's Wife; and when he flew up-hill it was for the same end. The Man was in the Plains, earning money for his Wife to spend on dresses and four-hundred-rupee bracelets, and inexpensive luxuries of that kind. He worked very hard, and sent her a letter or a post-card daily. She also wrote to him daily, and said that she was longing for him to come up to Simla. The Tertium Quid used to lean over her shoulder and laugh as she wrote the notes. Then the two would ride to the Post Office together.

Now, Simla is a strange place and its customs are peculiar; nor is any man who has not spent at least ten seasons there qualified to pass judgment on circumstantial evidence, which is the most untrustworthy in the Courts. For these reasons, and for others which need not appear, I decline to state positively whether there was anything irretrievably wrong in the relations between the Man's Wife and the Tertium Quid. If there was, and hereon you must form your own opinion, it was the Man's Wife's fault. She was kittenish in her man-

"She was taken out of the saddle a limp heap."

At the Pit's Mouth, p. 51

ners, wearing generally an air of soft and fluffy innocence. But she was deadly learned and evil-instructed; and now and again, when the mask dropped, men saw this, shuddered and—almost drew back. Men are occasionally particular, and the least particular men are always the most exacting.

Simla is eccentric in its fashion of treating friendships. Certain attachments which have set and crystallized through half a dozen seasons acquire almost the sancity of the marriage bond, and are revered as such. Again, certain attachments equally old, and, to all appearance, equally venerable, never seem to win any recognized official status; while a chance-sprung acquaintance, not two months born, steps into the place which by right belongs to the senior. There is no law reducible to print which regulates these affairs.

Some people have a gift which secures them infinite toleration, and others have not. The Man's Wife had not. If she looked over the garden wall, for instance, women taxed her with stealing their husbands. She complained pathetically that she was not allowed to choose her own friends. When she put up her big white muff to her lips, and gazed over it and under her eyebrows at you as she said this thing, you felt that she had been infamously misjudged, and that all the other women's instincts were all wrong; which was absurd. She was not allowed to own the Tertium Quid in peace; and was so strangely constructed that she would not have enjoyed peace had she been so permitted. She preferred some semblance of intrigue to cloak even her most commonplace actions.

After two months of riding first round Jakko, then Elysium, then Summer Hill, then Observatory Hill, then under Jutogh, and lastly up and down the Cart Road as far as the Tara Devi gap in the dusk, she said to the Tertium Quid, "Frank, people say we are too much together, and people are so horrid."

The Tertium Quid pulled his moustache, and replied that horrid people were unworthy of the consideration of nice people.

"But they have done more than talk—they have written—written to my hubby—I'm sure of it," said the Man's Wife, and she pulled a letter from her husband out of her saddle-pocket and gave it to the Tertium Quid.

It was an honest letter, written by an honest man, then stewing in the Plains on two hundred rupees a month (for he allowed his wife eight hundred and fifty), and in a silk banian and cotton trousers. It is said that, perhaps, she had not thought of the unwisdom of allowing her name to be so generally coupled with the Tertium Quid's; that she was too much of a child to understand the dangers of that sort of thing; that he, her husband, was the last man in the world to interfere jealously with her little amusements and interests, but that it would be better were she to drop the Tertium Quid quietly and for her husband's sake. The letter was sweetened with many pretty little pet names, and it amused the Tertium Quid considerably. He and She laughed over it, so that you, fifty yards away, could see their shoulders shaking while the horses slouched along side by side.

Their conversation was not worth reporting. The upshot of it was that, next day, no one saw the Man's Wife and the Tertium Quid together. They had both gone down to the Cemetery, which, as a rule, is only visited officially by the inhabitants of Simla.

A Simla funeral with the clergyman riding, the mourners riding, and the coffin creaking as it swings between the bearers, is one of the most depressing things on this earth, particularly when the procession passes under the wet, dank dip beneath the Rockcliffe Hotel, where the sun is shut out, and all the hill streams are wailing and weeping together as they go down the valleys.

Occasionally, folk tend the graves, but we in India shift and are transferred so often that, at the end of the second year, the Dead have no friends—only acquaintances who are far too busy amusing themselves up the hill to attend to old partners. The idea of using a Cemetery as a rendezvous is distinctly a feminine one. A man would have said simply "Let people talk. We'll go down the Mall." A woman is made differently, especially if she be such a woman as the Man's Wife. She and the Tertium Quid enjoyed each other's society among the graves of men and women whom they had known and danced with aforetime.

They used to take a big horse-blanket and sit on the grass a little to the left of the lower end, where there is a dip in the ground, and where the occupied graves stop short and the ready-made ones are not ready. Each well-regulated Indian Cemetery keeps half a dozen graves permanently open for contingencies and incidental wear and tear. In the Hills these are more usually baby's size, because children who come up weakened and sick from the Plains often succumb to the effects of the Rains in the

Hills or get pneumonia from their *ayahs* taking them through damp pine-woods after the sun has set. In Cantonments, of course, the man's size is more in request; these arrangements varying with the climate and population.

One day when the Man's Wife and the Tertium Quid had just arrived in the Cemetery, they saw some coolies breaking ground. They had marked out a full-size grave, and the Tertium Quid asked them whether any *Sahib* was sick. They said that they did not know; but it was an order that they should dig a *Sahib's* grave.

"Work away," said the Tertium Quid, "and let's see how it's done."

The coolies worked away, and the Man's Wife and the Tertium Quid watched and talked for a couple of hours while the grave was being deepened. Then a coolie, taking the earth in baskets as it was thrown up, jumped over the grave.

"That's queer," said the Tertium Quid. "Where's my ulster?"

"What's queer?" said the Man's Wife.

"I have got a chill down my back—just as if a goose had walked over my grave."

"Why do you look at the thing, then?" said the Man's Wife. "Let us go."

The Tertium Quid stood at the head of the grave, and stared without answering for a space. Then he said, dropping a pebble down, "It is nasty—and cold; horribly cold. I don't think I shall come to the Cemetery any more. I don't think grave-digging is cheerful."

The two talked and agreed that the Cemetery was depressing. They also arranged for a ride next day out from the Cemetery through the Mashobra Tunnel up to Fagoo and back, because all the world was going to a garden-party at Viceregal Lodge, and all the people of Mashobra would go too.

Coming up the Cemetery road, the Tertium Quid's horse tried to bolt up-hill, being tired with standing so long, and managed to strain a back sinew.

"I shall have to take the mare to-morrow," said the Tertium Quid, "and she will stand nothing heavier than a snaffle."

They made their arrangements to meet in the Cemetery, after allowing all the Mashobra people time to pass into Simla. That night it rained heavily, and, next day, when the Tertium Quid came to the trysting-place, he saw that the new grave had a foot of water in it, the ground being a tough and sour clay.

"'Jove! That looks beastly," said the Tertium Quid. "Fancy being boarded up and dropped into that well!"

They then started off to Fagoo, the mare playing with the snaffle and picking her way as though she were shod with satin, and the sun shining divinely. The road below Mashobra to Fagoo is officially styled the Himalayan-Thibet Road; but in spite of its name it is not much more than six feet wide in most places, and the drop into the valley below may be anything between one and two thousand feet.

"Now we're going to Thibet," said the Man's Wife merrily, as the horses drew near to Fagoo. She was riding on the cliff-side.

"Into Thibet," said the Tertium Quid, "ever so far from people who say horrid things, and hubbies who write stupid letters. With you—to the end of the world!"

A coolie carrying a log of wood came round a corner, and the mare went wide to avoid him—forefeet in and haunches out, as a sensible mare should go.

"To the world's end," said the Man's Wife, and looked unspeakable things over her near shoulder at the Tertium Quid.

He was smiling, but, while she looked, the smile froze stiff as it were on his face, and changed to a nervous grin—the sort of grin men wear when they are not quite easy in their saddles. The mare seemed to be sinking by the stern, and her nostrils cracked while she was trying to realize what was happening. The rain of the night before had rotted the drop-side of the Himalayan-Thibet Road, and it was giving way under her. "What are you doing?" said the Man's Wife. The Tertium Quid gave no answer. He grinned nervously and set his spurs into the mare, who rapped with her forefeet on the road, and the struggle began. The Man's Wife screamed, "Oh, Frank, get off!"

But the Tertium Quid was glued to the saddle—his face blue and white—and he looked into the Man's Wife's eyes. Then the Man's Wife clutched at the mare's head and caught her by the nose instead of the bridle. The brute threw up her head and went down with a scream, the Tertium Quid upon her, and the nervous grin still set on his face.

The Man's Wife heard the tinkle-tinkle of little stones and loose earth falling off the roadway, and the sliding roar of the man and horse going down. Then everything was quiet, and she called on Frank to leave his mare and walk up. But Frank did not answer. He was underneath the mare, nine hundred feet below, spoiling a patch of Indian corn.

As the revellers came back from Viceregal Lodge in the mists of the evening, they met a temporarily insane woman, on a temporarily mad horse, swinging round the corners, with her eyes and her mouth open, and her head like the head of a Medusa. She was stopped by a man at the risk of his life, and taken out of the saddle, a limp heap, and put on the bank to explain herself. This wasted twenty minutes, and then she was sent home in a lady's *'rickshaw,* still with her mouth open and her hands picking at her riding-gloves.

She was in bed through the following three days, which were rainy; so she missed attending the funeral of the Tertium Quid, who was lowered into eighteen inches of water, instead of the twelve to which he had first objected.

A WAYSIDE COMEDY

A WAYSIDE COMEDY

Because to every purpose there is time and judgment,
therefore the misery of man is great upon him.
Eccles. viii. 6.

FATE and the Government of India have turned the Station of Kashima into a prison; and, because there is no help for the poor souls who are now lying there in torment, I write this story, praying that the Government of India may be moved to scatter the European population to the four winds.

Kashima is bounded on all sides by the rock-tipped circle of the Dosehri hills. In Spring, it is ablaze with roses; in Summer, the roses die and the hot winds blow from the hills; in Autumn, the white mists from the *jhils* cover the place as with water, and in Winter the frosts nip everything young and tender to earth-level. There is but one view in Kashima—a stretch of perfectly flat pasture and plough-land, running up to the grey-blue scrub of the Dosehri hills.

There are no amusements, except snipe and tiger shooting; but the tigers have been long since hunted from their lairs in the rock-caves, and the snipe only come once a year. Narkarra—one hundred and forty-three miles by road—is the nearest station to Kashima. But Kashima never goes to Narkarra, where there are at least twelve English people. It stays within the circle of the Dosehri hills.

All Kashima acquits Mrs. Vansuythen of any intention to do harm; but all Kashima knows that she, and she alone, brought about their pain.

Boulte, the Engineer, Mrs. Boulte, and Captain Kurrell know this. They are the English population of Kashima, if we except Major Vansuythen, who is of no importance whatever, and Mrs. Vansuythen, who is the most important of all.

You must remember, though you will not understand, that all laws weaken in a small and hidden community where there is no public opinion. When a man is absolutely alone in a Station he runs a certain risk of falling into evil ways. This risk is multiplied by every addition to the population up to twelve—the Jury number. After that, fear and consequent restraint begin, and human action becomes less grotesquely jerky.

There was deep peace in Kashima till Mrs.

Vansuythen arrived. She was a charming woman, every one said so everywhere; and she charmed every one. In spite of this, or, perhaps, because of this, since Fate is so perverse, she cared only for one man, and he was Major Vansuythen. Had she been plain or stupid, this matter would have been intelligible to Kashima. But she was a fair woman, with very still grey eyes, the color of a lake just before the light of the sun touches it. No man who had seen those eyes could, later on, explain what fashion of woman she was to look upon. The eyes dazzled him. Her own sex said that she was "not bad looking, but spoiled by pretending to be so grave." And yet her gravity was natural. It was not her habit to smile. She merely went through life, looking at those who passed; and the women objected while the men fell down and worshipped.

She knows and is deeply sorry for the evil she has done to Kashima; but Major Vansuythen cannot understand why Mrs. Boulte does not drop in to afternoon tea at least three times a week. "When there are only two women in one Station they ought to see a great deal of each other," says Major Vansuythen.

Long and long before ever Mrs. Vansuythen

came out of those far-away places where there is society and amusement, Kurrell had discovered that Mrs. Boulte was the one woman in the world for hm and—you dare not blame them. Kashima was as out of the world as Heaven or the Other Place, and the Dosehri hills kept their secret well. Boulte had no concern in the matter. He was in camp for a fortnight at a time. He was a hard, heavy man, and neither Mrs. Boulte nor Kurrell pitied him. They had all Kashima and each other for their very, very own; and Kashima was the Garden of Eden in those days. When Boulte returned from his wanderings he would slap Kurrell between the shoulders and call him "old fellow," and the three would dine together. Kashima was happy then when the judgment of God seemed almost as distant as Narkarra or the railway that ran down to the sea. But the Government sent Major Vansuythen to Kashima, and with him came his wife.

The etiquette of Kashima is much the same as that of a desert island. When a stranger is cast away there, all hands go down to the shore to make him welcome. Kashima assembled at the masonry platform close to the Narkarra Road, and spread tea for the Vansuythens. That ceremony was reckoned a formal call, and made them free of the Station, its rights and privileges. When the Vansuythens were settled down, they gave a tiny house-warming to all Kashima; and that made Kashima free of their house, according to the immemorial usage of the Station.

Then the Rains came, when no one could go into camp, and the Narkarra Road was washed away by the Kasun River, and in the cup-like pastures of Kashima the cattle waded knee-deep. The clouds dropped down from the Dosehri hills and covered everything.

At the end of the Rains, Boulte's manner toward his wife changed, and became demonstratively affectionate. They had been married twelve years, and the change startled Mrs. Boulte, who hated her husband with the hate of a woman who has met with nothing but kindness from her mate, and, in the teeth of this kindness, has done him a great wrong. Moreover, she had her own troubles to fight with—her watch to keep over her own property, Kurrell. For two months the Rains had hidden the Dosehri hills and many other things besides; but, when they lifted, they showed Mrs. Boulte that her man among men, her Ted—for she called him Ted in the old days when Boulte was out of earshot—was slipping the links of the allegiance.

"The Vansuythen Woman has taken him," Mrs. Boulte said to herself; and when Boulte was away, wept over her belief, in the face of the over-vehement blandishments of Ted. Sorrow in Kashima is as fortunate as Love, because there is nothing to weaken it save the flight of Time. Mrs. Boulte had never breathed her suspicion to Kurrell because she was not certain; and her nature led her to be very certain before she took steps in any direction. That is why she behaved as she did.

Boulte came into the house one evening, and leaned against the door-posts of the drawing-room, chewing his moustache. Mrs. Boulte was putting some flowers into a vase. There is a pretence of civilization even in Kashima.

"Little woman," said Boulte, quietly, "do you care for me?"

"Immensely," said she, with a laugh. "Can you ask me?"

"But I'm serious," said Boulte. "*Do* you care for me?"

Mrs. Boulte dropped the flowers, and turned round quickly. "Do you want an honest answer?"

"Ye-es, I've asked for it."

Mrs. Boulte spoke in a low, even voice for five minutes, very distinctly, that there might be no misunderstanding her meaning. When Samson broke the pillars of Gaza, he did a little thing, and one not to be compared to the deliberate pulling down of a woman's homestead about her own ears. There was no wise female friend to advise Mrs. Boulte, the singularly cautious wife, to hold her hand. She struck at Boulte's heart, because her own was sick with suspicion of Kurrell, and worn out with the long strain of watching alone through the Rains. There was no plan or purpose in her speaking. The sentences made themselves; and Boulte listened, leaning against the door-post with his hands in his pockets. When all was over, and Mrs. Boulte began to breathe through her nose before breaking out into tears, he laughed and stared straight in front of him at the Dosehri hills.

"Is that all?" he said. "Thanks, I only wanted to know, you know."

"What are you going to do?" said the woman, between her sobs.

"Do! Nothing. What should I do? Kill Kurrell or send you Home, or apply for leave to get a divorce? It's two days' *dak* into Narkarra." He laughed again and went on: "I'll tell you what *you* can do. You can ask Kurrell to dinner to-morrow—no, on Thursday, that will allow you time to pack—and you can bolt with him. I give you my word I won't follow."

He took up his helmet and went out of the room, and Mrs. Boulte sat till the moonlight streaked the floor, thinking and thinking and thinking. She had done her best upon the spur of the moment to pull the house down; but it would not fall. Moreover, she could not understand her husband, and she was afraid. Then the folly of her useless truthfulness struck her, and she was ashamed to write to Kurrell, saying: "I have gone mad and told everything. My husband says that I am free to elope with you. Get a *dak* for Thursday, and we will fly after dinner." There was a cold-bloodedness about that procedure which did not appeal to her. So she sat still in her own house and thought.

At dinner-time Boulte came back from his walk, white and worn and haggard, and the woman was touched at his distress. As the evening wore on, she muttered some expression of sorrow, something approaching to contrition. Boulte came out of a brown study, and said, "Oh, *that!* I wasn't thinking about that. By the way, what does Kurrell say to the elopement?"

"I haven't seen him," said Mrs. Boulte. "Good God! is that all?"

But Boulte was not listening, and her sentence ended in a gulp.

The next day brought no comfort to Mrs. Boulte, for Kurrell did not appear, and the new life that she, in the five minutes' madness of the previous evening, had hoped to build out of the ruins of the old, seemed to be no nearer.

Boulte ate his breakfast, advised her to see her Arab pony fed in the veranda, and went out. The morning wore through, and at midday the tension became unendurable. Mrs. Boulte could not cry. She had finished crying in the night, and now she did not want to be left alone. Perhaps the Vansuythen Woman would talk to her; and, since talking opens the heart, perhaps there might be some comfort to be found in her company. She was the only other woman in the Station.

In Kashima there are no regular calling-hours. Every one can drop in upon every one else at pleasure. Mrs. Boulte put on a big *terai* hat, and walked across to the Vansuythen's house to borrow last week's *Queen*. The two compounds touched, and instead of going up the drive, she crossed through the gap in the cactus-hedge, entering the house from the back. As she passed through the dining-room she heard, behind the *purdah* that cloaked the drawing-room door, her husband's voice, saying—

"But on my Honor! On my Soul and Honor, I tell you she doesn't care for me. She told me so last night. I would have told you then if Vansuythen hadn't been with you. If it is for *her* sake that you'll have nothing to say to me, you can make your mind easy. It's Kurrell"—

"What?" said Mrs. Vansuythen, with an hysterical little laugh. "Kurrell! Oh, it can't be! You two must have made some horrible mistake. Perhaps you—you lost your temper, or misunderstood, or something. Things *can't* be as wrong as you say."

Mrs. Vansuythen had shifted her defence to avoid the man's pleading, and was desperately trying to keep him to a side-issue.

"There must be some mistake," she insisted, "and it can be all put right again."

Boulte laughed grimly.

"It can't be Captain Kurrell! He told me that he had never taken the least—the least interest in your wife, Mr. Boulte. Oh, *do* listen! He said he had not. He swore he had not," said Mrs. Vansuythen.

The *purdah* rustled, and the speech was cut short by the entry of a little, thin woman, with big rings round her eyes. Mrs. Vansuythen stood up with a gasp.

"What was that you said?" asked Mrs. Boulte. "Never mind that man. What did Ted say to you? What did he say to you? What did he say to you?"

Mrs. Vansuythen sat down helplessly on the sofa, overborne by the trouble of her questioner.

"He said—I can't remember exactly what he said—but I understood him to say—that is — But, really, Mrs. Boulte, isn't it rather a strange question?"

"*Will* you tell me what he said?" repeated Mrs. Boulte. Even a tiger will fly before a bear robbed of her whelps, and Mrs. Vansuythen was only an ordinarily good woman. She began in a sort of desperation: "Well, he said that he never cared for you at all, and, of course, there was not the least reason why he should have, and—and—that was all."

"You said he *swore* he had not cared for me. Was that true?"

"Yes," said Mrs. Vansuythen, very softly.

Mrs. Boulte wavered for an instant where she stood, and then fell forward fainting.

"What did I tell you?" said Boulte, as though the conversation had been unbroken. "You can see for yourself. She cares for *him.*" The light began to break into his dull mind, and he went on—"And he—what was *he* saying to you?"

But Mrs. Vansuythen, with no heart for explanations or impassioned protestations, was kneeling over Mrs. Boulte.

"Oh, you brute!" she cried. "Are *all* men like this? Help me to get her into my room—and her face is cut against the table. Oh, *will* you be quiet, and help me to carry her? I hate you, and I hate Captain Kurrell. Lift her up carefully and now—go! Go away!"

Boulte carried his wife into Mrs. Vansuythen's bedroom and departed before the storm of that lady's wrath and disgust, impenitent and burning with jealousy. Kurrell had been making love to Mrs. Vansuythen—would do Vansuythen as great a wrong as he had done Boulte, who caught himself considering whether Mrs. Vansuythen would faint if she discovered that the man she loved had foresworn her.

In the middle of these meditations, Kurrell came cantering along the road and pulled up with a cheery, "Good-mornin'. Been mashing Mrs. Vansuythen as usual, eh? Bad thing for a sober, married man, that. What will Mrs. Boulte say?"

Boulte raised his head and said, slowly, "Oh, you liar!" Kurrell's face changed. "What's that?" he asked, quickly.

"Nothing much," said Boulte. "Has my wife told you that you two are free to go off whenever you please? She has been good enough to explain the situation to me. You've been a true friend to me, Kurrell—old man—haven't you?"

Kurrell groaned, and tried to frame some sort of idiotic sentence about being willing to give "satisfaction." But his interest in the woman was dead, had died out in the Rains, and, mentally, he was abusing her for her amazing indiscretion. It would have been so easy to have broken off the thing gently and by degrees, and now he was saddled with—Boulte's voice recalled him.

"I don't think I should get any satisfaction from killing you, and I'm pretty sure you'd get none from killing me."

Then in a querulous tone, ludicrously disproportioned to his wrongs, Boulte added—

"Seems rather a pity that you haven't the decency to keep to the woman, now you've got her. You've been a true friend to *her* too, haven't you?"

Kurrell stared long and gravely. The situation was getting beyond him.

"What do you mean?" he said.

Boulte answered, more to himself than the questioner: "My wife came over to Mrs. Vansuythen's just now; and it seems you'd been telling Mrs. Vansuythen that you'd never cared for Emma. I suppose you lied, as usual. What had Mrs. Vansuythen to do with you, or you with her? Try to speak the truth for once in a way."

Kurrell took the double insult without wincing, and replied by another question: "Go on. What happened?"

"Emma fainted," said Boulte, simply. "But, look here, what had you been saying to Mrs. Vansuythen?"

Kurrell laughed. Mrs. Boulte had, with unbridled tongue, made havoc of his plans; and he could at least retaliate by hurting the man in whose eyes he was humiliated and shown dishonorable.

"Said to her? What does a man tell a lie like that for? I suppose I said pretty much what you've said, unless I'm a good deal mistaken."

"I spoke the truth," said Boulte, again more to himself than Kurrell. "Emma told me she hated me. She has no right in me."

"No! I suppose not. You're only her husband, y'know. And what did Mrs. Vansuythen say after you had laid your disengaged heart at her feet?"

Kurrell felt almost virtuous as he put the question.

"I don't think that matters," Boulte replied; "and it doesn't concern you."

"But it does! I tell you it does"—began Kurrell, shamelessly.

The sentence was cut by a roar of laughter from Boulte's lips. Kurrell was silent for an instant, and then he, too, laughed—laughed long and loudly, rocking in his saddle. It was an unpleasant sound—the mirthless mirth of these men on the long, white line of the Narkarra Road. There were no strangers in Kashima, or they might have thought that captivity within the Dosehri hills had driven half the European population mad. The laughter ended abruptly, and Kurrell was the first to speak.

"Well, what are you going to do?"

Boulte looked up the road, and at the hills.

"Nothing," said he, quietly; "what's the use? It's too ghastly for anything. We must let the old life go on. I can only call you a hound and a liar, and I can't go on calling you names forever. Besides which, I don't feel that I'm much better. We can't get out of this place. What *is* there to do"

Kurrell looked round the rat-pit of Kashima and made no reply. The injured husband took up the wondrous tale.

"Ride on, and speak to Emma if you want to. God knows *I* don't care what you do."

He walked forward, and left Kurrell gazing blankly after him. Kurrell did not ride on either to see Mrs. Boulte or Mrs. Vansuythen. He sat in his saddle and thought, while his pony grazed by the roadside.

The whir of approaching wheels roused him. Mrs. Vansuythen was driving home Mrs. Boulte, white and wan, with a cut on her forehead.

"Stop, please," said Mrs. Boulte, "I want to speak to Ted."

Mrs. Vansuythen obeyed, but as Mrs. Boulte leaned forward, putting her hand upon the splash-board of the dog-cart, Kurrell spoke.

"I've seen your husband, Mrs. Boulte."

There was no necessity for any further explanation. The man's eyes were fixed, not upon Mrs. Boulte, but her companion. Mrs. Boulte saw the look.

"Speak to him!" she pleaded, turning to the woman at her side. "Oh, speak to him! Tell him what you told me just now. Tell him you hate him. Tell him you hate him!"

She bent forward and wept bitterly, while the *sais*, impassive, went forward to hold the horse. Mrs. Vansuythen turned scarlet and dropped the reins. She wished to be no party to such unholy explanations.

"I've nothing to do with it," she began, coldly; but Mrs. Boulte's sobs overcame her, and she addressed herself to the man. "I don't know what I am to say, Captain Kurrell. I don't know what I can call you. I think you've—you've behaved abominably, and she has cut her forehead terribly aaginst the table."

"It doesn't hurt. It isn't anything," said Mrs. Boulte, feebly. "*That* doesn't matter. Tell him what you told me. Say you don't care for him. Oh, Ted, *won't* you believe her?"

"Mrs. Boulte has made me understand that you were—that you were fond of her once upon a time," went on Mrs. Vansuythen.

"Well!" said Kurrell, brutally. "It seems to

me that Mrs. Boulte had better be fond of her own husband first."

"Stop!" said Mrs. Vansuythen. "Hear me first. I don't care—I don't want to know anything about you and Mrs. Boulte; but I want *you* to know that I hate you, that I think you are a cur, and that I'll never, *never* speak to you again. Oh, I don't dare to say what I think of you, you—man!"

"I want to speak to Ted," moaned Mrs. Boulte, but the dog-cart rattled on, and Kurrell was left on the road, shamed, and boiling with wrath against Mrs. Boulte.

He waited till Mrs. Vansuythen was driving back to her own house, and, she being freed from the embarrassment of Mrs. Boulte's presence, learned for the second time her opinion of himself and his actions.

In the evenings, it was the wont of all Kashima to meet at the platform on the Narkarra Road, to drink tea, and discuss the trivialities of the day. Major Vansuythen and his wife found themselves alone at the gathering-place for almost the first time in their remembrance; and the cheery Major, in the teeth of his wife's remarkably reasonable suggestion that the rest of the Station might be sick, insisted upon driving round to the two bungalows and unearthing the population.

"Sitting in the twilight!" said he, with great indignation, to the Boultes. "That'll never do! Hang it all, we're one family here! You *must* come out, and so must Kurrell. I'll make him bring his banjo."

So great is the power of honest simplicity and a good digestion over guilty consciences that all Kashima did turn out, even down to the banjo; and the Major embraced the company in one expansive grin. As he grinned, Mrs. Vansuythen raised her eyes for an instant and looked at all Kashima. Her meaning was clear. Major Vansuythen would never know anything. He was to be the outsider in that happy family whose cage was the Dosehri hills.

"You're singing villainously out of tune, Kurrell," said the Major, truthfully. "Pass me that banjo."

And he sang in excruciating-wise till the stars came out and all Kashima went to dinner.

* * * * * *

That was the beginning of the New Life of Kashima—the life that Mrs. Boulte made when her tongue was loosened in the twilight.

Mrs. Vansuythen has never told the Major; and since he insists upon keeping up a burdensome geniality, she has been compelled to break her vow of not speaking to Kurrell. This speech, which must of necessity preserve the semblance of politeness and interest, serves admirably to keep alight the flame of jealousy and dull hatred in Boulte's bosom, as it awakens the same passions in his wife's heart. Mrs. Boulte hates Mrs. Vansuythen because she has taken Ted from her, and, in some curious fashion, hates her because Mrs. Vansuythen—and here the wife's eyes see far more clearly than the husband's—detests Ted. And Ted—that gallant captain and honorable man—knows now that it is possible to hate a woman once loved, to the verge of wishing to silence her forever with blows. Above all, is he shocked that Mrs. Boulte cannot see the error of her ways.

Boulte and he go out tiger-shooting together in all friendship. Boulte has put their relationship on a most satisfactory footing.

"You're a blackguard," he says to Kurrell, "and I've lost any self-respect I may ever have had; but when you're with me, I can feel certain that you are not with Mrs. Vansuythen, or making Emma miserable."

Kurrell endures anything that Boulte may say to him. Sometimes they are away for three days together, and then the Major insists upon his wife going over to sit with Mrs. Boulte; although Mrs. Vansuythen has repeatedly declared that she prefers her husband's company to any in the world. From the way in which she clings to him, she would certainly seem to be speaking the truth.

But, of course, as the Major says, "in a little Station we must all be friendly."

THE HILL OF ILLUSION

THE HILL OF ILLUSION.

What rendered vain their deep desire?
A God, a God their severance ruled,
And bade between their shores to be
The unplumbed, salt, estranging sea.
Matthew Arnold.

HE. Tell your *jhampanis* not to hurry so, dear. They forget I'm fresh from the Plains.

SHE. Sure proof that *I* have not been going out with any one. Yes, they *are* an untrained crew. Where do we go?

HE. As usual—to the world's end. No, Jakko.

SHE. Have your pony led after you, then. It's a long round.

HE. And for the last time, thank Heaven.

SHE. Do you mean *that* still? I didn't dare to write to you about it—all these months.

HE. Mean it! I've been shaping my affairs to that end since Autumn. What makes you speak as though it had occurred to you for the first time?

SHE. I! Oh! I don't know. I've had long enough to think, too.

HE. And you've changed your mind?

SHE. No. You ought to know that I am a miracle of constancy. What are your—arrangements?

HE. *Ours,* Sweetheart, please.

SHE. Ours, be it then. My poor boy, how the prickly heat has marked your forehead! Have you ever tried sulphate of copper in water?

HE. It'll go away in a day or two up here. The arrangements are simple enough. Tonga in the early morning—reach Kalka at twelve—Umballa at seven—down, straight by night train, to Bombay, and the steamer of the 21st for Rome. That's my idea. The Continent and Sweden—a ten-week honeymoon.

SHE. Ssh! Don't talk of it in that way. It makes me afraid. Guy, how long have we two been insane?

HE. Seven months and fourteen days, I forget the odd hours exactly, but I'll think.

SHE. I only wanted to see if you remembered. Who are those two on the Blessington Road?

HE. Eabrey and the Penner woman. What do they matter to *us?* Tell me everything that you've been doing and saying and thinking.

SHE. Doing little, saying less, and thinking a great deal. I've hardly been out at all.

HE. That was wrong of you. You haven't been moping?

SHE. Not very much. Can you wonder that I'm disinclined for amusement?

HE. Frankly, I do. Where was the difficulty?

SHE. In this only. The more people I know and the more I'm known here, the wider spread will be the news of the crash when it comes. I don't like that.

HE. Nonsense. We shall be out of it.

SHE. You think so?

HE. I'm sure of it, if there is any power in steam or horse-flesh to carry us away. Ha! ha!

SHE. And the *fun* of the situation comes in —where, my Lancelot?

HE. Nowhere, Guinevere. I was only thinking of something.

SHE. They say men have a keener sense of humor than women. Now *I* was thinking of the scandal.

HE. Don't think of anything so ugly. We shall be beyond it.

SHE. It will be there all the same—in the mouths of Simla—telegraphed over India, and talked of at the dinners—and when He goes out they will stare at Him to see how He takes it. And we shall be dead, Guy dear—dead and cast into the outer darkness where there is—

HE. Love at least. Isn't that enough?

SHE. I have said so.

HE. And you think so still?

SHE. What do *you* think?

HE. What have I *done?* It means equal ruin to me, as the world reckons it—outcasting, the loss of my appointment, the breaking off my life's work. I pay my price.

SHE. And are you so much above the world that you can afford to pay it? Am I?

HE. My Divinity—what else?

SHE. A very ordinary woman I'm afraid, but, so far, respectable. How'd you do, Mrs. Middleditch? Your husband? I think he's riding down to Annandale with Colonel Statters. Yes, isn't it divine after the rain?—Guy, how long am I to be allowed to bow to Mrs. Middleditch? Till the 17th?

HE. Frowsy Scotchwoman! What is the use of bringing her into the discussion? You were saying?

SHE. Nothing. Have you ever seen a man hanged?

HE. Yes. Once.

SHE. What was it for?

HE. Murder, of course.

SHE. Murder. Is *that* so great a sin after all? I wonder how he felt before the drop fell.

HE. I don't think he felt much. What a gruesome little woman it is this evening. You're shivering. Put on your cape, dear.

SHE. I think I will. Oh! Look at the mist coming over Sanjaoli; and I thought we should have sunshine on the Ladies' Mile! Let's turn back.

HE. What's the good? There's a cloud on Elysium Hill, and that means it's foggy all down the Mall. We'll go on. It'll blow away before we get to the Convent, perhaps. 'Jove! It *is* chilly.

SHE. You feel it, fresh from below. Put on your ulster. What do you think of my cape?

HE. Never ask a man his opinion of a woman's dress when he is desperately and abjectly in love with the wearer. Let me look. Like everything else of yours, it's perfect. Where did you get it from?

SHE. He gave it me, on Wednesday—our wedding-day, you know.

HE. The Deuce he did! He's growing generous in his old age. D'you like all that frilly, bunchy stuff at the throat? I don't.

SHE. Don't you?

Kind Sir, o' your courtesy,
As you go by the town, Sir,

'Pray you o' your love for me,
Buy me a russet gown, Sir.

HE. I won't say: "Keek into the draw-well, Janet, Janet." Only wait a little, darling, and you shall be stocked with russet gowns and everything else.

SHE. And when the frocks wear out, you'll get me new ones—and everything else?

HE. Assuredly.

SHE. I wonder!

HE. Look here, Sweetheart, I didn't spend two days and two nights in the train to hear you wonder. I thought we'd settled all that at Shaifazehat.

SHE. (*dreamily.*) At Shaifazehat? Does the Station go on still? That was ages and *ages* ago. It must be crumbling to pieces. All except the Amirtollah *kutcha* road. I don't believe *that* could crumble till the Day of Judgment.

HE. You think so? What *is* the mood now?

SHE. I can't tell. How cold it is! Let us get on quickly.

HE. Better walk a little. Stop your *jhampanis* and get out. What's the matter with you this evening, dear?

SHE. Nothing. You must grow accustomed to my ways. If I'm boring you I can go home.

Here's Captain Congleton coming, I dare say he'll be willing to escort me.

HE. *Goose!* Between *us,* too! *Damn* Captain Congleton!

SHE. Chivalrous Knight. Is it your habit to swear much in talking? It jars a little, and you might swear at me.

HE. My angel! I didn't know what I was saying; and you changed so quickly that I couldn't follow. I'll apologize in dust and ashes.

SHE. There'll be enough of those later on—Good-night, Captain Congleton. Going to the singing-quadrilles already? What dances am I giving you next week? No! You must have written them down wrong. Five and Seven, *I* said. If you've made a mistake, I certainly don't intend to suffer for it. You must alter your programme.

HE. I thought you told me that you had not been going out much this season.

SHE. Quite true, but when I do I dance with Captain Congleton. He dances very nicely.

HE. And sit out with him, I suppose?

SHE. Yes. Have you any objection? Shall I stand under the chandelier in future?

HE. What does he talk to you about?

SHE. What do men talk about when they sit out?

HE. Ugh! Don't! Well now I'm up, you must dispense with the fascinating Congleton for a while. I don't like him.

SHE (*after a pause*). Do you know what you have said?

HE. 'Can't say that I do exactly. I'm not in the best of tempers.

SHE. So I see,—and feel. My true and faithful lover, where is your "eternal constancy," "unalterable trust," and "reverent devotion"? I remember those phrases; you seem to have forgotten them. I mention a man's name—

HE. A good deal more than that.

SHE. Well, speak to him about a dance—perhaps the last dance that I shall ever dance in my life before I,—before I go away; and you at once distrust and insult me.

HE. I never said a word.

SHE. How much did you imply. Guy, is *this* amount of confidence to be our stock to start the new life on?

HE. No, of course not. I didn't mean that. On my word and honor, I didn't. Let it pass, dear. Please let it pass.

SHE. This once—yes—and a second time, and again and again, all through the years when I shall be unable to resent it. You want too much, my Lancelot, and,—you know too much.

HE. How do you mean?

SHE. That is a part of the punishment. There *cannot* be perfect trust between us.

HE. In Heaven's name, why not?

SHE. Hush! The Other Place is quite enough. Ask yourself.

HE. I don't follow.

SHE. You trust me so implicitly that when I look at another man— Never mind, Guy. Have you ever made love to a girl—a *good* girl?

HE. Something of the sort. Centuries ago —in the Dark Ages, before I ever met you, dear.

SHE. Tell me what you said to her.

HE. What does a man say to a girl? I've forgotten.

SHE. I remember. He tells her that he trusts her and worships the ground she walks on, and that he'll love and honor and protect her till her dying day; and so she marries him in that belief. At least, I speak of one girl who was *not* protected.

HE. Well, and then?

SHE. And then, Guy, and then, that girl needs *ten* times the love and trust and honor—

yes, *honor*—that was enough when she was only a mere wife if—if—the other life she chooses to lead is to be made even bearable. Do you understand?

HE. Even bearable! It'll be Paradise.

SHE. Ah! Can you give me all I've asked for—not now, nor a few months later, but when you begin to think of what you might have done if you had kept your own appointment and your caste here—when you begin to look upon me as a drag and a burden? I shall want it most, then, Guy, for there will be no one in the wide world but you.

HE. You're a little over-tired to-night, Sweetheart, and you're taking a stage view of the situation. After the necessary business in the Courts, the road is clear to—

SHE. "The holy state of matrimony!" Ha! ha! ha!

HE. Ssh! Don't laugh in that horrible way.

SHE. I—I c-c-c-can't help it! Isn't it too absurd! Ah! Ha! ha! ha! Guy, stop me quick or I shall—l-l-laugh till we get to the Church.

HE. For goodness' sake, stop! Don't make an exhibition of yourself. What *is* the matter with you?

SHE. N-nothing. I'm better now.

HE. That's all right. One moment, dear.

There's a little wisp of hair got loose from behind your right ear and it's straggling over your cheek. So!

SHE. Thank'oo. I'm 'fraid my hat's on one side, too.

HE. What do you wear these huge dagger bonnet-skewers for? They're big enough to kill a man with.

SHE. Oh! Don't kill *me*, though. You're sticking it into my head. Let *me* do it. You men are so clumsy.

HE. Have you had many opportunities of comparing us—in this sort of work?

SHE. Guy, what is my name?

HE. Eh! I don't follow.

SHE. Here's my cardcase. Can you read?

HE. Yes. Well?

SHE. Well, that answers your question. You know the other man's name. Am I sufficiently humbled, or would you like to ask me if there is any one else?

HE. I see now. My darling, I never meant that for an instant. I was only joking. There! Lucky there's no one on the road. They'd be scandalized.

SHE. They'll be more scandalized before the end.

HE. Do-on't! I don't like you to talk in that way.

SHE. Unreasonable man! Who asked me to face the situation and accept it?—Tell me, do I look like Mrs. Penner? *Do* I look like a naughty woman? *Swear* I don't! Give me your word of honor, my *honorable* friend, that I'm not like Mrs. Buzgago. That's the way she stands, with her hands clasped at the back of her head. D'you like that?

HE. Don't be affected.

SHE. I'm not. I'm Mrs. Buzgago. Listen!

> Pendant une anne' toute entière
> Le régiment n'a pas r'paru.
> Au Ministère de la Guerre
> On le r'porta comme perdu.
>
> On se r'noncait à r'trouver sa trace,
> Quand un matin subitement,
> On le vit r'paraître sur la place,
> L'Colonel toujours en avant.

That's the way she rolls her r's. *Am* I like her?

HE. No, but I object when you go on like an actress and sing stuff of that kind. Where in the world did you pick up the *Chanson du Colonel?* It isn't a drawing-room song. It isn't proper.

SHE. Mrs. Buzgago taught it me. She is both drawing-room and proper, and in another month she'll shut her drawing-room to me, and thank God she isn't as improper as I am. Oh, Guy, Guy! I wish I was like some women and had no scruples about—what is it Keene says?—"Wearing a corpse's hair and being false to the bread they eat."

HE. I am only a man of limited intelligence, and, just now, very bewildered. When you have *quite* finished flashing through all your moods tell me, and I'll try to understand the last one.

SHE. Moods, Guy! I haven't any. I'm sixteen years old, and you're just twenty, and you've been waiting for two hours outside the school in the cold. And now I've met you, and now we're walking home together. Does *that* suit you, my Imperial Majesty?

HE. No. We aren't children. Why can't you be rational?

SHE. He asks me that when I'm going to commit suicide for his sake, and, and—I don't want to be French and rave about my mother, but have I ever told you that I have a mother, and a brother who was my pet before I married? He's married now. Can't you imagine the pleasure that the news of the elopement will give him? Have *you* any people at Home, Guy, to be pleased with your performances?

HE. One or two. One can't make omelets

without breaking eggs.

SHE (*slowly*). I don't see the necessity—

HE. Hah! What do you mean?

SHE. Shall I speak the truth?

HE. Under the circumstances, perhaps it *would* be as well.

SHE. Guy, I'm afraid.

HE. I thought we'd settled all that. What of?

SHE. Of you.

HE. Oh, damn it all! The old business! This is *too* bad!

SHE. Of *you*.

HE. And what now?

SHE. What do you think of me.

HE. Beside the question altogether. What do you intend to do?

SHE. I daren't risk it. I'm afraid. If I could only cheat—

HE. *A la Buzgago?* No, *thanks*. That's the one point on which I have any notion of Honor. I won't eat his salt and steal too. I'll loot openly or not at all.

SHE. I never meant anything else.

HE. Then, why in the world do you pretend not to be willing to come?

SHE. It's *not* pretence, Guy. I *am* afraid.

HE. Please explain.

SHE. It can't last, Guy. It can't last. You'll get angry, and then you'll swear, and then you'll get jealous, and then you'll mistrust me —you do *now*—and you yourself will be the best reason for doubting. And I—what shall *I* do? I shall be no better than Mrs. Buzgago found out—no better than any one. And you'll *know* that. Oh, Guy, can't you *see?*

HE. I can see that you are desperately unreasonable, little woman.

SHE. There! The moment I begin to object, you get angry. What will you do when I am only your property—stolen property? It can't be, Guy. It can't be! I thought it could, but it *can't*. You'll get tired of me.

HE. I tell you I shall *not*. Won't anything make you understand that?

SHE. There, can't you see? If you speak to me like that now, you'll call me horrible names later, if I don't do everything as you like. And if you were cruel to me, Guy, where should I go—where should I go? I can't trust you. Oh! I *can't* trust you!

HE. I suppose I ought to say that I *can* trust you. I've ample reason.

SHE. Please don't, dear. It hurts as much as if you hit me.

HE. It isn't exactly pleasant for *me*.

SHE. I can't help it. I wish I were dead! I can't trust you, and I don't trust myself. Oh, Guy, let it die away and be forgotten!

HE. Too late now. I don't understand you —I won't—and I can't trust myself to talk this evening. May I call to-morrow?

SHE. Yes. *No!* Oh, give me time! The day after. I get into my *'rickshaw* here and meet Him at Peliti's. You ride.

HE. I'll go on to Peliti's too. I think I want a drink. My world's knocked about my ears and the stars are falling. Who are those brutes howling in the Old Library?

SHE. They're rehearsing the singing-quadrilles for the Fancy Ball. Can't you hear Mrs. Buzgago's voice? She has a solo. It's quite a new idea. Listen.

MRS. BUZGAGO. (*In the Old Library, con molt. exp.*).

> See saw! Margery Daw!
> Sold her bed to lie upon straw.
> Wasn't she a silly slut
> To sell her bed and lie upon dirt?

Captain Congleton, I'm going to alter that to "flirt." It sounds better.

HE. No, I've changed my mind about the drink. Good-night, little lady. I shall see you to-morrow?

SHE. Ye—es. Good-night, Guy. *Don't* be angry with me.

HE. Angry! You *know* I trust you absolutely. Good-night and—God bless you!

(*Three seconds later. Alone.*) Hmm! I'd give something to discover whether there's another man at the back of all this.

A SECOND-RATE WOMAN

A SECOND-RATE WOMAN

Est fuga, volvitur rota,
On we drift; where looms the dim port?
One Two Three Four Five contribute their quota:
Something is gained if one caught but the import,
Show it us, Hugues of Saxe-Gotha.
—*Master Hugues of Saxe-Gotha.*

DRESSED! Don't tell me that woman ever dressed in her life. She stood in the middle of the room while her *ayah*—no, her husband—it *must* have been a man—threw her clothes at her. She then did her hair with her fingers, and rubbed her bonnet in the flue under the bed. I *know* she did, as well as if I had assisted at the orgie. Who is she?" said Mrs. Hauksbee.

"Don't!" said Mrs. Mallowe, feebly. "You make my head ache. I'm miserable to-day. Stay me with *fondants,* comfort me with chocolates, for I am— Did you bring anything from Peliti's?"

"Questions to begin with. You shall have the sweets when you have answered them. Who and what is the creature? There were at least half a dozen men round her, and she appeared to be going to sleep in their midst."

"Delville," said Mrs. Mallowe, " 'Shady' Delville, to distinguish her from Mrs. Jim of that ilk. She dances as untidily as she dresses, I believe, and her husband is somewhere in Madras. Go and call, if you are so interested."

"What have I to do with Shigramitish women? She merely caught my attention for a minute, and I wondered at the attraction that a dowd has for a certain type of man. I expected to see her walk out of her clothes—until I looked at her eyes."

"Hooks and eyes, surely," drawled Mrs. Mallowe.

"Don't be clever, Polly. You make my head ache. And round this hayrick stood a crowd of men—a positive crowd!"

"Perhaps *they* also expected"—

"Polly, don't be Rabelaisian!"

Mrs. Mallowe curled herself up comfortably on the sofa, and turned her attention to the sweets. She and Mrs. Hauksbee shared the same house at Simla; and these things befell two seasons after the matter of Otis Yeere, which has been already recorded.

Mrs. Hauksbee stepped into the veranda and looked down upon the Mall, her forehead puckered with thought.

"Hah!" said Mrs. Hauksbee, shortly. "Indeed!"

"What is it?" said Mrs. Mallowe, sleepily.

"That dowd and The Dancing Master—to whom I object."

"Why to The Dancing Master? He is a middle-aged gentleman, of reprobate and romantic tendencies, and tries to be a friend of mine."

"Then make up your mind to lose him. Dowds cling by nature, and I should imagine that this animal—how terrible her bonnet looks from above!—is specially clingsome."

"She is welcome to The Dancing Master so far as I am concerned. I never could take an interest in a monotonous liar. The frustrated aim of his life is to persuade people that he is a bachelor."

"O-oh! I think I've met that sort of man before. And isn't he?"

"No. He confided that to me a few days ago. Ugh! Some men ought to be killed."

"What happened then?"

"He posed as the horror of horrors—a misunderstood man. Heaven knows the *femme incomprise* is sad enough and bad enough—but the other thing!"

"And so fat too! *I* should have laughed in his face. Men seldom confide in me. How is it they come to you?"

"For the sake of impressing me with their

careers in the past. Protect me from men with confidences!"

"And yet you encourage them!"

"What can I do? They talk, I listen, and they vow that I am sympathetic. I know I always profess astonishment even when the plot is—of the most old possible."

"Yes. Men are so unblushingly explicit if they are once allowed to talk, whereas women's confidences are full of reservations and fibs, except"—

"When they go mad and babble of the Unutterabilities after a week's acquaintance. Really, if you come to consider, we know a great deal more of men than of our own sex."

"And the extraordinary thing is that men will never believe it. They say we are trying to hide something."

"They are generally doing that on their own account. Alas! These chocolates pall upon me, and I haven't eaten more than a dozen. I think I shall go to sleep."

"Then you'll get fat, dear. If you took more exercise and a more intelligent interest in your neighbors you would"—

"Be as much loved as Mrs. Hauksbee. You're a darling in many ways and I like you—you are not a woman's woman—but *why* do you trouble yourself about mere human beings?"

"Because in the absence of angels, who I am sure would be horribly dull, men and women are the most fascinating things in the whole wide world, lazy one. I am interested in The Dowd—I am interested in The Dancing Master—I am interested in the Hawley Boy—and I am interested in *you.*"

"Why couple me with the Hawley Boy? He is your property."

"Yes, and in his own guileless speech, I'm making a good thing out of him. When he is slightly more reformed, and has passed his Higher Standard, or whatever the authorities think fit to exact from him, I shall select a pretty little girl, the Holt girl, I think, and"—here she waved her hands airily—"'whom Mrs. Hauksbee hath joined together let no man put asunder.' That's all."

"And when you have yoked May Holt with the most notorious detrimental in Simla, and earned the undying hatred of Mamma Holt, what will you do with me, Dispenser of the Destinies of the Universe?"

Mrs. Hauksbee dropped into a low chair in front of the fire, and, chin in hand, gazed long and steadfastly at Mrs. Mallowe.

"I do not know," she said, shaking her head, "*what* I shall do with you, dear. It's obviously impossible to marry you to some one else—your husband would object and the experiment might not be successful after all. I think I shall begin by preventing you from—what is it?—'sleeping on ale-house benches and snoring in the sun.'"

"Don't! I don't like your quotations. They are so rude. Go to the Library and bring me new books."

"While you sleep? *No!* If you don't come with me, I shall spread your newest frock on my *'rickshaw*-bow, and when any one asks me what I am doing, I shall say that I am going to Phelps's to get it let out. I shall take care that Mrs. McNamara sees me. Put your things on, there's a good girl."

Mrs. Mallowe groaned and obeyed, and the two went off to the Library, where they found Mrs. Delville and the man who went by the nickname of The Dancing Master. By that time Mrs. Mallowe was awake and eloquent.

"That is the Creature!" said Mrs. Hauksbee, with the air of one pointing out a slug in the road.

"No," said Mrs. Mallowe. "The man is the Creature. Ugh! Good-evening, Mr. Bent.

I thought you were coming to tea this evening."

"Surely it was for to-morrow, was it not?" answered The Dancing Master. "I understood . . . I fancied . . . I'm so sorry . . . How very unfortunate!" . . . . . .

But Mrs. Mallowe had passed on.

"For the practiced equivocator you said he was," murmured Mrs. Hauksbee, "he strikes *me* as a failure. Now wherefore should he have preferred a walk with The Dowd to tea with us? Elective affinities, I suppose—both grubby. Polly, I'd never forgive that woman as long as the world rolls."

"I forgive every woman everything," said Mrs. Mallowe. "He will be sufficient punishment for her. What a common voice she has!"

Mrs. Delville's voice was not pretty, her carriage was even less lovely, and her raiment was strikingly neglected. All these things Mrs. Mallowe noticed over the top of a magazine.

"Now *what* is there in her?" said Mrs. Hauksbee. "Do you see what I meant about the clothes falling off? If I were a man I would perish sooner than be seen with that rag-bag. And yet, she has good eyes, but—Oh!"

"What is it?"

"She doesn't know how to use them! On my Honor, she does not. Look! Oh, look! Untidiness I can endure, but ignorance never! The woman's a fool."

"Hsh! She'll hear you."

"All the women in Simla are fools. She'll think I mean some one else. Now she's going out. What a thoroughly objectionable couple she and The Dancing Master make! Which reminds me. Do you suppose they'll ever dance together?"

"Wait and see. I don't envy her the conversation of The Dancing Master—loathly man! His wife ought to be up here before long."

"Do you know anything about him?"

"Only what he told me. It may be all a fiction. He married a girl bred in the country, I think, and, being an honorable, chivalrous soul, told me that he repented his bargain and sent her to her mother as often as possible—a person who has lived in the Doon since the memory of man and goes to Mussoorie when other people go Home. The wife is with her at present. So he says."

"Babies?"

"One only, but he talks of his wife in a revolting way. I hated him for it. *He* thought he was being epigrammatic and brilliant."

"That is a vice peculiar to men. I dislike him because he is generally in the wake of some girl, disappointing the Eligibles. He will persecute May Holt no more, unless I am much mistaken."

"No. I think Mrs. Delville may occupy his attention for a while."

"Do you suppose she knows that he is the head of a family?"

"Not from his lips. He swore me to eternal secrecy. Wherefore I tell you. Don't you know that type of man?"

"Not intimately, thank goodness! As a general rule, when a man begins to abuse his wife to me, I find that the Lord gives me wherewith to answer him according to his folly; and we part with a coolness between us. I laugh."

"I'm different. I've no sense of humor."

"Cultivate it, then. It has been my mainstay for more years than I care to think about. A well-educated sense of Humor will save a woman when Religion, Training, and Home influences fail; and we may all need salvation sometimes."

"Do you suppose that the Delville woman has humor?"

"Her dress bewrays her. How can a Thing who wears her *supplément* under her left arm have any notion of the fitness of things—much less their folly? If she discards The Dancing Master after having once seen him dance, I may respect her. Otherwise"—

"But are we not both assuming a great deal too much, dear? You saw the woman at Peliti's—half an hour later you saw her walking with The Dancing Master—an hour later you met her here at the Library."

"Still with The Dancing Master, remember."

"Still with The Dancing Master, I admit, but why on the strength of that should you imagine"—

"I imagine nothing. I have no imagination. I am only convinced that The Dancing Master is attracted to The Dowd because he is objectionable in every way and she in every other. If I know the man as you have described him, he holds his wife in slavery at present."

"She's twenty years younger than he."

"Poor wretch! And, in the end, after he has posed and swaggered and lied—he has a mouth under that ragged moustache simply made for lies—he will be rewarded according to his merits."

"I wonder what those really are," said Mrs. Mallowe.

But Mrs. Hauksbee, her face close to the shelf of the new books, was humming softly: *"What shall he have who killed the Deer!"* She was a lady of unfettered speech.

One month later, she announced her intention of calling upon Mrs. Delville. Both Mrs. Hauksbee and Mrs. Mallowe were in morning wrappers, and there was a great peace in the land.

"I should go as I was," said Mrs. Mallowe. "It would be a delicate compliment to her style."

Mrs. Hauksbee studied herself in the glass.

"Assuming for a moment that she ever darkened these doors, I should put on this robe, after all the others, to show her what a morning wrapper ought to be. It might enlighten her. As it is, I shall go in the dove-colored——sweet emblem of youth and innocence—and shall put on my new gloves."

"If you really are going, dirty tan would be too good; and you know that dove-color spots with the rain."

"I care not. I may make her envious. At

least I shall try, though one cannot expect very much from such a woman, who puts a lace tucker into her habit."

"Just Heavens! When did she do that?"

"Yesterday—riding with The Dancing Master. I met them at the back of Jakko, and the rain had made the lace lie down. To complete the effect, she was wearing an unclean *terai* with the elastic under her chin. I felt almost too well content to take the trouble to despise her."

"The Hawley Boy was riding with you. What did he think?"

"Does a boy ever notice these things? Should I like him if he did? He stared in the rudest way, and just when I thought he had seen the elastic, he said, 'There's something very taking about that face.' I rebuked him on the spot. I don't approve of boys being taken by faces."

"Other than your own. I shouldn't be in the least surprised if the Hawley Boy immediately went to call."

"I forbade him. Let her be satisfied with The Dancing Master, and his wife when she comes up. I'm rather curious to see Mrs. Bent and the Delville woman together."

Mrs. Hauksbee departed and, at the end of an hour, returned slightly flushed.

"There is no limit to the treachery of youth! I *ordered* the Hawley Boy, as he valued my patronage, not to call. The first person I stumble over—literally stumble over—in her poky, dark, little drawing-room is, of course, the Hawley Boy. She kept us waiting ten minutes, and then emerged as though she had been tipped out of the dirty-clothes basket. You know my way, dear, when I am at all put out. I was Superior, *crrrrushingly* Superior! 'Lifted my eyes to Heaven, and had heard of nothing—dropped my eyes on the carpet and 'really didn't know'—played with my card-case and 'supposed so.' The Hawley Boy giggled like a girl, and I had to freeze him with scowls between the sentences."

"And she?"

"She sat in a heap on the edge of a couch, and managed to convey the impression that she was suffering from stomach-ache, at the very least. It was all I could do not to ask after her symptoms. When I rose she grunted just like a buffalo in the water—too lazy to move."

"Are you certain?"—

"Am I blind, Polly? Laziness, sheer laziness, nothing else—or her garments were only constructed for sitting down in. I stayed for a quarter of an hour trying to penetrate the gloom, to guess what her surroundings were like, while she stuck out her tongue."

"Lu—*cy!*"

"Well—I'll withdraw the tongue, though I'm sure if she didn't do it when I was in the room, she did the minute I was outside. At any rate, she lay in a lump and grunted. Ask the Hawley Boy, dear. I believe the grunts were meant for sentences, but she spoke so indistinctly that I can't swear to it."

"You are incorrigible, simply."

"I am *not!* Treat me civilly, give me peace with honor, don't put the only available seat facing the window, and a child may eat jam in my lap before Church. But I resent being grunted at. Wouldn't you? Do you suppose that she communicates her views on life and love to The Dancing Master in a set of modulated 'Grmphs'?"

"You attach too much importance to The Dancing Master."

"He came as we went, and The Dowd grew almost cordial at the sight of him. He smiled greasily, and moved about that darkened dog-kennel in a suspiciously familiar way."

"Don't be uncharitable. Any sin but that I'll forgive."

"Listen to the voice of History. I am only describing what I saw. He entered, the heap on the sofa revived slightly, and the Hawley Boy and I came away together. *He* is disillusioned, but I felt it my duty to lecture him severely for going there. And that's all."

"Now for Pity's sake leave the wretched creature and The Dancing Master alone. They never did you any harm."

"No harm? To dress as an example and a stumbling-block for half Simla, and then to find this Person who is dressed by the hand of God—not that I wish to disparage *Him* for a moment, but you know the *tikka dhurzie* way He attires those lilies of the field—this Person draws the eyes of men—and some of them nice men! It's almost enough to make one discard clothing. I told the Hawley Boy so."

"And what did that sweet youth do?"

"Turned shell-pink and looked across the far blue hills like a distressed cherub. *Am* I talking wildly, Polly? Let me say my say, and I shall be calm. Otherwise I may go abroad and disturb Simla with a few original reflections. Excepting always your own sweet self, there isn't a single woman in the land who understands me when I am—what's the word?"

"*Tête-félée,*" suggested Mrs. Mallowe.

"Exactly! And now let us have tiffin. The demands of Society are exhausting, and as Mrs. Delville says"— Here Mrs. Hauksbee, to the horror of the *khitmatgars,* lapsed into a series of grunts, while Mrs. Mallowe stared in lazy surprise.

"'God gie us a gude conceit of oorselves.'" said Mrs. Hauksbee, piously, returning to her natural speech. "Now, in any other woman that would have been vulgar. I am consumed with curiosity to see Mrs. Bent. I expect complications."

"Woman of one idea," said Mrs. Mallowe, shortly; "all complications are as old as the hills! I have lived through or near all—*all*—ALL!"

"And yet do not understand that men and women never behave twice alike. I am old who was young—if ever I put my head in your lap, you dear, big sceptic, you will learn that my parting is gauze—but never, no never, have I lost my interest in men and women. Polly, I shall see this business out to the bitter end."

"I am going to sleep," said Mrs. Mallowe, calmly. "I never interfere with men or women unless I am compelled," and she retired with dignity to her own room.

Mrs. Hauksbee's curiosity was not long left ungratified, for Mrs. Bent came up to Simla a few days after the conversation faithfully reported above, and pervaded the Mall by her husband's side.

"Behold!" said Mrs. Hauksbee, thoughtfully rubbing her nose. "That is the last link of the chain, if we omit the husband of the Delville, whoever he may be. Let me consider. The Bents and the Delvilles inhabit the same hotel; and the Delville is detested by the Waddy—do you know the Waddy?—who is almost as big a dowd. The Waddy also abominates the male Bent, for which, if her other sins do not weigh too heavily, she will eventually go to Heaven."

"Don't be irreverent," said Mrs. Mallowe, "I like Mrs. Bent's face."

"I am discussing the Waddy," returned Mrs. Hauksbee, loftily. "The Waddy will take the female Bent apart, after having borrowed—yes!—everything that she can, from hairpins to babies' bottles. Such, my dear, is life in a hotel. The Waddy will tell the female Bent facts and fictions about The Dancing Master and The Dowd."

"Lucy, I should like you better if you were not always looking into people's back-bedrooms."

"Anybody can look into their front drawing-rooms; and remember whatever I do, and wherever I look, I never talk—as the Waddy will. Let us hope that The Dancing Master's greasy smile and manner of the pedagogue will soften the heart of that cow, his wife. If mouths speak truth, I should think that little Mrs. Bent could get very angry on occasion."

"But what reason has she for being angry?"

"What reason! The Dancing Master in himself is a reason. How does it go? 'If in his life some trivial errors fall, Look in his face and you'll believe them all.' I am prepared to credit *any* evil of The Dancing Master, because I hate him so. And The Dowd is so disgustingly badly dressed"—

"That she, too, is capable of every iniquity? I always prefer to believe the best of everybody. It saves so much trouble."

"Very good. I prefer to believe the worst. It saves useless expenditure of sympathy. And you may be quite certain that the Waddy believes with me."

Mrs. Mallowe sighed and made no answer.

The conversation was holden after dinner while Mrs. Hauksbee was dressing for a dance.

"I am too tired to go," pleaded Mrs. Mallowe, and Mrs. Hauksbee left her in peace till two in the morning, when she was aware of emphatic knocking at her door.

"Don't be *very* angry, dear," said Mrs. Hauksbee. "My idiot of an *ayah* has gone home, and, as I hope to sleep to-night, there isn't a soul in the place to unlace me."

"Oh, this is too bad!" said Mrs. Mallowe, sulkily.

"'Can't help it. I'm a lone, lorn grass-widow, dear, but I will *not* sleep in my stays. And such news, too! Oh, *do* unlace me, there's a darling! The Dowd—The Dancing Master—I and the Hawley Boy— You know the North veranda?"

"How can I do anything if you spin round like this?" protested Mrs. Mallowe, fumbling with the knot of the laces.

"Oh, I forget. I must tell my tale without the aid of your eyes. Do you know you've lovely eyes, dear? Well, to begin with, I took the Hawley Boy to a *kala juggah*."

"Did he want much taking?"

"Lots! There was an arrangement of loose-boxes in *kanats*, and *she* was in the next one talking to *him*."

"Which? How? Explain."

"You know what I mean—The Dowd and The Dancing Master. We could hear every word, and we listened shamelessly—'specially the Hawley Boy. Polly, I quite love that woman!"

"This is interesting. There! Now turn round. What happened?"

"One moment. Ah—h! Blessed relief. I've been looking forward to taking them off for the last half-hour—which is ominous at my time of life. But, as I was saying, we listened and heard The Dowd drawl worse than ever. She drops her final g's like a barmaid or a blue-blooded Aide-de-Camp. 'Look he-ere, you're gettin' too fond o' me,' she said, and The Dancing Master owned it was so in language that nearly made me ill. The Dowd reflected for a while. Then we heard her say, 'Look he-ere, Mister Bent, why are you such an aw-ful liar?' I nearly exploded while The Dancing Master denied the charge. It seems that he never told her he was a married man."

"I said he wouldn't."

"And she had taken this to heart, on personal grounds, I suppose. She drawled along for four or five minutes, reproaching him with his perfidy, and grew quite motherly. 'Now you've got a nice little wife of your own—you have,' she said. 'She's ten times too good for a fat old man like you, and, look he-ere, you never told me a word about her, and I've been thinkin' about it a good deal, and I think you're a liar.' Wasn't that delicious? The Dancing Master maundered and raved till the Hawley Boy suggested that he should burst in and beat him. His voice runs up into an impassioned squeak when he is afraid. The Dowd must be an extraordinary woman. She explained that had he been a bachelor she might not have objected to his devotion; but since he was a married man and the father of a very nice baby, she considered him a hypocrite, and this she repeated twice. She wound up her drawl with: 'An' I'm tellin' you this because your wife is angry with me, an' I hate quarrelin' with any other woman, an' I like your wife. You know how you have behaved for the last six weeks. You shouldn't have done it, indeed you shouldn't. You're too old an' too fat.' Can't you imagine how The Dancing Master would wince at that! 'Now go away,' she said. 'I don't want to tell you what I think of you, because I think you are not nice. I'll stay he-ere till the next dance begins.' Did you think that the creature had so much in her?"

"I never studied her as closely as you did. It sounds unnatural. What happened?"

"The Dancing Master attempted blandishment, reproof, jocularity, and the style of the Lord High Warden, and I had almost to pinch the Hawley Boy to make him keep quiet. She grunted at the end of each sentence and, in the end *he* went away swearing to himself, quite like a man in a novel. He looked more objectionable than ever. I laughed. I love that woman—in spite of her clothes. And now I'm going to bed. What do you think of it?"

"I sha'n't begin to think till the morning," said Mrs. Mallowe, yawning. "Perhaps she spoke the truth. They do fly into it by accident sometimes."

Mrs. Hauksbee's account of her eavesdropping was an ornate one but truthful in the main. For reasons best known to herself, Mrs. "Shady" Delville had turned upon Mr. Bent and rent him limb from limb, casting him away limp and disconcerted ere she withdrew the light of her eyes from him permanently. Being a man of resource, and anything but pleased in that he had been called both old and fat, he gave Mrs. Bent to understand that he had, during her absence in the Doon, been the victim of unceasing persecution at the hands of Mrs. Delville, and he told the tale so often and with such eloquence that he ended in believing it, while his wife marvelled at the manners and customs of "some women." When the situation showed signs of languishing, Mrs. Waddy was always on hand to wake the smouldering fires of suspicion in Mrs. Bent's bosom and to contribute generally to the peace and comfort of the hotel. Mr. Bent's life was not a happy one, for if Mrs. Waddy's story were true, he was, argued his wife, untrustworthy to the last degree. If his own statement was true, his charms of manner and conversation were so great that he needed constant surveillance. And he received it till he repented genuinely of his marriage and neglected his personal appearance. Mrs. Delville alone in the hotel was unchanged. She removed her chair some six paces toward the head of the table, and occasionally in the twilight ventured on timid overtures of friendship to Mrs. Bent, which were repulsed.

"She does it for my sake," hinted the virtuous Bent.

"A dangerous and designing woman," purred Mrs. Waddy.

Worst of all, every other hotel in Simla was full!

* * * * * *

"Polly, are you afraid of diphtheria?"

"Of nothing in the world except smallpox. Diphtheria kills, but it doesn't disfigure. Why do you ask?"

"Because the Bent baby has got it, and the whole hotel is upside down in consequence. The Waddy has "set her five young on the rail" and fled. The Dancing Master fears for his precious throat, and that miserable little woman, his wife, has no notion of what ought to be done. She wanted to put it into a mustard bath—for croup!"

"Where did you learn all this?"

"Just now, on the Mall. Dr. Howlen told me. The Manager of the hotel is abusing the Bents, and the Bents are abusing the Manager. They *are* a feckless couple."

"Well. What's on your mind?"

"This; and I know it's a grave thing to ask. Would you seriously object to my bringing the child over here, with its mother?"

"On the most strict understanding that we see nothing of The Dancing Master."

"He will be only too glad to stay away. Polly, you're an angel. The woman really is at her wits' end."

"And you know nothing about her, careless, and would hold her up to public scorn if it gave you a minute's amusement. Therefore you risk your life for the sake of her brat. No, Loo, *I'm* not the angel. I shall keep to my rooms and avoid her. But do as you please—only tell me why you do it."

Mrs. Hauksbee's eyes softened; she looked out of the window and back into Mrs. Mallowe's face.

"I don't know," said Mrs. Hauksbee, simply.

"You dear!"

"Polly!—and for aught you knew you might have taken my fringe off. Never do that again without warning. Now we'll get the rooms ready. I don't suppose I shall be allowed to circulate in society for a month."

"And I also. Thank goodness I shall at last get all the sleep I want."

Much to Mrs. Bent's surprise she and the baby were brought over to the house almost before she knew where she was. Bent was devoutly and undisguisedly thankful, for he was afraid of the infection, and also hoped that a few weeks in the hotel alone with Mrs. Delville might lead to explanations. Mrs. Bent had thrown her jealousy to the winds in her fear for her child's life.

"We can give you good milk," said Mrs.

Hauksbee to her, "and our house is much nearer to the Doctor's than the hotel, and you won't feel as though you were living in a hostile camp. Where is the dear Mrs. Waddy? She seemed to be a particular friend of yours."

"They've all left me," said Mrs. Bent, bitterly. "Mrs. Waddy went first. She said I ought to be ashamed of myself for introducing diseases there, and I am *sure* it wasn't my fault that little Dora"—

"How nice!" cooed Mrs. Hauksbee. "The Waddy is an infectious disease herself—'more quickly caught than the plague and the taker runs presently mad.' I lived next door to her at the Elysium, three years ago. Now see, you won't give us the *least* trouble, and I've ornamented all the house with sheets soaked in carbolic. It smells comforting, doesn't it? Remember I'm always in call, and my *ayah's* at your service when yours goes to her meals and—and—if you cry I'll *never* forgive you."

Dora Bent occupied her mother's unprofitable attention through the day and the night. The Doctor called thrice in the twenty-four hours, and the house reeked with the smell of the Condy's Fluid, chlorine-water, and carbolic acid washes. Mrs. Mallowe kept to her own rooms—she considered that she had made sufficient concessions in the cause of humanity —and Mrs. Hauksbee was more esteemed by the Doctor as a help in the sick-room than the half-distraught mother.

"I know nothing of illness," said Mrs. Hauksbee to the Doctor. "Only tell me what to do, and I'll do it."

"Keep that crazy woman from kissing the child, and let her have as little to do with the nursing as you possibly can," said the Doctor; "I'd turn her out of the sick-room, but that I honestly believe she'd die of anxiety. She is less than no good, and I depend on you and the *ayahs,* remember."

Mrs. Hauksbee accepted the responsibility, though it painted olive hollows under her eyes and forced her to her oldest dresses. Mrs. Bent clung to her with more than childlike faith.

"I *know* you'll make Dora well, won't you?" she said at least twenty times a day; and twenty times a day Mrs. Hauksbee answered valiantly, "Of course I will."

But Dora did not improve, and the Doctor seemed to be always in the house.

"There's some danger of the thing taking a bad turn," he said; "I'll come over between three and four in the morning to-morrow."

"Good gracious!" said Mrs. Hauksbee. "He never told me what the turn would be! My education has been horribly neglected; and I have only this foolish mother-woman to fall back upon."

The night wore through slowly, and Mrs. Hauksbee dozed in a chair by the fire. There was a dance at the Viceregal Lodge, and she dreamed of it till she was aware of Mrs. Bent's anxious eyes staring into her own.

"Wake up! Wake up! Do something!" cried Mrs. Bent, piteously. "Dora's choking to death! Do you mean to let her die?"

Mrs. Hauksbee jumped to her feet and bent over the bed. The child was fighting for breath, while the mother wrung her hands despairing.

"Oh, what can I do? What can you do? She won't stay still! I can't hold her. Why didn't the Doctor say this was coming?" screamed Mrs. Bent. "*Won't* you help me? She's dying!"

"I—I've never seen a child die before!" stammered Mrs. Hauksbee, feebly, and then—let none blame her weakness after the strain of long watching—she broke down, and covered her face with her hands. The *ayahs* on the threshold snored peacefully.

There was a rattle of *'rickshaw* wheels below, the clash of an opening door, a heavy step on the stairs, and Mrs. Delville entered to find Mrs. Bent screaming for the Doctor as she ran round the room. Mrs. Hauksbee, her hands to her ears, and her face buried in the chintz of a chair, was quivering with pain at each cry from the bed, and murmuring, "Thank God, I never bore a child! Oh, thank God, I never bore a child!"

Mrs. Delville looked at the bed for an instant, took Mrs. Bent by the shoulders, and said, quietly, "Get me some caustic. Be quick."

The mother obeyed mechanically. Mrs. Delville had thrown herself down by the side of the child and was opening its mouth.

"Oh, you're killing her!" cried Mrs. Bent. "Where's the Doctor? Leave her alone!"

Mrs. Delville made no reply for a minute, but busied herself with the child.

"Now the caustic, and hold a lamp behind my shoulder. *Will* you do as you are told? The acid-bottle, if you don't know what I mean," she said.

A second time Mrs. Delville bent over the child. Mrs. Hauksbee, her face still hidden, sobbed and shivered. One of the *ayahs* staggered sleepily into the room, yawning: *"Doctor Sahib* come."

Mrs. Delville turned her head.

"You're only just in time," she said. "It was chokin' her when I came an' I've burned it."

"There was no sign of the membrane getting to the air-passages after the last steaming. It was the general weakness I feared," said the Doctor half to himself, and he whispered as he looked, "You've done what I should have been afraid to do without consultation."

"She was dyin'," said Mrs. Delville, under her breath. "Can you do anythin'? What a mercy it was I went to the dance!"

Mrs. Hauksbee raised her head.

"Is it all over?" she gasped. "I'm useless—I'm worse than useless! What are *you* doing here?"

She stared at Mrs. Delville, and Mrs. Bent, realizing for the first time who was the Goddess from the Machine, stared also.

Then Mrs. Delville made explanation, putting on a dirty long glove and smoothing a crumpled and ill-fitting ball-dress.

"I was at the dance, an' the Doctor was tellin' me about your baby bein' so ill. So I came away early, an' your door was open, an'

I—I—lost my boy this way six months ago, an' I've been tryin' to forget it ever since, an' I—I—I am very sorry for intrudin' an' anythin' that has happened."

Mrs. Bent was putting out the Doctor's eye with a lamp as he stooped over Dora.

"Take it away," said the Doctor. "I think the child will do, thanks to you, Mrs. Delville. *I* should have come too late, but, I assure you" —he was addressing himself to Mrs. Delville —"I had not the faintest reason to expect *this*. The membrane must have grown like a mushroom. Will one of you help me, please?"

He had reason for the last sentence. Mrs. Hauksbee had thrown herself into Mrs. Delville's arms, where she was weeping bitterly, and Mrs. Bent was unpicturesquely mixed up with both, while from the tangle came the sound of many sobs and much promiscuous kissing.

"Good gracious! I've spoilt all your beautiful roses!" said Mrs. Hauksbee, lifting her head from the lump of crushed gum and calico atrocities on Mrs. Delville's shoulder and hurrying to the Doctor.

Mrs. Delville picked up her shawl, and slouched out of the room, mopping her eyes with the glove that she had not put on.

"I always said she was more than a woman," sobbed Mrs. Hauksbee, hysterically, "and *that* proves it!"

* * * * * *

Six weeks later, Mrs. Bent and Dora had returned to the hotel. Mrs. Hauksbee had come out of the Valley of Humiliation, had ceased to reproach herself for her collapse in an hour of need, and was even beginning to direct the affairs of the world as before.

"So nobody died, and everything went off as it should, and I kissed The Dowd, Polly. I feel so old. Does it show in my face?"

"Kisses don't as a rule, do they? Of course you know what the result of The Dowd's providential arrival has been."

"They ought to build her a statue—only no sculptor dare copy those skirts."

"Ah!" said Mrs. Mallowe, quietly. "She has found another reward. The Dancing Master has been smirking through Simla, giving every one to understand that she came because of her undying love for him—for him—to save *his* child, and all Simla naturally believes this."

"But Mrs. Bent"—

"Mrs. Bent believes it more than any one else. She won't speak to The Dowd now. *Isn't* The Dancing Master an angel?"

Mrs. Hauksbee lifted up her voice and raged till bedtime. The doors of the two rooms stood open.

"Polly," said a voice from the darkness, "what did that American-heiress-globe-trotter girl say last season when she was tipped out of her *'rickshaw* turning a corner? Some absurd adjective that made the man who picked her up explode."

"'Paltry,'" said Mrs. Mallowe. "Through her nose—like this—'Ha-ow pahltry!'"

"Exactly," said the voice. "Ha-ow pahltry it all is!"

"Which?"

"Everything. Babies, Diphtheria, Mrs. Bent and The Dancing Master, I whooping in a chair, and The Dowd dropping in from the clouds. I wonder what the motive was—*all* the motives."

"Um!"

"What do *you* think?"

"Don't ask me. Go to sleep."

ONLY A SUBALTERN

ONLY A SUBALTERN

. . . Not only to enforce by command but to encourage by example the energetic discharge of duty and the steady endurance of the difficulties and privations inseparable from Military Service.—*Bengal Army Regulations.*

THEY made Bobby Wick pass an examination at Sandhurst. He was a gentleman before he was gazetted, so, when the Empress announced that "Gentleman-Cadet Robert Hanna Wick" was posted as Second Lieutenant to the Tyneside Tail Twisters at Krab Bokhar, he became an officer *and* a gentleman, which is an enviable thing; and there was joy in the house of Wick where Mamma Wick and all the little Wicks fell upon their knees and offered incense to Bobby by virtue of his achievements.

Papa Wick had been a Commissioner in his day, holding authority over three millions of men in the Chota-Buldana Division, building great works for the good of the land, and doing his best to make two blades of grass grow where there was but one before. Of course, nobody knew anything about this in the little English village where he was just "old Mr. Wick" and had forgotten that he was a Companion of the Order of the Star of India.

He patted Bobby on the shoulder and said: "Well done, my boy!"

There followed, while the uniform was being prepared, an interval of pure delight, during which Bobby took brevet-rank as a "man" at the women-swamped tennis-parties and tea-fights of the village, and, I dare say, had his joining-time been extended, would have fallen in love with several girls at once. Little country villages at Home are very full of nice girls, because all the young men come out to India to make their fortunes.

"India," said Papa Wick, "is the place. I've had thirty years of it and, begad, I'd like to go back again. When you join the Tail Twisters you'll be among friends, if every one hasn't forgotten Wick of Chota-Buldana, and a lot of people will be kind to you for our sakes. The mother will tell you more about outfit than I can, but remember this: Stick to your Regiment, Bobby—stick to your Regiment. You'll see men all round you going into the Staff Corps, and doing every possible sort of duty but regimental, and you may be tempted to follow suit. Now so long as you keep within your allowance, and I haven't stinted you there, stick to the Line, the whole Line and nothing but the Line. Be careful how you back another young fool's bill, and if you fall in love with a woman twenty years older than yourself, don't tell *me* about it, that's all."

With these counsels, and many others equally valuable, did Papa Wick fortify Bobby ere that last awful night at Portsmouth when the Officers' Quarters held more inmates than were provided for by the Regulations, and the liberty-men of the ships fell foul of the drafts for India, and the battle raged from the Dockyard Gates even to the slums of Longport, while the Drabs of Fratton came down and scratched the faces of the Queen's Officers.

Bobby Wick, with an ugly bruise on his freckled nose, a sick and shaky detachment to manœuvre inship and the comfort of fifty scornful females to attend to, had no time to feel homesick till the *Malabar* reached mid-Channel, when he doubled his emotions with a little guard-visiting and a great many other matters.

The Tail Twisters were a most particular

Regiment. Those who knew them least said that they were eaten up with "side." But their reserve and their internal arrangements generally were merely protective diplomacy. Some five years before, the Colonel commanding had looked into the fourteen fearless eyes of seven plump and juicy subalterns who had all applied to enter the Staff Corps, and had asked them why the three stars should he, a Colonel of the Line, command a dashed nursery for double-dashed bottle-suckers who put on condemned tin spurs and rode qualified mokes at the hiatused heads of forsaken Black Regiments. He was a rude man and a terrible. Wherefore the remnant took measures [with the half-butt as an engine of public opinion] till the rumor went abroad that young men who used the Tail Twisters as a crutch to the Staff Corps, had many and varied trials to endure. However, a regiment had just as much right to its own secrets as a woman.

When Bobby came up from Deolali and took his place among the Tail Twisters, it was gently but firmly borne in upon him that the Regiment was his father and his mother and his indissolubly wedded wife, and that there was no crime under the canopy of heaven blacker than that of bringing shame on the

Regiment, which was the best-shooting, best-drilled, best set-up, bravest, most illustrious, and in all respects most desirable Regiment within the compass of the Seven Seas. He was taught the legends of the Mess Plate, from the great grinning Golden Gods that had come out of the Summer Palace in Pekin to the silver-mounted markhorhorn snuff-mull presented by the last C. O. [he who spake to the seven subalterns]. And every one of those legends told him of battles fought at long odds, without fear as without support; of hospitality catholic as an Arab's; of friendships deep as the sea and steady as the fighting-line; of honor won by hard roads for honor's sake; and of instant and unquestioning devotion to the Regiment—the Regiment that claims the lives of all and lives forever.

More than once, too, he came officially into contact with the Regimental colors, which looked like the lining of a bricklayer's hat on the end of a chewed stick. Bobby did not kneel and worship them, because British subalterns are not constructed in that manner. Indeed, he condemned them for their weight at the very moment that they were filling him with awe and other more noble sentiments.

But best of all was the occasion when he

moved with the Tail Twisters in review order at the breaking of a November day. Allowing for duty-men and sick, the Regiment was one thousand and eighty strong, and Bobby belonged to them; for was he not a Subaltern of the Line—the whole Line and nothing but the Line—as the tramp of two thousand one hundred and sixty sturdy ammunition boots attested? He would not have changed places with Deighton of the Horse Battery, whirling by in a pillar of cloud to a chorus of "Strong right! Strong left!" or Hogan-Yale of the White Hussars, leading his squadron for all it was worth, with the price of horseshoes thrown in; or "Tick" Boileau, trying to live up to his fierce blue and gold turban while the wasps of the Bengal Cavalry stretched to a gallop in the wake of the long, lollopping Walers of the White Hussars.

They fought through the clear cool day, and Bobby felt a little thrill run down his spine when he heard the *tinkle-tinkle-tinkle* of the empty cartridge-cases hopping from the breech-blocks after the roar of the volleys; for he knew that he should live to hear that sound in action. The review ended in a glorious chase across the plain—batteries thundering after cavalry to the huge disgust of the White

Hussars, and the Tyneside Tail Twisters hunting a Sikh Regiment, till the lean lathy Singhs panted with exhaustion. Bobby was dusty and dripping long before noon, but his enthusiasm was merely focused—not diminished.

He returned to sit at the feet of Revere, his "skipper," that is to say, the Captain of his Company, and to be instructed in the dark art and mystery of managing men, which is a very large part of the Profession of Arms.

"If you haven't a taste that way," said Revere, between his puffs of his cheroot, "you'll never be able to get the hang of it, but remember, Bobby, 'tisn't the best drill, though drill is nearly everything, that hauls a Regiment through Hell and out on the other side. It's the man who knows how to handle men—goat-men, swine-men, dog-men, and so on."

"Dormer, for instance," said Bobby, "I think he comes under the head of fool-men. He mopes like a sick owl."

"That's where you make your mistake, my son. Dormer isn't a fool *yet,* but he's a dashed dirty soldier, and his room corporal makes fun of his socks before kit-inspection. Dormer, being two-thirds pure brute, goes into a corner and growls."

"How do you know?" said Bobby, admiringly.

"Because a Company commander has to know these things—because, if he does *not* know, he may have crime—ay, murder—brewing under his very nose and yet not see that it's there. Dormer is being badgered out of his mind—big as he is—and he hasn't intellect enough to resent it. He's taken to quiet boozing and, Bobby, when the butt of a room goes on the drink, or takes to moping by himself, measures are necessary to pull him out of himself."

"What measures? 'Man can't run round coddling his men forever."

"No. The men would precious soon show him that he was not wanted. You've got to"—

Here the Color-Sergeant entered with some papers; Bobby reflected for a while as Revere looked through the Company forms.

"Does Dormer do anything, Sergeant?" Bobby asked, with the air of one continuing an interrupted conversation.

"No, sir. Does 'is dooty like a hortomato," said the Sergeant, who delighted in long words. "A dirty soldier, and 'e's under full stoppages for new kit. It's covered with scales, sir."

"Scales? What scales?"

"Fish-scales, sir. 'E's always pokin' in the

mud by the river an' a-cleanin' them *muchly*-fish with 'is thumbs." Revere was still absorbed in the Company papers, and the Sergeant, who was sternly fond of Bobby, continued,—" 'E generally goes down there when 'e's got 'is skinful, beggin' your pardon, sir, an' they *do* say that the more lush—in-*he*-briated 'e is, the more fish 'e catches. They call 'im the Looney Fishmonger in the Comp'ny, sir."

Revere signed the last paper and the Sergeant retreated.

"It's a filthy amusement," sighed Bobby to himself. Then aloud to Revere: "Are you really worried about Dormer?"

"A little. You see he's never mad enough to send to hospital, or drunk enough to run in, but at any minute he may flare up, brooding and sulking as he does. He resents any interest being shown in him, and the only time I took him out shooting he all but shot *me* by accident."

"I fish," said Bobby, with a wry face. "I hire a country-boat and go down the river from Thursday to Sunday, and the amiable Dormer goes with me—if you can spare us both."

"You blazing young fool!" said Revere, but

his heart was full of much more pleasant words.

Bobby, the Captain of a *dhoni,* with Private Dormer for mate, dropped down the river on Thursday morning—the Private at the bow, the Subaltern at the helm. The Private glared uneasily at the Subaltern, who respected the reserve of the Private.

After six hours, Dormer paced to the stern, saluted, and said—"Bey y' pardon, sir, but *was* you ever on the Durh'm Canal?"

"No," said Bobby Wick. "Come and have some tiffin."

They ate in silence. As the evening fell, Private Dormer broke forth, speaking to himself—

"Hi was on the Durh'm Canal, jes' such a night, come next week twelve month, a-trailin' *of* my toes in the water." He smoked and said no more till bedtime.

The witchery of the dawn turned the grey river-reaches to purple, gold, and opal; and it was as though the lumbering *dhoni* crept across the splendors of a new heaven.

Private Dormer popped his head out of his blanket and gazed at the glory below and around.

"Well—damn—my eyes!" said Private

Dormer, in an awed whisper. "This 'ere is like a bloomin' gallantry-show!" For the rest of the day he was dumb, but achieved an ensanguined filthiness through the cleaning of big fish.

The boat returned on Saturday evening. Dormer had been struggling with speech since noon. As the lines and luggage were being disembarked, he found tongue.

"Beg y' pardon, sir," he said, "but would you—would you min' shakin' 'ands with me, sir?"

"Of course not," said Bobby, and he shook accordingly. Dormer returned to barracks and Bobby to mess.

"He wanted a little quiet and some fishing, I think," said Bobby. "My aunt, but he's a filthy sort of animal! Have you ever seen him clean 'them *muchly*-fish with 'is thumbs'?"

"Anyhow," said Revere, three weeks later "he's doing his best to keep his things clean."

When the spring died, Bobby joined in the general scramble for Hill leave, and to his surprise and delight secured three months.

"As good a boy as I want," said Revere, the admiring skipper.

"The best of the batch," said the Adjutant to the Colonel. "Keep back that young skrimshanker Porkiss, sir, and let Revere make him sit up."

So Bobby departed joyously to Simla Pahar with a tin box of gorgeous raiment.

"'Son of Wick—old Wick of Chota-Buldana? Ask him to dinner, dear," said the aged men.

"What a nice boy!" said the matrons and the maids.

"First-class place, Simla. Oh, ri—ipping!" said Bobby Wick, and ordered new white cord breeches on the strength of it.

"We're in a bad way," wrote Revere to Bobby at the end of two months. "Since you left, the Regiment has taken to fever and is fairly rotten with it—two hundred in hospital, about a hundred in cells—drinking deep to keep off fever—and the Companies on parade fifteen file strong at the outside. There's rather more sickness in the out-villages than I care for, but then I'm so blistered with prickly-heat that I'm ready to hang myself. What's the yarn about your mashing a Miss Haverley up there? Not serious, I hope? You're over-young to hang millstones round your neck, and the Colonel will turf you out of that in double-quick time if you attempt it."

It was not the Colonel that brought Bobby

out of Simla, but a much more to be respected Commandant. The sickness in the out-villages spread, the Bazar was put out of bounds, and then came the news that the Tail Twisters must go into camp. The message flashed to the Hill stations.—"Cholera—Leave stopped —Officers recalled." Alas, for the white gloves in the neatly soldered boxes, the rides and the dances and picnics that were to be, the loves half spoken, and the debts unpaid! Without demur and without question, fast as tonga could fly or pony gallop, back to their Regiments and their Batteries, as though they were hastening to their weddings, fled the subalterns.

Bobby received his orders on returning from a dance at Viceregal Lodge where he had—but only the Haverley girl knows what Bobby had said or how many waltzes he had claimed for the next ball. Six in the morning saw Bobby at the Tonga Office in the drenching rain, the whirl of the last waltz still in his ears, and an intoxication due neither to wine nor waltzing in his brain.

"Good man!" shouted Deighton of the Horse Battery, through the mists. "Whar you raise dat tonga? I'm coming with you. Ow! But I've a head and a half. *I* didn't sit out all night. They say the Battery's awful bad," and he hummed dolorously—

"Leave the what at the what's-its-name,
Leave the flock without shelter,
Leave the corpse uninterred.
Leave the bride at the altar!

"My faith! I'll be more bally corpse than bride, though, this journey. Jump in, Bobby. Get on, *Coachwan!*"

On the umbrella platform waited a detachment of officers discussing the latest news from the stricken cantonment, and it was here that Bobby learned the real condition of the Tail Twisters.

"They went into camp," said an elderly Major recalled from the whist-tables at Mussoorie to a sickly Native Regiment, "they went into camp with two hundred and ten sick in carts. Two hundred and ten fever cases only, and the balance looking like so many ghosts with sore eyes. A Madras Regiment could have walked through 'em."

"But they were as fit as be-damned when I left them!" said Bobby.

"Then you'd better make them as fit as be-damned when you rejoin," said the Major, brutally.

Bobby pressed his forehead against the rain-splashed windowpane as the train lumbered across the sodden Doab, and prayed for the health of the Tyneside Tail Twisters. Naini Tal had sent down her contingent with all speed; the lathering ponies of the Dalhousie Road staggered into Pathankot, taxed to the full stretch of their strength; while from cloudy Darjiling the Calcutta Mail whirled up the last straggler of the little army that was to fight a fight, in which was neither medal nor honor for the winning, against an enemy none other than "the sickness that destroyeth in the noonday."

And as each man reported himself, he said: "This is a bad business," and went about his own forthwith, for every Regiment and Battery in the cantonment was under canvas, the sickness bearing them company.

Bobby fought his way through the rain to the Tail Twisters' temporary mess, and Revere could have fallen on the boy's neck for the joy of seeing that ugly, wholesome phiz once more.

"Keep 'em amused and interested," said Revere. "They went on the drink, poor fools, after the first two cases, and there was no improvement. Oh, it's good to have you back, Bobby! Porkiss is a—never mind."

Deighton came over from the Artillery camp to attend a dreary mess dinner, and contributed to the general gloom by nearly weeping over the condition of his beloved Battery. Porkiss so far forgot himself as to insinuate that the presence of the officers could do no earthly good, and that the best thing would be to send the entire Regiment into hospital and "let the doctors look after them." Porkiss was demoralized with fear, nor was his peace of mind restored when Revere said coldly: "Oh! The sooner *you* go out the better, if that's your way of thinking. Any public school could send us fifty *good* men in your place, but it takes time, time, Porkiss, and money, and a certain amount of trouble, to make a Regiment. 'S'pose *you're* the person we go into camp for, eh?"

Whereupon Porkiss was overtaken with a great and chilly fear which a drenching in the rain did not allay, and, two days later, quitted this world for another where, men do fondly hope, allowances are made for the weaknesses of the flesh. The Regimental Sergeant-Major looked wearily across the Sergeants' Mess tent when the news was announced.

"There goes the worst of them," he said. "It'll take the best, and then, please God, it'll stop." The Sergeants were silent till one said: "It couldn't be *him!*" and all knew of whom Travis was thinking.

Bobby Wick stormed through the tents of his Company, rallying, rebuking, mildly, as is consistent with the Regulations, chaffing the faint-hearted; haling the sound into the watery sunlight when there was a break in the weather, and bidding them be of good cheer for their trouble was nearly at an end; scuttling on his dun pony round the outskirts of the camp and heading back men who, with the innate perversity of British soldiers, were always wandering into infected villages, or drinking deeply from rain-flooded marshes; comforting the panic-stricken with rude speech, and more than once tending the dying who had no friends—the men without "townies"; organizing, with banjos and burned cork, Sing-songs which should allow the talent of the Regiment full play; and generally, as he explained, "playing the giddy garden-goat all round."

"You're worth a half a dozen of us, Bobby," said Revere in a moment of enthusiasm. "How the devil do you keep it up?"

Bobby made no answer, but had Revere looked into the breast-pocket of his coat he might have seen there a sheaf of badly-written letters which perhaps accounted for the power that possessed the boy. A letter came to Bobby every other day. The spelling was not above reproach, but the sentiments must have been most satisfactory, for on receipt Bobby's eyes softened marvelously, and he was wont to fall into a tender abstraction for a while ere, shaking his cropped head, he charged into his work.

By what power he drew after him the hearts of the roughest, and the Tail Twisters counted in their ranks some rough diamonds indeed, was a mystery to both skipper and C. O., who learned from the regimental chaplain that Bobby was considerably more in request in the hospital tents than the Reverend John Emery.

"The men seem fond of you. Are you in the hospitals much?" said the Colonel, who did his daily round and ordered the men to get well with a hardness that did not cover his bitter grief.

"A little, sir," said Bobby.

"Shouldn't go there too often if I were you. They say it's not contagious, but there's no use in running unnecessary risks. We can't afford to have you down, y' know."

Six days later, it was with the utmost difficulty that the post-runner plashed his way out to the camp with the mail-bags, for the rain was falling in torrents. Bobby received a letter, bore it off to his tent, and, the programme for the next week's Sing-song being satisfactorily disposed of, sat down to answer it. For an hour the unhandy pen toiled over the paper, and where sentiment rose to more than normal tide-level, Bobby Wick stuck out his tongue and breathed heavily. He was not used to letter-writing.

"Beg y' pardon, sir," said a voice at the tent door; "but Dormer's 'orrid bad, sir, an' they've taken him orf, sir."

"Damn Private Dormer and you too!" said Bobby Wick, running the blotter over the half-finished letter. "Tell him I'll come in the morning."

"'E's awful bad, sir," said the voice, hesitatingly. There was an undecided squelching of heavy boots.

"Well?" said Bobby, impatiently.

"Excusin' 'imself before'and for takin' the liberty, 'e says it would be a comfort for to assist 'im, sir, if"—

"Tattoo lao! Get my pony! Here, come in out of the rain till I'm ready. What blasted

nuisances you are! That's brandy. Drink some; you want it. Hang on to my stirrup and tell me if I go too fast."

Strengthened by a four-finger "nip" which he swallowed without a wink, the Hospital Orderly kept up with the slipping, mud-stained, and very disgusted pony as it shambled to the hospital tent.

Private Dormer was certainly " 'orrid bad." He had all but reached the stage of collapse and was not pleasant to look upon.

"What's this, Dormer?" said Bobby, bending over the man. "You're not going out this time. You've got to come fishing with me once or twice more yet."

The blue lips parted and in the ghost of a whisper said—"Beg y' pardon, sir, disturbin' of you now, but would you min' 'oldin' my 'and, sir?"

Bobby sat on the side of the bed, and the icy cold hand closed on his own like a vice, forcing a lady's ring which was on the little finger deep into the flesh. Bobby set his lips and waited, the water dripping from the hem of his trousers. An hour passed and the grasp of the hand did not relax, nor did the expression of the drawn face change. Bobby with infinite craft lit himself a cheroot with the left hand,

"'Beg y' pardon, Sir, but Dormer's 'orrid bad.'"

Only a Subaltern, p. 153

his right arm was numbed to the elbow, and resigned himself to a night of pain.

Dawn showed a very white-faced Subaltern sitting on the side of a sick man's cot, and a Doctor in the doorway using language unfit for publication.

"Have you been here all night, you young ass?" said the Doctor.

"There or thereabouts," said Bobby, ruefully. "He's frozen on to me."

Dormer's mouth shut with a click. He turned his head and sighed. The clinging hand opened, and Bobby's arm fell useless at his side.

"He'll do," said the Doctor, quietly. "It must have been a toss-up all through the night. 'Think you're to be congratulated on this case."

"Oh, bosh!" said Bobby. "I thought the man had gone out long ago—only—only I didn't care to take my hand away. Rub my arm down, there's a good chap. What a grip the brute has! I'm chilled to the marrow!" He passed out of the tent shivering.

Private Dormer was allowed to celebrate his repulse of Death by strong waters. Four days later, he sat on the side of his cot and said to the patients mildly: "I'd 'a' liken to 'a' spoken to 'im—so I should."

But at that time Bobby was reading yet another letter—he had the most persistent correspondent of any man in camp—and was even then about to write that the sickness had abated, and in another week at the outside would be gone. He did not intend to say that the chill of a sick man's hand seemed to have struck into the heart whose capacities for affection he dwelt on at such length. He did intend to enclose the illustrated programme of the forthcoming Sing-song whereof he was not a little proud. He also intended to write on many other matters which do not concern us, and doubtless would have done so but for the slight feverish headache which made him dull and unresponsive at mess.

"You are overdoing it, Bobby," said his skipper. "'Might give the rest of us credit of doing a little work. You go on as if you were the whole Mess rolled into one. Take it easy."

"I will," said Bobby. "I'm feeling done up, somehow." Revere looked at him anxiously and said nothing.

There was a flickering of lanterns about the camp that night, and a rumor that brought men out of their cots to the tent doors, paddling of the naked feet of doolie-bearers and the rush of a galloping horse.

"Wot's up?" asked twenty tents; and through twenty tents ran the answer—"Wick, 'e's down."

They brought the news to Revere and he groaned. "Any one but Bobby and I shouldn't have cared! The Sergeant-Major was right."

"Not going out this journey," gasped Bobby, as he was lifted from the doolie. "Not going out this journey." Then with an air of supreme conviction—"I *can't,* you see."

"Not if I can do anything!" said the Surgeon-Major, who had hastened over from the mess where he had been dining.

He and the Regimental Surgeon fought together with Death for the life of Bobby Wick. Their work was interrupted by a hairy apparition in a blue-grey dressing-gown who stared in horror at the bed and cried—"Oh, my Gawd! It can't be *'im!*" until an indignant Hospital Orderly whisked him away.

If care of man and a desire to live could have done aught, Bobby would have been saved. As it was, he made a fight of three days, and the Surgeon-Major's brow uncreased. "We'll save him yet," he said; and the Surgeon, who, though he ranked with the Captain, had a very youthful heart, went out upon the word and pranced joyously in the mud.

"Not going out this journey," whispered Bobby Wick, gallantly, at the end of the third day.

"Bravo!" said the Surgeon-Major. "That's the way to look at it, Bobby."

As evening fell a grey shade gathered round Bobby's mouth, and he turned his face to the tent wall wearily. The Surgeon-Major frowned.

"I'm awfully tired," said Bobby, very faintly. "What's the use of bothering me with medicine? I—don't—want—it. Let me alone."

The desire for life had departed, and Bobby was content to drift away on the easy tide of Death.

"It's no good," said the Surgeon-Major. "He doesn't want to live. He's meeting it, poor child." And he blew his nose.

Half a mile away, the regimental band was playing the overture to the Sing-song, for the men had been told that Bobby was out of danger. The clash of the brass and the wail of the horns reached Bobby's ears.

> Is there a single joy or pain
> That I should never kno-ow?
> You do not love me, 'tis in vain,
> Bid me good-bye and go!

An expression of hopeless irritation crossed the boy's face, and he tried to shake his head.

The Surgeon-Major bent down—"What is it? Bobby?"—"Not that waltz," muttered Bobby. "That's our own—our very ownest own. . . . Mummy dear."

With this he sank into the stupor that gave place to death early next morning.

Revere, his eyes red at the rims and his nose very white, went into Bobby's tent to write a letter to Papa Wick which should bow the white head of the ex-Commissioner of Chota-Buldana in the keenest sorrow of his life. Bobby's little store of papers lay in confusion on the table, and among them a half-finished letter. The last sentence ran: "So you see, darling, there is really no fear, because as long as I know you care for me and I care for you, nothing can touch me."

Revere stayed in the tent for an hour. When he came out his eyes were redder than ever.

* * * * * *

Private Conklin sat on a turned-down bucket, and listened to a not unfamiliar tune. Private Conklin was a convalescent and should have been tenderly treated.

"Ho!" said Private Conklin. "There's another bloomin' orf'cer da—ed."

The bucket shot from under him, and his eyes filled with a smythyful of sparks. A tall man in a blue-grey bedgown was regarding him with deep disfavor.

"You ought to take shame for yourself, Conky! Orf'cer—bloomin' orf'cer? I'll learn you to misname the likes of 'im. Hangel! *Bloomin'* Hangel! That's wot 'e is!"

And the Hospital Orderly was so satisfied with the justice of the punishment that he did not even order Private Dormer back to his cot.

IN THE MATTER OF A PRIVATE.

IN THE MATTER OF A PRIVATE

Hurrah! hurrah! a soldier's life for me!
Shout, boys, shout! for it makes you jolly and free.
—*The Ramrod Corps.*

PEOPLE who have seen, say that one of the quaintest spectacles of human frailty is an outbreak of hysterics in a girls' school. It starts without warning, generally on a hot afternoon, among the elder pupils. A girl giggles till the giggle gets beyond control. Then she throws up her head, and cries, *"Honk, honk, honk,"* like a wild goose, and tears mix with the laughter. If the mistress be wise, she will rap out something severe at this point to check matters. If she be tender-hearted, and send for a drink of water, the chances are largely in favor of another girl laughing at the afflicted one and herself collapsing. Thus the trouble spreads, and may end in half of what answers to the Lower Sixth of a boys' school rocking and whooping together. Given a week of warm weather, two stately promenades per diem, a heavy mutton and rice meal in the middle of the day, a certain amount of nagging from the teachers, and a few other things, some amazing effects develop. At least, this is what folk say who have had experience.

Now, the Mother Superior of a Convent and the Colonel of a British Infantry Regiment would be justly shocked at any comparison being made between their respective charges. But it is a fact that, under certain circumstances, Thomas in bulk can be worked up into dithering, rippling hysteria. He does not weep, but he shows his trouble unmistakably, and the consequences get into the newspapers, and all the good people who hardly know a Martini from a Snider say: "Take away the brute's ammunition!"

Thomas isn't a brute, and his business, which is to look after the virtuous people, demands that he shall have his ammunition to his hand. He doesn't wear silk stockings, and he really ought to be supplied with a new Adjective to help him to express his opinions: but, for all that, he is a great man. If you call him "the heroic defender of the national honor" one day, and "a brutal and licentious soldiery" the next, you naturally bewilder him, and he looks upon you with suspicion. There is nobody to speak for Thomas except people who have theories to work off on him; and nobody understands Thomas except Thomas, and he does not always know what is the matter with himself.

That is the prologue. This is the story:

Corporal Slane was engaged to be married to Miss Jhansi M'Kenna, whose history is well known in the regiment and elsewhere. He had his Colonel's permission, and, being popular with the men, every arrangement had been made to give the wedding what Private Ortheris called "eeklar." It fell in the heart of the hot weather, and, after the wedding, Slane was going up to the Hills with the bride. None the less, Slane's grievance was that the affair would be only a hired-carriage wedding, and he felt that the "eeklar" of that was meagre. Miss M'Kenna did not care so much. The Sergeant's wife was helping her to make her wedding dress, and she was very busy. Slane was, just then, the only moderately contented man in barracks. All the rest were more or less miserable.

And they had so much to make them happy, too. All their work was over at eight in the morning, and for the rest of the day they could lie on their backs and smoke Canteen-plug and swear at the punkah-coolies. They enjoyed a fine, full flesh meal in the middle of the day, and then threw themselves down on their cots and sweated and slept till it was cool enough to go out with their "towny," whose vocabulary contained less than six hundred words, and the Adjective, and whose views on every conceivable question they had heard many times before.

There was the Canteen, of course, and there was the Temperance Room with the second-hand papers in it; but a man of any profession cannot read for eight hours a day in a temperature of 96° or 98° in the shade, running up sometimes to 103° at midnight. Very few men, even though they get a pannikin of flat, stale, muddy beer and hide it under their cots, can continue drinking for six hours a day. One man tried, but he died, and nearly the whole regiment went to his funeral because it gave them something to do. It was too early for the excitement of fever or cholera. The men could only wait and wait and wait, and watch the shadow of the barrack creeping across the blinding white dust. That was a gay life.

They lounged about cantonments—it was too hot for any sort of game, and almost too hot for vice—and fuddled themselves in the evening, and filled themselves to distension with the healthy nitrogenous food provided for them, and the more they stoked the less exercise they took and more explosive they grew. Then tempers began to wear away, and men fell a-brooding over insults real or imaginary, for they had nothing else to think of. The tone of the repartees changed, and instead of saying light-heartedly: "I'll knock your silly face in," men grew laboriously polite and hinted that the cantonments were not big enough for themselves and their enemy, and that there would be more space for one of the two in another Place.

It may have been the Devil who arranged the thing, but the fact of the case is that Losson had for a long time been worrying Simmons in an aimless way. It gave him occupation. The two had their cots side by side, and would sometimes spend a long afternoon swearing at each other; but Simmons was afraid of Losson and dared not challenge him to a fight. He thought over the words in the hot still nights, and half the hate he felt toward Losson he vented on the wretched punkah-coolie.

Losson bought a parrot in the bazar, and

put it into a little cage, and lowered the cage into the cool darkness of a well, and sat on the well-curb, shouting bad language down to the parrot. He taught it to say: "Simmons, ye *so-oor,*" which means swine, and several other things entirely unfit for publication. He was a big gross man, and he shook like a jelly when the parrot had the sentence correctly. Simmons, however, shook with rage, for all the room were laughing at him—the parrot was such a disreputable puff of green feathers and it looked so human when it chattered. Losson used to sit, swinging his fat legs, on the side of the cot, and ask the parrot what it thought of Simmons. The parrot would answer: "Simmons, ye *so-oor.*" "Good boy," Losson used to say, scratching the parrot's head; "ye 'ear that, Sim?" And Simmons used to turn over on his stomach and make answer: "I 'ear. Take 'eed *you* don't 'ear something one of these days."

In the restless nights, after he had been asleep all day, fits of blind rage came upon Simmons and held him till he trembled all over, while he thought in how many different ways he would slay Losson. Sometimes he would picture himself trampling the life out of the man, with heavy ammunition-boots, and at others smashing in his face with the butt, and at others jumping on his shoulders and dragging the head back till the neckbone cracked. Then his mouth would feel hot and fevered, and he would reach out for another sup of the beer in the pannikin.

But the fancy that came to him most frequently and stayed with him longest was one connected with the great roll of fat under Losson's right ear. He noticed it first on a moonlight night, and thereafter it was always before his eyes. It was a fascinating roll of fat. A man could get his hand upon it and tear away one side of the neck; or he could place the muzzle of a rifle on it and blow away all the head in a flash. Losson had no right to be sleek and contented and well-to-do, when he, Simmons, was the butt of the room. Some day, perhaps, he would show those who laughed at the "Simmons, ye *so-oor*" joke, that he was as good as the rest, and held a man's life in the crook of his forefinger. When Losson snored, Simmons hated him more bitterly than ever. Why should Losson be able to sleep when Simmons had to stay awake hour after hour, tossing and turning on the tapes, with the dull liver pain gnawing into his right side and his head throbbing and aching after Canteen? He thought over this for many many nights, and the world became unprofitable to him. He even blunted his naturally fine appetite with beer and tobacco; and all the while the parrot talked at and made a mock of him.

The heat continued and the tempers wore away more quickly than before. A Sergeant's wife died of heat-apoplexy in the night, and the rumor ran abroad that it was cholera. Men rejoiced openly, hoping that it would spread and send them into camp. But that was a false alarm.

It was late on a Tuesday evening, and the men were waiting in the deep double verandas for "Last Posts," when Simmons went to the box at the foot of his bed, took out his pipe, and slammed the lid down with a bang that echoed through the deserted barrack like the crack of a rifle. Ordinarily speaking, the men would have taken no notice; but their nerves were fretted to fiddle-strings. They jumped up, and three or four clattered into the barrack-room only to find Simmons kneeling by his box.

"Ow! It's you, is it?" they said and laughed foolishly. "We thought 'twas"—

Simmons rose slowly. If the accident had

"Blind with rage and rushed at Slane."

In the Matter of a Private, p. 176

so shaken his fellows, what would not the reality do?

"You thought it was—did you? And what makes you think?" he said, lashing himself into madness as he went on; "to Hell with your thinking, ye dirty spies."

"Simmons, ye *so-oor,*" chuckled the parrot in the veranda, sleepily, recognizing a well-known voice. Now that was absolutely all.

The tension snapped. Simmons fell back on the arm-rack deliberately,—the men were at the far end of the room,—and took out his rifle and packet of ammunition. "Don't go playing the goat, Sim!" said Losson. "Put it down," but there was a quaver in his voice. Another man stooped, slipped his boot and hurled it at Simmons's head. The prompt answer was a shot which, fired at random, found its billet in Losson's throat. Losson fell forward without a word, and the others scattered.

"You thought it was!" yelled Simmons. "You're drivin' me to it! I tell you you're drivin' me to it! Get up, Losson, an' don't lie shammin' there—you an' your blasted parrit that druv me to it!"

But there was an unaffected reality about Losson's pose that showed Simmons what he had done. The men were still clamoring in the veranda. Simmons appropriated two more packets of ammunition and ran into the moonlight, muttering: "I'll make a night of it. Thirty roun's, an' the last for myself. Take you that, you dogs!"

He dropped on one knee and fired into the brown of the men on the veranda, but the bullet flew high, and landed in the brickwork with a vicious *pwhit* that made some of the younger ones turn pale. It is, as musketry theorists observe, one thing to fire and another to be fired at.

Then the instinct of the chase flared up. The news spread from barrack to barrack, and the men doubled out intent on the capture of Simmons, the wild beast, who was heading for the Cavalry parade-ground, stopping now and again to send back a shot and a curse in the direction of his pursuers.

"I'll learn you to spy on me!" he shouted; "I'll learn you to give me dorg's names! Come on the 'ole lot o' you! Colonel John Anthony Deever, C.B.!"—he turned toward the Infantry Mess and shook his rifle—"you think yourself the devil of a man—but I tell you that if you put your ugly old carcass outside o' that door, I'll make you the poorest-lookin' man in the army. Come out, Colonel John Anthony

Deever, C.B.! Come out and see me practiss on the rainge. I'm the crack shot of the 'ole bloomin' battalion." In proof of which statement Simmons fired at the lighted windows of the mess-house.

"Private Simmons, E Comp'ny, on the Cavalry p'rade-ground, Sir, with thirty rounds," said a Sergeant breathlessly to the Colonel. "Shootin' right and lef', Sir. Shot Private Losson. What's to be done, Sir?"

Colonel John Anthony Deever, C.B., sallied out, only to be saluted by a spurt of dust at his feet.

"Pull up!" said the Second in Command; "I don't want my step in that way, Colonel. He's as dangerous as a mad dog."

"Shoot him like one, then," said the Colonel, bitterly, "if he won't take his chance. *My* regiment, too! If it had been the Towheads I could have understood."

Private Simmons had occupied a strong position near a well on the edge of the parade-ground, and was defying the regiment to come on. The regiment was not anxious to comply, for there is small honor in being shot by a fellow-private. Only Corporal Slane, rifle in hand, threw himself down on the ground, and wormed his way toward the well.

"Don't shoot," said he to the men round him; "like as not you'll 'it me. I'll catch the beggar, livin'."

Simmons ceased shouting for a while, and the noise of trap-wheels could be heard across the plain. Major Oldyne, Commanding the Horse Battery, was coming back from a dinner in the Civil Lines; was driving after his usual custom—that is to say, as fast as the horse could go.

"A orf'cer! A blooming spangled orf'cer!" shrieked Simmons; "I'll make a scarecrow of that orf'cer!" The trap stopped.

"What's this?" demanded the Major of Gunners. "You there, drop your rifle."

"Why, it's Jerry Blazes! I ain't got no quarrel with you, Jerry Blazes. Pass frien', an' all's well!"

But Jerry Blazes had not the faintest intention of passing a dangerous murderer. He was, as his adoring Battery swore long and fervently, without knowledge of fear, and they were surely the best judges, for Jerry Blazes, it was notorious, had done his possible to kill a man each time the Battery went out.

He walked toward Simmons, with the intention of rushing him, and knocking him down. "Don't make me do it, Sir," said Simmons;

"I ain't got nothing agin you. Ah! you would?"—the Major broke into a run—"Take that then!"

The Major dropped with a bullet through his shoulder, and Simmons stood over him. He had lost the satisfaction of killing Losson in the desired way: but here was a helpless body to his hand. Should he slip in another cartridge, and blow off the head, or with the butt smash in the white face? He stopped to consider, and a cry went up from the far side of the parade-ground: "He's killed Jerry Blazes!" But in the shelter of the well-pillars Simmons was safe, except when he stepped out to fire. "I'll blow yer 'andsome 'ead off, Jerry Blazes," said Simmons, reflectively. "Six an' three is nine an' one is ten, an' that leaves me another nineteen, an' one for myself." He tugged at the string of the second packet of ammunition. Corporal Slane crawled out of the shadow of a bank into the moonlight.

"I see you!" said Simmons. "Come a bit furder on an' I'll do for you."

"I'm comin'," said Corporal Slane, briefly; "you've done a bad day's work, Sim. Come out 'ere an' come back with me."

"Come to,"—laughed Simmons, sending a

cartridge home with his thumb. "Not before I've settled you an' Jerry Blazes."

The Corporal was lying at full length in the dust of the parade-ground, a rifle under him. Some of the less-cautious men in the distance shouted: "Shoot 'im! Shoot 'im, Slane!"

"You move 'and or foot, Slane," said Simmons, "an' I'll kick Jerry Blazes' 'ead in, and shoot you after."

"I ain't movin'," said the Corporal, raising his head; "you daren't 'it a man on 'is legs. Let go o' Jerry Blazes an' come out o' that with your fistes. Come an' 'it me. You daren't, you bloomin' dog-shooter!"

"I dare."

"You lie, you man-sticker. You sneakin', Sheeny butcher, you lie. See there!" Slane kicked the rifle away, and stood up in the peril of his life. "Come on, now!"

The temptation was more than Simmons could resist, for the Corporal in his white clothes offered a perfect mark.

"Don't misname me," shouted Simmons, firing as he spoke. The shot missed, and the shooter, blind with rage, threw his rifle down and rushed at Slane from the protection of the well. Within striking distance, he kicked savagely at Slane's stomach, but the weedy

Corporal knew something of Simmons's weakness, and knew, too, the deadly guard for that kick. Bowing forward and drawing up his right leg till the heel of the right foot was set some three inches above the inside of the left knee-cap, he met the blow standing on one leg—exactly as Gonds stand when they meditate—and ready for the fall that would follow. There was an oath, the Corporal fell over to his own left as shinbone met shinbone, and the Private collapsed, his right leg broken an inch above the ankle.

"'Pity you don't know that guard, Sim," said Slane, spitting out the dust as he rose. Then raising his voice—"Come an' take him orf. I've bruk 'is leg." This was not strictly true, for the Private had accomplished his own downfall, since it is the special merit of that leg-guard that the harder the kick the greater the kicker's discomfiture.

Slane walked to Jerry Blazes and hung over him with ostentatious anxiety, while Simmons, weeping with pain, was carried away. "'Ope you ain't 'urt badly, Sir," said Slane. The Major had fainted, and there was an ugly, ragged hole through the top of his arm. Slane knelt down and murmured: "S'elp me, I believe 'e's dead. Well, if that ain't my blooming luck all over!"

But the Major was destined to lead his Battery afield for many a long day with unshaken nerve. He was removed, and nursed and petted into convalescence, while the Battery discussed the wisdom of capturing Simmons, and blowing him from a gun. They idolized their Major, and his reappearance on parade brought about a scene nowhere provided for in the Army Regulations.

Great, too, was the glory that fell to Slane's share. The Gunners would have made him drunk thrice a day for at least a fortnight. Even the Colonel of his own regiment complimented him upon his coolness, and the local paper called him a hero. These things did not puff him up. When the Major offered him money and thanks, the virtuous Corporal took the one and and put aside the other. But he had a request to make and prefaced it with many a "Beg y' pardon, Sir." Could the Major see his way to letting the Slane-M'Kenna wedding be adorned by the presence of four Battery horses to pull a hired barouche? The Major could, and so could the Battery. Excessively so. It was a gorgeous wedding.

* * * * * *

"Wot did I do it for?" said Corporal Slane. "For the 'orses o' course. Jhansi ain't a beauty to look at, but I wasn't goin' to 'ave a hired turnout. Jerry Blazes? If I 'adn't 'a' wanted something, Sim might ha' blowed Jerry Blazes' blooming 'ead into Hirish stew for aught I'd 'a' cared."

And they hanged Private Simmons—hanged him as high as Haman in hollow square of the regiment; and the Colonel said it was Drink; and the Chaplain was sure it was the Devil; and Simmons fancied it was both, but he didn't know, and only hoped his fate would be a warning to his companions; and half a dozen "intelligent publicists" wrote six beautiful leading articles on "The Prevalence of Crime in the Army."

But not a soul thought of comparing the "bloody-minded Simmons" to the squawking, gaping schoolgirl with which this story opens.

THE ENLIGHTENMENTS OF PAGETT, M.P.

THE ENLIGHTENMENTS OF PAGETT, M.P.

"Because half a dozen grasshoppers under a fern make the field ring with their importunate chink while thousands of great cattle, reposed beneath the shadow of the British oak, chew the cud and are silent, pray do not imagine that those who make the noise are the only inhabitants of the field—that, of course, they are many in number—or that, after all, they are other than the little, shrivelled, meagre, hopping, though loud and troublesome insects of the hour."—*Burke:* "Reflections on the Revolution in France."

THEY were sitting in the veranda of "the splendid palace of an Indian Pro-Consul"; surrounded by all the glory and mystery of the immemorial East. In plain English it was a one-storied, ten-roomed, whitewashed, mud-roofed bungalow, set in a dry garden of dusty tamarisk trees and divided from the road by a low mud wall. The green parrots screamed overhead as they flew in battalions to the river for their morning drink. Beyond the wall, clouds of fine dust showed where the cattle and goats of the city were passing afield to graze. The remorseless white light of the winter sunshine of Northern India lay upon everything and improved nothing, from the whining Persian-wheel by the lawn-tennis court to the long perspective of level road and the blue, domed tombs of Mohammedan saints just visible above the trees.

"A Happy New Year," said Orde to his guest. "It's the first you've ever spent out of England, isn't it?"

"Yes. 'Happy New Year," said Pagett, smiling at the sunshine. "What a divine climate you have here! Just think of the brown cold fog hanging over London now!" And he rubbed his hands.

It was more than twenty years since he had last seen Orde, his schoolmate, and their paths in the world had divided early. The one had quitted college to become a cog-wheel in the machinery of the great Indian Government; the other, more blessed with goods, had been whirled into a similar position in the English scheme. Three successive elections had not affected Pagett's position with a loyal constituency, and he had grown insensibly to regard himself in some sort as a pillar of the Empire, whose real worth would be known later on. After a few years of conscientious attendance at many divisions, after newspaper battles innumerable and the publication of interminable correspondence, and more hasty oratory than in his calmer moments he cared to think upon, it occurred to him, as it had occurred to many of his fellows in Parliament, that a tour to India would enable him to sweep a larger lyre and address himself to the problems of Imperial administration with a firmer hand. Accepting, therefore, a general invitation extended to him by Orde some years before, Pagett had taken ship to Karachi, and only over-night had been received with joy by the Deputy-Commissioner of Amara. They had sat late, discussing the changes and chances of twenty years, recalling the names of the dead, and weighing the futures of the living, as is the custom of men meeting after intervals of action.

Next morning they smoked the after breakfast pipe in the veranda, still regarding each other curiously, Pagett, in a light grey frock-coat and garments much too thin for the time of the year, and a puggried sun-hat carefully and wonderfully made. Orde in a shooting coat, riding breeches, brown cowhide boots with spurs, and a battered flax helmet. He had ridden some miles in the early morning to inspect a doubtful river dam. The men's faces differed as much as their attire. Orde's worn and wrinkled about the eyes, and grizzled at the temples, was the harder and more square of the two, and it was with something like envy that the owner looked at the comfortable outlines of Pagett's blandly receptive countenance, the clear skin, the untroubled eye, and the mobile, clean-shaved lips.

"And this is India!" said Pagett for the twentieth time, staring long and intently at the grey feathering of the tamarisks.

"One portion of India only. It's very much like this for 300 miles in every direction. By the way, now that you have rested a little—I wouldn't ask the old question before—what d'you think of the country?"

" 'Tis the most pervasive country that ever yet was seen. I acquired several pounds of your country coming up from Karachi. The air is heavy with it, and for miles and miles along that distressful eternity of rail there's no horizon to show where the air and earth separate."

"Yes. It isn't easy to see truly or far in India. But you had a decent passage out, hadn't you?"

"Very good on the whole. Your Anglo-Indian may be unsympathetic about one's political views; but he has reduced ship life to a science."

"The Anglo-Indian is a political orphan, and if he's wise he won't be in a hurry to be adopted by your party grandmothers. But how were your companions unsympathetic?"

"Well, there was a man called Dawlishe, a judge somewhere in this country it seems, and a capital partner at whist by the way, and when I wanted to talk to him about the progress of India in a political sense (Orde hid a grin, which might or might not have been sympathetic), the National Congress movement, and other things in which, as a Member of Parliament, I'm of course interested, he shifted the subject, and when I once cornered him, he looked me calmly in the eye, and said: 'That's all Tommy Rot. Come and have a game at Bull.' You may laugh; but that isn't the way to treat a great and important question; and, knowing who I was, well, I thought it rather rude, don't you know; and yet Dawlishe is a thoroughly good fellow."

"Yes; he's a friend of mine, and one of the straightest men I know. I suppose, like many Anglo-Indians, he felt it was hopeless to give you any just idea of any Indian question without the documents before you, and in this case the documents you want are the country and the people."

"Precisely. That was why I came straight to you, bringing an open mind to bear on things. I'm anxious to know what popular feeling in India is really like y'know, now that it has wakened into political life. The National Congress, in spite of Dawlishe, must have caused great excitement among the masses?"

"On the contrary, nothing could be more tranquil than the state of popular feeling; and as to excitement, the people would as soon be excited over the 'Rule of Three' as over the Congress."

"Excuse me, Orde, but do you think you are a fair judge? Isn't the official Anglo-Indian naturally jealous of any external influences that might move the masses, and so much opposed to liberal ideas, truly liberal ideas, that he can scarcely be expected to regard a popular movement with fairness?"

"What did Dawlishe say about Tommy Rot? Think a moment, old man. You and I were brought up together; taught by the same tutors, read the same books, lived the same life, and thought, as you may remember, in parallel lines. *I* come out here, learn new languages, and work among new races; while, you, more fortunate, remain at home. Why should I change my mind—our mind—because I change my sky? Why should I and the few hundred Englishmen in my service become unreasonable, prejudiced fossils, while you and your newer friends alone remain bright and open-minded? You surely don't fancy civilians are members of a Primrose League?"

"Of course not, but the mere position of an English official gives him a point of view which cannot but bias his mind on this question." Pagett moved his knee up and down a little uneasily as he spoke.

"That sounds plausible enough, but, like more plausible notions on Indian matters, I believe it's a mistake. You'll find when you come to consult the unofficial Briton that our fault, as a class—I speak of the civilian now—is rather to magnify the progress that has been made toward liberal institutions. It is of English origin, such as it is, and the stress of our work since the Mutiny—only thirty years ago—has been in that direction. No, I think you will get no fairer or more dispassionate view of the Congress business than such men as I can give you. But I may as well say at once that those who know most of India, from the inside, are inclined to wonder at the noise our scarcely begun experiment makes in England."

"But surely the gathering together of Congress delegates is of itself a new thing."

"There's nothing new under the sun. When Europe was a jungle half Asia flocked to the canonical conferences of Buddhism; and for centuries the people have gathered at Puri, Hurdwar, Trimbak, and Benares in immense numbers. A great meeting, what you call a mass meeting, is really one of the oldest and most popular of Indian institutions. In the case of the Congress meetings, the only notable fact is that the priests of the altar are British, not Buddhist, Jain or Brahmanical, and that the whole thing is a British contrivance kept alive by the efforts of Messrs. Hume, Eardley, Norton, and Digby."

"You mean to say, then, it's not a spontaneous movement?"

"What movement was ever spontaneous in any true sense of the word? This seems to be more factitious than usual. You seem to know a great deal about it; try it by the touchstone of subscriptions, a coarse but fairly trustworthy criterion, and there is scarcely the color of money in it. The delegates write from England that they are out of pocket for working expenses, railway fares, and stationery—the mere pasteboard and scaffolding of their show. It is, in fact, collapsing from mere financial inanition."

"But you cannot deny that the people of India, who are, perhaps, too poor to subscribe, are mentally and morally moved by the agitation," Pagett insisted.

"That is precisely what I *do* deny. The native side of the movement is the work of a limited class, a microscopic minority, as Lord Dufferin described it, when compared with the people proper, but still a very interesting class, seeing that it is of our own creation. It is composed almost entirely of those of the literary or clerkly castes who have received an English education."

"Surely that's a very important class. Its members must be the ordained leaders of popular thought."

"Anywhere else they might be leaders, but they have no social weight in this topsy-turvy land, and though they have been employed in clerical work for generations they have no practical knowledge of affairs. A ship's clerk is a useful person, but he is scarcely the captain; and an orderly-room writer, however smart he may be, is not the colonel. You see, the writer class in India has never till now aspired to anything like command. It wasn't allowed to. The Indian gentleman, for thousands of years past, has resembled Victor Hugo's noble:

> 'Un vrai sire
> Chatelain
> Laisse ecrire
> Le vilain.
> Sa main digne
> Quand il signe
> Égratigne
> Le velin.'

And the little *egratignures* he most likes to make have been scored pretty deeply by the sword."

"But this is childish and mediæval nonsense!"

"Precisely; and from your, or rather our, point of view the pen *is* mightier than the sword. In this country it's otherwise. The fault lies in our Indian balances, not yet adjusted to civilized weights and measures."

"Well, at all events, this literary class represents the natural aspirations and wishes of the people at large, though it may not exactly lead them, and, in spite of all you say, Orde, I defy you to find a really sound English Radical who would not sympathize with those aspirations."

Pagett spoke with some warmth, and he had scarcely ceased when a well-appointed dog-cart turned into the compound gates, and Orde rose saying:

"Here is Edwards, the Master of the Lodge I neglect so diligently, come to talk about accounts, I suppose."

As the vehicle drove up under the porch Pagett also rose, saying with the trained effusion born of much practice:

"But this is also *my* friend, my old and valued friend Edwards. I'm delighted to see you. I knew you were in India, but not exactly where."

"Then it isn't accounts, Mr. Edwards," said Orde, cheerily.

"Why, no, sir; I heard Mr. Pagett was coming, and as our works were closed for the New Year I thought I would drive over and see him."

"A very happy thought. Mr. Edwards, you may not know, Orde, was a leading member of our Radical Club at Switchton when I was beginning political life, and I owe much to his exertions. There's no pleasure like meeting an old friend, except, perhaps, making a new one. I suppose, Mr. Edwards, you stick to the good old cause?"

"Well, you see, sir, things are different out here. There's precious little one can find to say against the Government, which, was the main of our talk at home, and them that do say things are not the sort o' people a man who respects himself would like to be mixed up with. There are no politics, in a manner of speaking, in India. It's all work."

"Surely you are mistaken, my good friend. Why I have come all the way from England just to see the working of this great National movement."

"I don't know where you're going to find the nation as moves to begin with, and then you'll be hard put to it to find what they are moving about. It's like this, sir," said Edwards, who had not quite relished being called "my good friend." "They haven't got any grievance—nothing to hit with, don't you see, sir; and then there's not much to hit against, because the Government is more like a kind of general Providence, directing an old-established state of things, than that at home, where there's something new thrown down for us to fight about every three months."

"You are probably, in your workshops, full

of English mechanics, out of the way of learning what the masses think."

"I don't know so much about that. There are four of us English foremen, and between seven and eight hundred native fitters, smiths, carpenters, painters, and such like."

"And they are full of the Congress, of course?"

"Never hear a word of it from year's end to year's end, and I speak the talk, too. But I wanted to ask how things are going on at home—old Tyler and Brown and the rest?"

"We will speak of them presently, but your account of the indifference of your men surprises me almost as much as your own. I fear you are a backslider from the good old doctrine, Edwards." Pagett spoke as one who mourned the death of a near relative.

"Not a bit, sir, but I should be if I took up with a parcel of baboos, pleaders, and schoolboys, as never did a day's work in their lives, and couldn't if they tried. And if you was to poll us English railway men, mechanics, trades-people, and the like of that all up and down the country from Peshawur to Calcutta, you would find us mostly in a tale together. And yet you know we're the same English you pay some respect to at home at 'lection time, and we have the pull o' knowing something about it."

"This is very curious, but you will let me come and see you, and perhaps you will kindly show me the railway works, and we will talk things over at leisure. And about all old friends and old times," added Pagett, detecting with quick insight a look of disappointment in the mechanic's face.

Nodding briefly to Orde, Edwards mounted his dog-cart and drove off.

"It's very disappointing," said the Member to Orde, who, while his friend discoursed with Edwards, had been looking over a bundle of sketches drawn on grey paper in purple ink, brought to him by a Chuprassee.

"Don't let it trouble you, old chap," said Orde, sympathetically. "Look here a moment, here are some sketches by the man who made the carved wood screen you admired so much in the dining-room, and wanted a copy of, and the artist himself is here too."

"A native?" said Pagett.

"Of course," was the reply, "Bishen Singh is his name, and he has two brothers to help him. When there is an important job to do, the three go into partnership, but they spend most of their time and all their money in litigation over an inheritance, and I'm afraid they are getting involved. Thoroughbred Sikhs of the old rock, obstinate, touchy, bigoted, and cunning, but good men for all that. Here is Bishen Singh—shall we ask *him* about the Congress?"

But Bishen Singh, who approached with a respectful salaam had never heard of it, and he listened with a puzzled face and obviously feigned interest to Orde's account of its aims and objects, finally shaking his vast white turban with great significance when he learned that it was promoted by certain pleaders named by Orde, and by educated natives. He began with labored respect to explain how he was a poor man with no concern in such matters, which were all under the control of God, but presently broke out of Urdu into familiar Punjabi, the mere sound of which had a rustic smack of village smoke-reek and plough-tail, as he denounced the wearers of white coats, the jugglers with words who filched his field from him, the men whose backs were never bowed in honest work; and poured ironical scorn on the Bengali. He and one of his brothers had seen Calcutta, and being at work there had Bengali carpenters given to them as assistants.

"Those carpenters!" said Bishen Singh. "Black apes were more efficient workmates, and as for the Bengali babu—tchick!" The guttural click needed no interpretation, but Orde translated the rest, while Pagett gazed with interest at the wood-carver.

"He seems to have a most illiberal prejudice against the Bengali," said the M.P.

"Yes, it's very sad that for ages outside Bengal there should be so bitter a prejudice. Pride of race, which also means race-hatred, is the plague and curse of India and it spreads far," Orde pointed with his riding-whip to the large map of India on the veranda wall.

"See! I begin with the North," said he. "There's the Afghan, and, as a highlander, he despises all the dwellers in Hindoostan—with the exception of the Sikh, whom he hates as cordially as the Sikh hates him. The Hindu loathes Sikh and Afghan, and the Rajput—that's a little lower down across this yellow blot of desert—has a strong objection, to put it mildly, to the Maratha who, by the way, poisonously hates the Afghan. Let's go North a minute. The Sindhi hates everybody I've mentioned. Very good, we'll take less warlike races. The cultivator of Northern India domineers over the man in the next province, and the Behari of the Northwest ridicules the Bengali. They are all at one on that point. I'm giving you merely the roughest possible outlines of the facts, of course."

Bishen Singh, his clean cut nostrils still quivering, watched the large sweep of the whip as it traveled from the frontier, through Sindh, the Punjab and Rajputana, till it rested by the valley of the Jumna.

"Hate—eternal and inextinguishable hate," concluded Orde, flicking the lash of the whip across the large map from East to West as he sat down. "Remember Canning's advice to Lord Granville. 'Never write or speak of Indian things without looking at a map.' "

Pagett opened his eyes, Orde resumed. "And the race-hatred is only a part of it. What's really the matter with Bishen Singh is class-hatred, which, unfortunately, is even more intense and more widely spread. That's one of the little drawbacks of caste, which some of your recent English writers find an impeccable system."

The wood-carver was glad to be recalled to the business of his craft, and his eyes shone as he received instructions for a carved wooden doorway for Pagett, which he promised should be splendidly executed and despatched to England in six months. It is an irrelevant detail, but in spite of Orde's reminders, fourteen months elapsed before the work was finished. Business over, Bishen Singh hung about, reluctant to take his leave, and at last joining his hands and approaching Orde with bated breath and whispering humbleness, said he had a petition to make. Orde's face suddenly lost all trace of expression. "Speak on, Bishen Singh," said he, and the carver in a whining tone explained that his case against his brothers was fixed for hearing before a native judge and—here he dropped his voice still lower till he was summarily stopped by Orde, who sternly pointed to the gate with an emphatic "Begone!"

Bishen Singh, showing but little sign of discomposure, salaamed respectfully to the friends and departed.

Pagett looked inquiry; Orde with complete recovery of his usual urbanity, replied: "It's nothing, only the old story, he wants his case to be tried by an English judge—they all do that—but when he began to hint that the other side were in improper relations with the native judge I had to shut him up. Gunga Ram, the man he wanted to make insinuations about, may not be very bright; but he's as honest as daylight on the bench. But that's just what one can't get a native to believe."

"Do you really mean to say these people prefer to have their cases tried by English judges?"

"Why, certainly."

Pagett drew a long breath. "I didn't know that before." At this point a phaeton entered the compound, and Orde rose with "Confound it, there's old Rasul Ali Khan come to pay one of his tiresome duty calls. I'm afraid we shall never get through our little Congress discussion."

Pagett was an almost silent spectator of the grave formalities of a visit paid by a punctilious old Mohammedan gentleman to an Indian official; and much impressed by the distinction of manner and fine appearance of the Mohammedan landholder. When the exchange of polite banalities came to a pause, he expressed a wish to learn the courtly visitor's opinion of the National Congress.

Orde reluctantly interpreted, and with a smile which even Mohammedan politeness could not save from bitter scorn, Rasul Ali Khan intimated that he knew nothing about it and cared still less. It was a kind of talk encouraged by the Government for some mysterious purpose of its own and for his own part he wondered and held his peace.

Pagett was far from satisfied with this, and wished to have the old gentleman's opinion on the propriety of managing all Indian affairs on the basis of an elective system.

Orde did his best to explain, but it was plain the visitor was bored and bewildered. Frankly, he didn't think much of committees; they had a Municipal Committee at Lahore and had elected a menial servant, an orderly, as a member. He had been informed of this on good authority, and after that, committees had ceased to interest him. But all was according to the rule of Government, and, please God, it was all for the best.

"What an old fossil it is!" cried Pagett, as Orde returned from seeing his guest to the door; "just like some old blue-blooded hidalgo of Spain. What does he really think of the Congress after all, and of the elective system?"

"Hates it all like poison. When you are sure of a majority, election is a fine system; but you can scarcely expect the Mohammedans, the most masterful and powerful minority in the country, to contemplate their own extinction with joy. The worst of it is that he and his co-religionists, who are many, and the landed proprietors, also, of Hindu race, are frightened and put out by this election business and by the importance we have bestowed on lawyers, pleaders, writers, and the like, who have, up to now, been in abject submission to them. They say little, but after all they are the most important fagots in the great bundle of communities, and all the glib bunkum in the world would not pay for their estrangement. They have controlled the land."

"But I am assured that experience of local self-government in your municipalities has been most satisfactory, and when once the principle is accepted in your centres, don't you know, it is bound to spread, and these important—ah'm—people of yours would learn it like the rest. I see no difficulty at all," and the smooth lips closed with the complacent snap habitual to Pagett, M.P., the "man of cheerful yesterdays and confident to-morrows."

Orde looked at him with a dreary smile.

"The privilege of election has been most reluctantly withdrawn from scores of municipalities, others have had to be summarily suppressed, and, outside the Presidency towns, the actual work done has been badly performed. This is of less moment, perhaps—it only sends up the local death-rates—than the fact that the public interest in municipal elections, never very strong, has waned, and is waning, in spite of careful nursing on the part of Government servants."

"Can you explain this lack of interest?" said Pagett, putting aside the rest of Orde's remarks.

"You may find a ward of the key in the fact that only one in every thousand of our population can spell. Then they are infinitely more interested in religion and caste questions than in any sort of politics. When the business of mere existence is over, their minds are occupied by a series of interests, pleasures, rituals, superstitions, and the like, based on centuries of tradition and usage. You, perhaps, find it hard to conceive of people absolutely devoid of curiosity, to whom the book, the daily paper, and the printed speech are unknown, and you would describe their life as blank. That's a profound mistake. You are in another land, another century, down on the bed-rock of society, where the family merely, and not the community, is all-important. The average Oriental cannot be brought to look beyond his clan. His life, too, is more complete and self-sufficing, and less sordid and low-thoughted than you might imagine. It is bovine and slow in some respects, but it is never empty. You and I are inclined to put the cart before the horse, and to forget that it is the man that is elemental, not the book.

> 'The corn and the cattle are all my care,
> And the rest is the will of God.'

Why should such folk look up from their immemorially appointed round of duty and interests to meddle with the unknown and fuss with voting-papers. How would you, atop of all your interests care to conduct even one-tenth of your life according to the manners and customs of the Papuans, let's say? That's what it comes to."

"But if they won't take the trouble to vote, why do you anticipate that Mohammedans, proprietors, and the rest would be crushed by majorities of them?"

Again Pagett disregarded the closing sentence.

"Because, though the landholders would not move a finger on any purely political question, they could be raised in dangerous excitement by religious hatreds. Already the first note of this has been sounded by the people who are trying to get up an agitation on the cow-killing question, and every year there is trouble over the Mohammedan Muharrum processions."

"But who looks after the popular rights, being thus unrepresented?"

"The Government of Her Majesty the Queen, Empress of India, in which, if the Congress promoters are to be believed the people have an implicit trust; for the Congress circular, specially prepared for rustic comprehension, says the movement is *'for the remission of tax, the advancement of Hindustan, and the strengthening of the British Government.'* This paper is headed in large letters—'MAY THE PROSPERITY OF THE EMPRESS OF INDIA ENDURE.' "

"Really!" said Pagett, "that shows some cleverness. But there are things better worth imitation in our English methods of—er—political statement than this sort of amiable fraud."

"Anyhow," resumed Orde, "you perceive that not a word is said about elections and the elective principle, and the reticence of the Congress promoters here shows they are wise in their generation."

"But the elective principle must triumph in the end, and the little difficulties you seem to anticipate would give way on the introduction of a well-balanced scheme, capable of indefinite extension."

"But is it possible to devise a scheme which, always assuming that the people took any interest in it, without enormous expense, ruinous dislocation of the administration and danger to the public peace, can satisfy the aspirations of Mr. Hume and his following, and yet safeguard the interests of the Mohammedans, the landed and wealthy classes, the Conservative Hindus, the Eurasians, Parsees, Sikhs, Rajputs, native Christians, domiciled Europeans and others, who are each important and powerful in their way?"

Pagett's attention, however, was diverted to the gate, where a group of cultivators stood in apparent hesitation.

"Here are the twelve Apostles, by Jove!—come straight out of Raffaele's cartoons," said the M.P., with the fresh appreciation of a newcomer.

Orde, loth to be interrupted, turned impatiently toward the villagers, and their leader, handing his long staff to one of his companions, advanced to the house.

"It is old Jelloo, the Lumberdar, or headman of Pind Sharkot, and a very intelligent man for a villager."

The Jat farmer had removed his shoes and stood smiling on the edge of the veranda. His strongly marked features glowed with russet bronze, and his bright eyes gleamed under deeply set brows, contracted by lifelong exposure to sunshine. His beard and moustache streaked with grey swept from bold cliffs of brow and cheek in the large sweeps one sees drawn by Michael Angelo, and strands of long black hair mingled with the irregularly piled wreaths and folds of his turban. The drapery of stout blue cotton cloth thrown over his broad shoulders and girt round his narrow loins, hung from his tall form in broadly sculptured folds, and he would have made a superb model for an artist in search of a patriarch.

Orde greeted him cordially, and after a polite pause the countryman started off with a long story told with impressive earnestness. Orde listened and smiled, interrupting the speaker at times to argue and reason with him in a tone which Pagett could hear was kindly, and finally checking the flux of words was about to dismiss him, when Pagett suggested that he should be asked about the National Congress.

But Jelloo had never heard of it. He was a poor man, and such things, by the favor of his Honor, did not concern him.

"What's the matter with your big friend that he was so terribly in earnest?" asked Pagett, when he had left.

"Nothing much. He wants the blood of the people in the next village, who have had smallpox and cattle plague prettly badly, and by the help of a wizard, a currier, and several pigs have passed it on to his own village. 'Wants to know if they can't be run in for this awful crime. It seems they made a dreadful charivari at the village boundary, threw a quantity of spell-bearing objects over the border, a buffalo's skull and other things; then branded a *chamár*—what you would call a currier—on his hinder parts and drove him and a number of pigs over into Jelloo's village. Jelloo says he can bring evidence to prove that the wizard directing these proceedings, who is a Sansi, has been guilty of theft, arson, cattle-killing, perjury and murder, but would prefer to have him punished for bewitching them and inflicting smallpox."

"And how on earth did you answer such a lunatic?"

"Lunatic! The old fellow is as sane as you or I; and he has some ground of complaint against those Sansis. I asked if he would like a native superintendent of police with some men to make inquiries, but he objected on the grounds the police were rather worse than smallpox and criminal tribes put together."

"Criminal tribes—er—I don't quite understand," said Pagett.

"We have in India many tribes of people who in the slack anti-British days became robbers, in various kind, and preyed on the people. They are being restrained and reclaimed little by little, and in time will become useful citizens, but they still cherish hereditary traditions of crime, and are a difficult lot to deal with. By the way what about the political rights of these folk under your schemes? The country people call them vermin, but I suppose they would be electors with the rest."

"Nonsense—special provision would be made for them in a well-considered electoral scheme, and they would doubtless be treated with fitting severity," said Pagett, with a magisterial air.

"Severity, yes—but whether it would be fitting is doubtful. Even those poor devils have rights. and, after all, they only practice what they have been taught."

"But criminals, Orde!"

"Yes, criminals with codes and rituals of crime, gods and godlings of crime, and a hundred songs and sayings in praise of it. Puzzling, isn't it?"

"It's simply dreadful. They ought to be put down at once. Are there many of them?"

"Not more than about sixty thousand in this province, for many of the tribes broadly described as criminal are really vagabond and criminal only on occasion, while others are being settled and reclaimed. They are of great antiquity, a legacy from the past, the golden, glorious Aryan past of Max Müller, Birdwood and the rest of your spindrift philosophers."

An orderly brought a card to Orde, who took it with a movement of irritation at the interruption, and handed it to Pagett; a large card with a ruled border in red ink, and in the centre in schoolboy copper plate, *Mr. Dina Nath.* "Give salaam," said the civilian, and there entered in haste a slender youth, clad in closely fitting coat of grey homespun, tight trousers, patent-leather shoes, and a small black velvet cap. His thin cheek twitched, and his eyes wandered restlessly, for the young man was evidently nervous and uncomfortable, though striving to assume a free and easy air.

"Your honor may perhaps remember me," he said in English, and Orde scanned him keenly.

"I know your face somehow. You belonged to the Shershah district I think, when I was in charge there?"

"Yes, sir, my father is writer at Shershah, and your honor gave me a prize when I was first in the Middle School examination five years ago. Since then I have prosecuted my studies, and I am now second year's student in the Mission College."

"Of course: you are Kedar Nath's son—the boy who said he liked geography better than play or sugar cakes, and I didn't believe you. How is your father getting on?"

"He is well, and he sends his salaam, but his circumstances are depressed, and he also is down on his luck."

"You learn English idioms at the Mission College, it seems."

"Yes, sir, they are the best idioms, and my father ordered me to ask your honor to say a word for him to the present incumbent of your honor's shoes, the latchet of which he is not worthy to open, and who knows not Joseph; for things are different at Shershah now, and my father wants promotion."

"Your father is a good man, and I will do what I can for him."

At this point a telegram was handed to

Orde, who, after glancing at it, said he must leave his young friend whom he introduced to Pagett, "a member of the English House of Commons who wishes to learn about India."

Orde had scarcely retired with his telegram when Pagett began:

"Perhaps you can tell me something of the National Congress movement?"

"Sir, it is the greatest movement of modern times, and one in which all educated men like us *must* join. All our students are for the Congress."

"Excepting, I suppose, Mohammedans, and the Christians?" said Pagett, quick to use his recent instruction.

"These are some *mere* exceptions to the universal rule."

"But the people outside the College, the working classes, the agriculturists; your father and mother, for instance."

"My mother," said the young man, with a visible effort to bring himself to pronounce the word, "has no ideas, and my father is not agriculturist, nor working class; he is of the Kayeth caste; but he had not the advantage of a collegiate education, and he does not know much of the Congress. It is a movement for the educated young-man"—connecting adjective and noun in a sort of vocal hyphen.

"Ah, yes," said Pagett, feeling he was a little off the rails, " and what are the benefits you expect to gain by it?"

"Oh, sir, everything. England owes its greatness to Parliamentary institutions, and we should *at once* gain the same high position in scale of nations. Sir, we wish to have the sciences, the arts, the manufactures, the industrial factories, with steam engines, and other motive powers, and public meetings, and debates. Already we have a debating club in connection with the college, and elect a Mr. Speaker. Sir, the progress *must* come. You also are a Member of Parliament and worship the great Lord Ripon," said the youth, breathlessly, and his black eyes flashed as he finished his commaless sentences.

"Well," said Pagett, drily, "it has not yet occurred to me to worship his Lordship, although I believe he is a very worthy man, and I am not sure that England owes quite all the things you name to the House of Commons. You see, my young friend, the growth of a nation like ours is slow, subject to many influences, and if you have read your history aright"—

"Sir, I know it all—all! Norman Conquest, Magna Charta, Runnymede, Reformation, Tudors, Stuarts, Mr. Milton and Mr. Burke, and I have read something of Mr. Herbert Spencer and Gibbon's 'Decline and Fall,' Reynold's 'Mysteries of the Court,' and"—

Pagett felt like one who had pulled the string of a shower-bath unawares, and hastened to stop the torrent with a question as to what particular grievances of the people of India the attention of an elected assembly should be first directed. But young Mr. Dina Nath was slow to particularize. There were many, very many demanding consideration. Mr. Pagett would like to hear of one or two typical examples. The Repeal of the Arms Act was at last named, and the student learned for the first time that a license was necessary before an Englishman could carry a gun in England. Then natives of India ought to be allowed to become Volunteer Riflemen if they chose, and the absolute equality of the Oriental with his European fellow-subject in civil status should be proclaimed on principle, and the Indian Army should be considerably reduced. The student was not, however, prepared with answers to Mr. Pagett's mildest questions on these points, and he returned to vague generalities, leaving the M.P. so much impressed with the crudity of his views that he was glad on Orde's return to say good-bye to his "very interesting" young friend.

"What do you think of young India?" asked Orde.

"Curious, very curious—and callow."

"And yet," the civilian replied, "one can scarcely help sympathizing with him for his mere youth's sake. The young orators of the Oxford Union arrived at the same conclusions and showed doubtless just the same enthusiasm. If there were any political analogy between India and England, if the thousand races of this Empire were one, if there were any chance even of their learning to speak one language, if, in short, India were a Utopia of the debating-room, and not a real land, this kind of talk might be worth listening to, but it is all based on false analogy and ignorance of the facts."

"But he is a native and knows the facts."

"He is a sort of English schoolboy, but married three years, and the father of two weaklings, and knows less than most English schoolboys. You saw all he is and knows, and such ideas as he has acquired are directly hostile to the most cherished convictions of the vast majority of the people."

"But what does he mean by saying he is a

student of a mission college. Is he a Christian?"

"He meant just what he said, and he is not a Christian, nor ever will he be. Good people in America, Scotland, and England, most of whom would never dream of collegiate education for their own sons, are pinching themselves to bestow it in pure waste on Indian youths. Their scheme is an oblique, subterranean attack on heathenism; the theory being that with the jam of secular education, leading to a University degree, the pill of moral or religious instruction may be coaxed down the heaten gullet."

"But does it succeed; do they make converts?"

"They make no converts, for the subtle Oriental swallows the jam and rejects the pill; but the mere example of the sober, righteous, and godly lives of the principals and professors, who are most excellent and devoted men, must have a certain moral value. Yet, as Lord Lansdowne pointed out the other day, the market is dangerously overstocked with graduates of our Universities who look for employment in the administration. An immense number are employed, but year by year the college mills grind out increasing lists of youths foredoomed to failure and disappointment, and meanwhile, trade, manufactures, and the industrial arts are neglected, and in fact regarded with contempt by our new literary mandarins *in posse*."

"But our young friend said he wanted steam-engines and factories," said Pagett.

"Yes, he would like to direct such concerns. He wants to begin at the top, for manual labor is held to be discreditable, and he would never defile his hands by the apprenticeship which the architects, engineers, and manufacturers of England cheerfully undergo; and he would be aghast to learn that the leading names of industrial enterprise in England belonged a generation or two since, or now belong, to men who wrought with their own hands. And, though he talks glibly of manufacturers, he refuses to see that the Indian manufacturer of the future will be the despised workman of the present. It was proposed, for example, a few weeks ago, that a certain municipality in this province should establish an elementary technical school for the sons of workmen. The stress of the opposition to the plan came from a pleader who owed all he had to a college education bestowed on him gratis by Government and missions. You would have fancied some fine old crusted Tory squire of the last generation was speaking. 'These people,' he said, 'want no education, for they learn their trades from their fathers, and to teach a workman's son the elements of mathematics and physical science would give him ideas above his business. They must be kept in their place, and it is idle to imagine that there is any science in wood or iron work.' And he carried his point. But the Indian workman will rise in the social scale in spite of the new literary caste."

"In England we have scarcely begun to realize that there is an industrial class in this country, yet, I suppose, the example of men, like Edwards, for instance, must tell," said Pagett, thoughtfully.

"That you shouldn't know much about it is natural enough, for there are but few sources of information. India in this, as in other respects, is like a badly kept ledger—not written up to date. And men like Edwards are, in reality, missionaries, who by precept and example are teaching more lessons than they know. Only a few, however, of their crowds of subordinates seem to care to try to emulate them, and aim at individual advancement; the rest drop into the ancient Indian caste groove."

"How do you mean?" asked Pagett.

"Well, it is found that the new railway and factory workmen, the fitter, the smith, the engine-driver, and the rest are already forming separate hereditary castes. You may notice this down at Jamalpur in Bengal, one of the oldest railway centres; and at other places, and in other industries, they are following the same inexorable Indian law."

"Which means?"—queried Pagett.

"It means that the rooted habit of the people is to gather in small self-contained, self-sufficing family groups with no thought or care for any interests but their own—a habit which is scarcely compatible with the right acceptation of the elective principle."

"Yet you must admit, Orde, that though our young friend was not able to expound the faith that is in him, your Indian army is too big."

"Not nearly big enough for its main purpose. And, as a side issue, there are certain powerful minorities of fighting folk whose interests an Asiatic Government is bound to consider. Arms is as much a means of livelihood as civil employ under Government and law. And it would be a heavy strain on British bayonets to hold down Sikhs, Jats, Bilochis, Rohillas, Rajputs, Bhils, Dogras, Pathans, and

Gurkhas to abide by the decisions of a numerical majority opposed to their interests. Leave the 'numerical majority' to itself without the British bayonets—a flock of sheep might as reasonably hope to manage a troop of collies."

"This complaint about excessive growth of the army is akin to another contention of the Congress party. They protest against the malversation of the whole of the moneys raised by additional taxes as a Famine Insurance Fund to other purposes. You must be aware that this special Famine Fund has all been spent on frontier roads and defences and strategic railway schemes as a protection against Russia."

"But there was never a special famine fund raised by special taxation and put by as in a box. No sane administrator would dream of such a thing. In a time of prosperity a finance minister, rejoicing in a margin, proposed to annually apply a million and a half to the construction of railways and canals for the protection of districts liable to scarcity, and to the reduction of the annual loans for public works. But times were not always prosperous, and the finance minister had to choose whether he would hang up the insurance scheme for a year or impose fresh taxation. When a farmer hasn't got the little surplus he hoped to have for buying a new wagon and draining a low-lying field corner, you don't accuse him of malversation, if he spends what he has on the necessary work of the rest of his farm."

A clatter of hoofs was heard, and Orde looked up with vexation, but his brow cleared as a horseman halted under the porch.

"Hello, Orde! just looked in to ask if you are coming to polo on Tuesday: we want you badly to help to crumple up the Krab Bokhar team."

Orde explained that he had to go out into the District, and while the visitor complained that though good men wouldn't play, duffers were always keen, and that his side would probably be beaten, Pagett rose to look at his mount, a red, lathered Biloch mare, with a curious lyrelike incurving of the ears. "Quite a little thoroughbred in all other respects," said the M.P., and Orde presented Mr. Reginald Burke, Manager of the Sind and Sialkote Bank to his friend.

"Yes, she's as good as they make 'em, and she's all the female I possess and spoiled in consequence, aren't you, old girl?" said Burke, patting the mare's glossy neck as she backed and plunged.

"Mr. Pagett," said Orde, "has been asking

me about the Congress. What is your opinion?" Burke turned to the M.P. with a frank smile.

"Well, if it's all the same to you, sir, I should say, 'Damn the Congress,' but then I'm no politician, but only a business man."

"You find it a tiresome subject?"

"Yes, it's all that, and worse than that, for this kind of agitation is anything but wholesome for the country."

"How do you mean?"

"It would be a long job to explain, and *Sara* here won't stand, but you know how sensitive capital is, and how timid investors are. All this sort of rot is likely to frighten them, and we can't afford to frighten them. The passengers aboard an ocean steamer don't feel reassured when the ship's way is stopped, and they hear the workmen's hammers tinkering at the engines down below. The old Ark's going on all right as she is, and only wants quiet and room to move. Them's my sentiments, and those of some other people who have to do with money and business."

"Then you are a thick-and-thin supporter of the Government as it is."

"Why, no! The Indian Government is much too timid with its money—like an old maiden aunt of mine—always in a funk about her investments. They don't spend half enough on railways for instance, and they are slow in a general way, and ought to be made to sit up in all that concerns the encouragement of private enterprise, and coaxing out into use the millions of capital that lie dormant in the country."

The mare was dancing with impatience, and Burke was evidently anxious to be off, so the men wished him good-bye.

"Who is your genial friend who condemns both Congress and Government in a breath?" asked Pagett, with an amused smile.

"Just now he is Reggie Burke, keener on polo than on anything else, but if you go to the Sind and Sialkote Bank to-morrow you would find Mr. Reginald Burke a very capable man of business, known and liked by an immense constituency North and South of this."

"Do you think he is right about the Government's want of enterprise?"

"I should hesitate to say. Better consult the merchants and chambers of commerce in Cawnpore, Madras, Bombay, and Calcutta. But though these bodies would like, as Reggie puts it, to make Government sit up, it is an elementary consideration in governing a country like India, which must be administered for the benefit of the people at large, that the counsels of those who resort to it for the sake of making money should be judiciously weighed and not allowed to overpower the rest. They are welcome guests here, as a matter of course, but it has been found best to restrain their influence. Thus the rights of plantation laborers, factory operatives, and the like, have been protected, and the capitalist, eager to get on, has not always regarded Government action with favor. It is quite conceivable that under an elective system the commercial communities of the great towns might find means to secure majorities on labor questions and on financial matters."

"They would act at least with intelligence and consideration."

"Intelligence, yes; but as to consideration, who at the present moment most bitterly resents the tender solicitude of Lancashire for the welfare and protection of the Indian factory operative? English and native capitalists running cotton mills and factories."

"But is the solitude of Lancashire in this matter entirely disinterested?"

"It is no business of mine to say. I merely indicate an example of how a powerful commercial interest might hamper a Government intent in the first place on the larger interests of humanity."

Orde broke off to listen a moment. "There's Dr. Lathrop talking to my wife in the drawing-room," said he.

"Surely not; that's a lady's voice, and if my ears don't deceive me, an American."

"Exactly, Dr. Eva McCreery Lathrop, chief of the new Women's Hospital here, and a very good fellow forbye. Good-morning, Doctor," he said, as a graceful figure came out on the veranda, "you seem to be in trouble. I hope Mrs. Orde was able to help you."

"Your wife is real kind and good, I always come to her when I'm in a fix, but I fear it's more than comforting I want."

"You work too hard and wear yourself out," said Orde, kindly. "Let me introduce my friend, Mr. Pagett, just fresh from home, and anxious to learn his India. You could tell him something of that more important half of which a mere man knows so little."

"Perhaps I could if I'd any heart to do it, but I'm in trouble, I've lost a case that was doing well, through nothing in the world but inattention on the part of a nurse I had begun to trust. And when I spoke only a small piece of my mind she collapsed in a whining heap on the floor. It is hopeless!"

The men were silent, for the blue eyes of the lady doctor were dim. Recovering herself she looked up with a smile, half sad, half humorous, "And I am in a whining heap, too; but what phase of Indian life are you particularly interested in, sir?"

"Mr. Pagett intends to study the political aspect of things and the possibility of bestowing electoral institutions on the people."

"Wouldn't it be as much to the purpose to bestow point-lace collars on them? They need many things more urgently than votes. Why it's like giving a bread-pill for a broken leg."

"Er—I don't quite follow," said Pagett, uneasily.

"Well, what's the matter with this country is not in the least political, but an all round entanglement of physical, social, and moral evils and corruptions, all more or less due to the unnatural treatment of women. You can't gather figs from thistles, and so long as the system of infant marriage, the prohibition of the remarriage of widows, the lifelong imprisonment of wives and mothers in a worse than penal confinement, and the withholding from them of any kind of education or treatment as rational beings continues, the country can't advance a step. Half of it is morally dead, and worse than dead, and that's just the half from which we have a right to look for the best impulses. It's right here where the trouble is, and not in any political considerations whatsoever."

"But do they marry so early?" said Pagett, vaguely.

"The average age is seven, but thousands are married still earlier. One result is that girls of twelve and thirteen have to bear the burden of wifehood and motherhood, and, as might be expected, the rate of mortality both for mothers and children is terrible. Pauperism, domestic unhappiness, and a low state of health are only a few of the consequences of this. Then, when, as frequently happens, the boy-husband dies prematurely, his widow is condemned to worse than death. She may not re-marry, must live a secluded and despised life, a life so unnatural, that she sometimes prefers suicide; more often she goes astray. You don't know in England what such words as 'infant-marriage, baby-wife, girl-mother, and virgin-widow' mean; but they mean unspeakable horrors here."

"Well, but the advanced political party here

will surely make it their business to advocate social reforms as well as political ones," said Pagett.

"Very surely they will do no such thing," said the lady doctor, emphatically. "I *wish* I could make you understand. Why, even of the funds devoted to the Marchioness of Dufferin's organization for medical aid to the women of India, it was said in print and in speech, that they would be better spent on more college scholarships for men. And in all the advanced parties' talk—God forgive them—and in all their programmes, they carefully avoid all such subjects. They will talk about the protection of the cow, for that's an ancient superstition—they can all understand that; but the protection of the women is a new and dangerous idea." She turned to Pagett impulsively:

"You are a member of the English Parliament. Can you do nothing? The foundations of their life are rotten—utterly and bestially rotten. I could tell your wife things that I couldn't tell you. I know the life—the inner life that belongs to the native, and I know nothing else; and believe me you might as well try to grow golden-rod in a mushroom-pit as to make anything of a people that are born and reared as these—these things are. The men talk of their rights and privileges. I have seen the women that bear these very men, and again—may God forgive the men!"

Pagett's eyes opened with a large wonder. Dr. Lathrop rose tempestuously.

"I must be off to lecture," said she, "and I'm sorry that I can't show you my hospital; but you had better believe, sir, that it's more necessary for India than all the elections in creation."

"That's a woman with a mission, and no mistake," said Pagett, after a pause.

"Yes; she believes in her work, and so do I," said Orde. "I've a notion that in the end it will be found that the most helpful work done for India in this generation was wrought by Lady Dufferin in drawing attention—what work that was, by the way, even with her husband's great name to back it!—to the needs of women here. In effect, native habits and beliefs are an organized conspiracy against the laws of health and happy life—but there is some dawning of hope now."

"How d' you account for the general indifference, then?"

"I suppose it's due in part to their fatalism and their utter indifference to all human suffering. How much do you imagine the great province of the Punjab with over twenty million people and half a score rich towns has contributed to the maintenance of civil dispensaries last year? About seven thousand rupees."

"That's seven hundred pounds," said Pagett, quickly.

"I wish it was," replied Orde; "but anyway, it's an absurdly inadequate sum, and shows one of the blank sides of Oriental character."

Pagett was silent for a long time. The question of direct and personal pain did not lie within his researches. He preferred to discuss the weightier matters of the law, and contented himself with murmuring: "They'll do better later on." Then, with a rush, returning to his first thought:

"But, my dear Orde, if it's merely a class movement of a local and temporary character, how d' you account for Bradlaugh, who is at least a man of sense, taking it up?"

"I know nothing of the champion of the New Brahmins but what I see in the papers. I suppose there is something tempting in being hailed by a large assemblage as the representative of the aspirations of two hundred and fifty millions of people. Such a man looks 'through all the roaring and the wreaths,' and does not reflect that it is a false perspective, which, as a matter of fact, hides the real complex and manifold India from his gaze. He can scarcely be expected to distinguish between the ambitions of a new oligarchy and the real wants of the people of whom he knows nothing. But it's strange that a professed Radical should come to be the chosen advocate of a movement which has for its aim the revival of an ancient tyranny. Shows how even Radicalism can fall into academic grooves and miss the essential truths of its own creed. Believe me, Pagett, to deal with India you want first-hand knowledge and experience. I wish he would come and live here for a couple of years or so."

"Is not this rather an *ad hominem* style of argument?"

"Can't help it in a case like this. Indeed, I am not sure you ought not to go further and weigh the whole character and quality and upbringing of the man. You must admit that the monumental complacency with which he trotted out his ingenious little Constitution for India showed a strange want of imagination and the sense of humor."

"No, I don't quite admit it," said Pagett.

"Well, you know him and I don't, but that's how it strikes a stranger." He turned on his heel and paced the veranda thoughtfully. "And, after all, the burden of the actual, daily unromantic toil falls on the shoulders of the men out here, and not on his own. He enjoys all the privileges of recommendation without responsibility, and we—well, perhaps, when you've seen a little more of India you'll understand. To begin with, our death rate's five times higher than yours—I speak now for the brutal bureaucrat—and we work on the refuse of worked-out cities and exhausted civilizations, among the bones of the dead."

Pagett laughed. "That's an epigrammatic way of putting it, Orde."

"Is it? Let's see," said the Deputy Commissioner of Amara, striding into the sunshine toward a half-naked gardener potting roses. He took the man's hoe, and went to a rain-scarped bank at the bottom of the garden.

"Come here, Pagett," he said, and cut at the sun-baked soil. After three strokes there rolled from under the blade of the hoe the half of a clanking skeleton that settled at Pagett's feet in an unseemly jumble of bones. The M.P. drew back.

"Our houses are built on cemeteries," said

Orde. "There are scores of thousands of graves within ten miles."

Pagett was contemplating the skull with the awed fascination of a man who has but little to do with the dead. "India's a very curious place," said he, after a pause.

"Ah? You'll know all about it in three months. Come in to lunch," said Orde.

AMERICAN NOTES

AT THE GOLDEN GATE

I

AT THE GOLDEN GATE

"Serene, indifferent to fate,
Thou sittest at the Western Gate;
Thou seest the white seas fold their tents,
Oh, warder of two continents;
Thou drawest all things, small and great,
To thee, beside the Western Gate."

THIS is what Bret Harte has written of the great city of San Francisco, and for the past fortnight I have been wondering what made him do it.

There is neither serenity nor indifference to be found in these parts; and evil would it be for the continents whose wardship were intrusted to so reckless a guardian.

Behold me pitched neck-and-crop from twenty days of the high seas into the whirl of California, deprived of any guidance, and left to draw my own conclusions. Protect me from the wrath of an outraged community if these letters be ever read by American eyes! San Francisco is a mad city—inhabited for the most part by perfectly insane people, whose women are of a remarkable beauty.

When the "City of Pekin" steamed through the Golden Gate, I saw with great joy that the blockhouse which guarded the mouth of the "finest harbor in the world, sir," could be silenced by two gunboats from Hong Kong with safety, comfort, and despatch. Also, there was not a single American vessel of war in the harbor.

This may sound bloodthirsty; but remember, I had come with a grievance upon me—the grievance of the pirated English books.

Then a reporter leaped aboard, and ere I could gasp held me in his toils. He pumped me exhaustively while I was getting ashore, demanding of all things in the world news about Indian journalism. It is an awful thing to enter a new land with a new lie on your lips. I spoke the truth to the evil-minded Custom House man who turned my most sacred raiment on a floor composed of stable refuse and pine splinters; but the reporter overwhelmed me not so much by his poignant audacity as his beautiful ignorance. I am sorry now that I did not tell him more lies as I passed into a city of three hundred thousand white men. Think of it! Three hundred thousand white men and women gathered in one spot, walking upon real pavements in front of plate-glass-windowed shops, and talking something that at first hearing was not very different from English. It was only when I had tangled myself up in a hopeless maze of small wooden houses, dust, street refuse, and children who played with empty kerosene tins, that I discovered the difference of speech.

"You want to go to the Palace Hotel?" said an affable youth on a dray. "What in hell are you doing here, then? This is about the lowest ward in the city. Go six blocks north to corner of Geary and Markey, then walk around till you strike corner of Gutter and Sixteenth, and that brings you there."

I do not vouch for the literal accuracy of these directions, quoting but from a disordered memory.

"Amen," I said. "But who am I that I should strike the corners of such as you name? Peradventure they be gentlemen of repute, and might hit back. Bring it down to dots, my son."

I thought he would have smitten me, but he didn't. He explained that no one ever used the word "street," and that every one was supposed to know how the streets ran, for sometimes the names were upon the lamps and sometimes they weren't. Fortified with these directions, I proceeded till I found a mighty street, full of sumptuous buildings four and five stories high, but paved with rude cobblestones, after the fashion of the year 1.

Here a tram-car, without any visible means of support, slid stealthily behind me and nearly struck me in the back. This was the famous cable car of San Francisco, which runs by gripping an endless wire rope sunk in the ground, and of which I will tell you more anon. A hundred yards further there was a slight commotion in the street, a gathering together of three or four, something that glittered as it moved very swiftly. A ponderous Irish gentleman, with priest's cords in his hat and a small nickel-plated badge on his fat bosom, emerged from the knot supporting a Chinaman who had been stabbed in the eye and was bleeding like a pig. The bystanders went their ways, and the Chinaman, assisted by the policeman, his own. Of course this was none of my business, but I rather wanted to know what had happened to the gentleman who had dealt the stab. It said a great deal for the excellence of the municipal arrangement of the town that a surging crowd did not at once block the street to see what was going forward. I was the sixth man and the last who assisted at the performance, and my curiosity was six times the greatest. Indeed, I felt ashamed of showing it.

There were no more incidents till I reached the Palace Hotel, a seven-storied warren of humanity with a thousand rooms in it. All the travel books will tell you about hotel arrangements in this country. They should be seen to be appreciated. Understand clearly—and this letter is written after a thousand miles of experiences—that money will not buy you service in the West. When the hotel clerk—the man who awards your room to you and who is supposed to give you information—when that resplendent individual stoops to attend to your wants, he does so whistling or humming or picking his teeth, or pauses to converse with some one he knows. These performances, I gather, are to impress upon you that he is a free man and your equal. From his general appearance and the size of his diamonds he ought to be your superior. There is no necessity for this swaggering self-consciousness of freedom. Business is business, and the man who is paid to attend to a man might reasonably devote his whole attention to the job. Out of office hours he can take his coach and four and pervade society if he pleases.

In a vast marble-paved hall, under the glare of an electric light, sat forty or fifty men, and for their use and amusement were provided spittoons of infinite capacity and generous gape. Most of the men wore frock-coats and top-hats—the things that we in India put on at a wedding-breakfast, if we possess them—but they all spat. They spat on principle. The spittoons were on the staircases, in each bedroom—yea, and in chambers even more sacred than these. They chased one into retirement, but they blossomed in chiefest splendor round the bar, and they were all used, every reeking one of them.

Just before I began to feel deathly sick another reporter grappled me. What he wanted to know was the precise area of India in square miles. I referred him to Whitaker. He had never heard of Whitaker. He wanted it from my own mouth, and I would not tell him. Then he swerved off, just like the other man, to details of journalism in our own country. I ventured to suggest that the interior economy of a paper most concerned the people who worked it.

"That's the very thing that interests us," he said. "Have you got reporters anything like our reporters on Indian newspapers?"

"We have not," I said, and suppressed the "thank God" rising to my lips.

"Why haven't you?" said he.

"Because they would die," I said.

It was exactly like talking to a child—a very rude little child. He would begin almost every sentence with, "Now tell me something about India," and would turn aimlessly from one question to the other without the least continuity. I was not angry, but keenly interested. The man was a revelation to me. To his questions I returned answers mendacious and evasive. After all, it really did not matter what I said. He could not understand. I can only hope and pray that none of the readers of the *Pioneer* will ever see that portentous interview. The man made me out to be an idiot several sizes more driveling than my destiny intended, and the rankness of his ignorance managed to distort the few poor facts with which I supplied him into large and elaborate lies. "Then," thought I, "the matter of American journalism shall be looked into later on. At present I will enjoy myself."

No man rose to tell me what were the lions of the place. No one volunteered any sort of conveyance. I was absolutely alone in this big city of white folk. By instinct I sought refreshment, and came upon a bar-room full of bad Salon pictures in which men with hats on the backs of their heads were wolfing food from a counter. It was the institution of the "free lunch" I had struck. You paid for a drink and got as much as you wanted to eat. For something less than a rupee a day a man can feed himself sumptuously in San Francisco, even though he be a bankrupt. Remember this if ever you are stranded in these parts.

Later I began a vast but unsystematic exploration of the streets. I asked for no names. It was enough that the pavements were full of white men and women, the streets clanging with traffic, and that the restful roar of a great city rang in my ears. The cable cars glided to all points of the compass at once. I took them one by one till I could go no further. San Francisco has been pitched down on the sand bunkers of the Bikaneer desert. About one-fourth of it is ground reclaimed from the sea—any old-timers will tell you all about that. The remainder is just ragged, unthrifty sand hills, to-day pegged down by houses.

From an English point of view there has not been the least attempt at grading those hills, and indeed you might as well try to grade the hillocks of Sind. The cable cars have for all practical purposes made San Francisco a dead level. They take no count of rise or fall, but slide equably on their appointed courses from one end to the other of a six-mile street. They turn corners almost at right angles, cross other lines, and for aught I know may run up the sides of houses. There is no visible agency of their flight, but once in a while you shall pass a five-storied building humming with machinery that winds up an everlasting wire cable, and the initiated will tell you that here is the mechanism. I gave up asking questions. If it pleases Providence to make a car run up and down a slit in the ground for many miles, and if for twopence halfpenny I can ride in that car, why shall I seek the reasons of the miracle? Rather let me look out of the windows till the shops give place to thousands and thousands of little houses made of wood (to imitate stone), each house just big enough for a man and his family. Let me watch the people in the cars and try to find out in what manner they differ from us, their ancestors.

It grieves me now that I cursed them (in the matter of book piracy), because I perceived that my curse is working and that their speech is becoming a horror already. They delude themselves into the belief that they talk English—the English—and I have already been pitied for speaking with "an English accent." The man who pitied me spoke, so far as I was concerned, the language of thieves. And they all do. Where we put the accent forward they throw it back, and *vice versâ;* where we give the long "a" they use the short, and words so simple as to be past mistaking they pronounce somewhere up in the dome of their heads. How do these things happen?

Oliver Wendell Holmes says that the Yankee school-marm, the cider and the salt codfish of the Eastern States, are responsible for what he calls a nasal accent. I know better. They stole books from across the water without paying for 'em, and the snort of delight was fixed in their nostrils forever by a just Providence. That is why they talk a foreign tongue to-day.

"Cats is dogs, and rabbits is dogs, and so's parrots. But this 'ere tortoise is an insect, so there ain't no charge," as the old porter said.

A Hindoo is a Hindoo and a brother to the man who knows his vernacular. And a Frenchman is French because he speaks his own language. But the American has no language. He is dialect, slang, provincialism, accent, and so forth. Now that I have heard their voices, all the beauty of Bret Harte is being ruined for me, because I find myself catching through the roll of his rhythmical prose the cadence of his peculiar fatherland. Get an American lady to read to you "How Santa Clause Came to Simpson's Bar," and see how much is, under her tongue, left of the beauty of the original.

But I am sorry for Bret Harte. It happened this way. A reporter asked me what I thought of the city, and I made answer suavely that it was hallowed ground to me, because of Bret Harte. That was true.

"Well," said the reporter, "Bret Harte claims California, but California don't claim Bret Harte. He's been so long in England that he's quite English. Have you seen our cracker factories or the new offices of the *Examiner*.

He could not understand that to the outside world the city was worth a great deal less than the man. I never intended to curse the people with a provincialism so vast as this.

But let us return to our sheep—which means the sea-lions of the Cliff House. They are the great show of San Francisco. You take a train which pulls up the middle of the street (it killed two people the day before yesterday, being unbraked and driven absolutely regardless of consequences), and you pull up somewhere at the back of the city on the Pacific beach. Originally the cliffs and their approaches must have been pretty, but they have been so carefully defiled with advertisements that they are now one big blistered abomination. A hundred yards from the shore stood a big rock covered with the carcasses of the sleek sea-beasts, who roared and rolled and walloped in the spouting surges. No bold man had painted the creatures sky-blue or advertised newspapers on their backs, wherefore they did not match the landscape, which was chiefly hoarding. Some day, perhaps, whatever sort of government may obtain in this country will make a restoration of the place and keep it clean and neat. At present the sovereign people, of whom I have heard so much already, are vending cherries and painting the virtues of "Little Bile Beans" all over it.

Night fell over the Pacific, and the white sea-fog whipped through the streets, dimming the splendors of the electric lights. It is the use of this city, her men and women folk, to parade between the hours of eight and ten a certain street called Kearney Street, where the finest shops are situated. Here the click of high heels on the pavement is loudest, here the lights are brightest, and here the thunder of the traffic is most overwhelming. I watched Young California, and saw that it was, at least, expensively dressed, cheerful in manner, and self-asserting in conversation. Also the women were very fair. Perhaps eighteen days aboard ship had something to do with my unreserved admiration. The maidens were of generous build, large, well groomed, and attired in raiment that even to my inexperienced eyes must have cost much. Kearney Street at nine o'clock levels all distinctions of rank as impartially as the grave. Again and again I loitered at the heels of a couple of resplendent beings, only to overhear, when I expected the level voice of culture, the staccato "Sez he," "Sez I" that is the mark of the white servant-girl all the world over.

This was depressing because, in spite of all that goes to the contrary, fine feathers ought to make fine birds. There was wealth—unlimited wealth—in the streets, but not an accent that would not have been dear at fifty cents. Wherefore, revolving in my mind that these folk were barbarians, I was presently enlightened and made aware that they also were the heirs of all the ages, and civilized after all. There appeared before me an affable stranger of prepossessing appearance, with a blue and an innocent eye. Addressing me by name, he claimed to have met me in New York, at the Windsor, and to this claim I gave qualified assent. I did not remember the fact, but since he was so certain of it, why, then—I waited developments.

"And what did you think of Indiana when you came through?" was the next question.

It revealed the mystery of previous acquaintance and one or two other things. With reprehensible carelessness my friend of the light-blue eye had looked up the name of his victim in the hotel register, and read "Indiana" for India.

The provincialism with which I had cursed his people extended to himself. He could not imagine an Englishman coming through the States from west to east instead of by the regularly ordained route. My fear was that in his delight in finding me so responsive he would make remarks about New York and the Windsor which I could not understand. And, indeed, he adventured in this direction once or twice, asking me what I thought of such and such streets, which from his tone I gathered to be anything but respectable. It is trying to talk unknown New York in almost unknown San Francisco. But my friend was merciful. He protested that I was one after his own heart, and pressed upon me rare and curious drinks at more than one bar. These drinks I accepted with gratitude, as also the cigars with which his pockets were stored. He would show me the life of the city. Having no desire to watch a weary old play again, I evaded the offer and received in lieu of the devil's instruction much coarse flattery. Curiously constituted is the soul of man. Knowing how and where this man lied, waiting idly for the finale, I was distinctly conscious, as he bubbled compliments in my ear, of soft thrills of gratified pride stealing from hat-rim to boot-heels. I was wise, quoth he—any body could see that with half an eye; sagacious, versed in the ways of the world, an acquaintance to be desired; one who had tasted the cup of life with discretion.

All this pleased me, and in a measure numbed the suspicion that was thoroughly aroused. Eventually the blue-eyed one discovered, nay, insisted, that I had a taste for cards (this was clumsily worked in, but it was my fault, for in that I met him half-way and allowed him no chance of good acting).

Hereupon I laid my head upon one side and simulated unholy wisdom quoting odds and ends of poker talk, all ludicrously misapplied. My friend kept his countenance admirably, and well he might, for five minutes later we arrived, always by the purest of chance, at a place where we could play cards and also frivol with Louisiana State Lottery tickets. Would I play?

"Nay," said I, "for to me cards have neither meaning nor continuity; but let us assume that I am going to play. How would you and your friends get to work? Would you play a straight game, or make me drunk, or—well, the fact is, I'm a newspaper man, and I'd be much obliged if you'd let me know something about bunco steering."

My blue-eyed friend erected himself into an obelisk of profanity. He cursed me by his gods—the right and left bower; he even cursed the very good cigars he had given me. But, the storm over, he quieted down and explained. I apologized for causing him to waste an evening, and we spent a very pleasant time together.

Inaccuracy, provincialism, and a too hasty rushing to conclusions, were the rocks that he had split on, but he got his revenge when he said:

"How would I play with you? From all the poppy-cock (*Anglice* bosh) you talked about poker, I'd ha' played a straight game, and skinned you. I wouldn't have taken the trouble to make you drunk. You never knew anything of the game, but how I was mistaken in going to work on you, makes me sick."

He glared at me as though I had done him an injury. To-day I know how it is that year after year, week after week, the bunco steerer, who is the confidence trick and the card-sharper man of other climes, secures his prey. He clavers them over with flattery as the snake clavers the rabbit. The incident depressed me because it showed I had left the innocent East far behind and was come to a country where a man must look out for himself. The very hotels bristled with notices about keeping my door locked and depositing my valuables in a safe. The white man in a lump is bad. Weeping softly for O-Toyo (little I knew that my heart was to be torn afresh from my bosom) I fell asleep in the clanging hotel.

Next morning I had entered upon the deferred inheritance. There are no princes in America—at least with crowns on their heads—but a generous-minded member of some royal family received my letter of introduction.

Ere the day closed I was a member of the two clubs, and booked for many engagements to dinner and party. Now, this prince, upon whose financial operations be continual increase, had no reason, nor had the others, his friends, to put himself out for the sake of one Briton more or less, but he rested not till he had accomplished all in my behalf that a mother could think of for her *débutante* daughter.

Do you know the Bohemian Club of San Francisco? They say its fame extends over the world. It was created, somewhat on the lines of the Savage, by men who wrote or drew things, and has blossomed into most unrepublican luxury. The ruler of the place is an owl—an owl standing upon a skull and crossbones, showing forth grimly the wisdom of the man of letters and the end of his hopes for immortality. The owl stands on the staircase, a statue four feet high; is carved in the woodwork, flutters on the frescoed ceiling, is stamped on the note-paper, and hangs on the walls. He is an ancient and honorable bird. Under his wing 'twas my privilege to meet with white men whose lives were not chained down to routine of toil, who wrote magazine articles instead of reading them hurriedly in the pauses of office-work, who painted pictures instead of contenting themselves with cheap etchings picked up at another man's sale of effects. Mine were all the rights of social intercourse, craft by craft, that India, stony-hearted stepmother of collectors, has swindled us out of. Treading soft carpets and breathing the incense of superior cigars, I wandered from room to room studying the paintings in which the members of the club had caricatured themselves, their associates, and their aims. There was a slick French audacity about the workmanship of these men of toil unbending that went straight to the heart of the beholder. And yet it was not altogether French. A dry grimness of treatment, almost Dutch, marked the difference. The men painted as they spoke —with certainty. The club indulges in revelries which it calls "jinks"—high and low, at intervals—and each of these gatherings is faithfully portrayed in oils by hands that know their business. In this club were no amateurs spoiling canvas, because they fancied they could handle oils without knowledge of shadows or anatomy—no gentleman of leisure ruining the temper of publishers and an already ruined market with attempts to write, "because everybody writes something these days."

My hosts were working, or had worked for their daily bread with pen or paint, and their talk for the most part was of the shop—shoppy—that is to say, delightful. They extended a large hand of welcome, and were as brethren, and I did homage to the owl and listened to their talk. An Indian club about Christmas-time will yield, if properly worked, an abundant harvest of queer tales; but at a gathering of Americans from the uttermost ends of their own continent, the tales are larger, thicker, more spinous, and even more azure than any Indian variety. Tales of the war I heard told by an ex-officer of the South over his evening drink to a colonel of the Northern army, my introducer, who had served as a trooper in the Northern Horse, throwing in emendations from time to time. "Tales of the Law," which in this country is an amazingly elastic affair, followed from the lips of a judge. Forgive me for recording one tale that struck me as new. It may interest the up-country Bar in India.

Once upon a time there was Samuelson, a young lawyer, who feared not God, neither regarded the Bench. (Name, age, and town of the man were given at great length.) To him no case had ever come as a client, partly because he lived in a district where lynch law prevailed, and partly because the most desperate prisoner shrunk from intrusting himself to the mercies of a phenomenal stammerer. But in time there happened an aggravated murder —so bad, indeed, that by common consent the citizens decided, as a prelude to lynching, to give the real law a chance. They could, in fact, gambol round that murder. They met— the court in its shirt-sleeves—and against the raw square of the Court House window a temptingly suggestive branch of a tree fretted the sky. No one appeared for the prisoner, and, partly in jest, the court advised young Samuelson to take up the case.

"The prisoner is undefended, Sam," said the court. "The square thing to do would be for you to take him aside and do the best you can for him."

Court, jury, and witness then adourned to the veranda, while Samuelson led his client aside to the Court House cells. An hour passed ere the lawyer returned alone. Mutely the audience questioned.

"May it p-p-please the c-court," said Samuelson, "my client's case is a b-b-b-bad one—a d-d-amn bad one. You told me to do the b-b-best I c-could for him, judge, so I've jest given him y-your b-b-bay gelding, an' told him to light out for healthier c-climes, my p-p-professional opinion being he'd be hanged quicker'n h-h-hades if he dallied here. B-by this time my client's 'bout fifteen mile out yonder somewheres. That was the b-b-best I could do for him, may it p-p-please the court."

The young man, escaping punishment in lieu of the prisoner, made his fortune ere five years.

Other voices followed, with equally wondrous tales of riata-throwing in Mexico and Arizona, of gambling at army posts in Texas, of newspaper wars waged in godless Chicago (I could not help being interested, but they were not pretty tricks), of deaths sudden and violent in Montana and Dakota, of the loves of half-breed maidens in the South, and fantastic huntings for gold in mysterious Alaska. Above all, they told the story of the building of old San Francisco, when the "finest collection of humanity on God's earth, sir, started this town, and the water came up to the foot of Market Street." Very terrible were some of the tales, grimly humorous the others, and the men in broadcloth and fine linen who told them had played their parts in them.

"And now and again when things got too

bad they would toll the city bell, and the Vigilance Committee turned out and hanged the suspicious characters. A man didn't begin to be suspected in those days till he had committed at least one unprovoked murder," said a calm-eyed, portly old gentleman.

I looked at the pictures around me, the noiseless, neat-uniformed waiter behind me, the oak-ribbed ceiling above, the velvet carpet beneath. It was hard to realize that even twenty years ago you could see a man hanged with great pomp. Later on I found reason to change my opinion. The tales gave me a headache and set me thinking. How in the world was it possible to take in even one thousandth of this huge, roaring, many-sided continent? In the tobacco-scented silence of the sumptuous library lay Professor Bryce's book on the American Republic.

"It is an omen," said I. "He has done all things in all seriousness, and he may be purchased for half a guinea. Those who desire information of the most undoubted, must refer to his pages. For me is the daily round of vagabondage, the recording of the incidents of the hour and intercourse with the traveling-companion of the day. I will not 'do' this country at all."

And I forgot all about India for fen days while I went out to dinners and watched the social customs of the people, which are entirely different from our customs, and was introduced to men of many millions. These persons are harmless in their earlier stages—that is to say, a man worth three or four million dollars may be a good talker, clever, amusing, and of the world; a man with twice that amount is to be avoided, and a twenty million man is—just twenty millions. Take an instance. I was speaking to a newspaper man about seeing the proprietor of his journal, as in my innocence I supposed newspaper men occasionally did. My friend snorted indignantly:

"See him! Great Scott! No. If he happens to appear in the office, I have to associate with him; but, thank Heaven! outside of that I move in circles where he cannot come."

And yet the first thing I have been taught to believe is that money was everything in America!

AMERICAN POLITICS

II

AMERICAN POLITICS

I HAVE been watching machinery in repose after reading about machinery in action.

An excellent gentleman, who bears a name honored in the magazine, writes, much as Disraeli orated, of "the sublime instincts of an ancient people," the certainty with which they can be trusted to manage their own affairs in their own way, and the speed with which they are making for all sorts of desirable goals. This he called a statement or purview of American politics.

I went almost directly afterward to a saloon where gentlemen interested in ward politics nightly congregate. They were not pretty persons. Some of them were bloated, and they all swore cheerfully till the heavy gold watch-chains on their fat stomachs rose and fell again; but they talked over their liquor as men who had power and unquestioned access to places of trust and profit.

The magazine writer discussed theories of

government; these men the practice. They had been there. They knew all about it. They banged their fists on the table and spoke of political "pulls," the vending of votes, and so forth. Theirs was not the talk of village babblers reconstructing the affairs of the nation, but of strong, coarse, lustful men fighting for spoil, and thoroughly understanding the best methods of reaching it.

I listened long and intently to speech I could not understand—or but in spots.

It was the speech of business, however. I had sense enough to know that, and to do my laughing outside the door.

Then I began to understand why my pleasant and well-educated hosts in San Francisco spoke with a bitter scorn of such duties of citizenship as voting and taking an interest in the distribution of offices. Scores of men have told me, without false pride, that they would as soon concern themselves with the public affairs of the city or state as rake muck with a steam-shovel. It may be that their lofty disdain covers selfishness, but I should be very sorry habitually to meet the fat gentlemen with shiny top-hats and plump cigars in whose society I have been spending the evening.

Read about politics as the cultured writer of

the magazine regards 'em, and then, and not till then, pay your respects to the gentlemen who run the grimy reality.

I'm sick of interviewing night editors who lean their chair against the wall, and, in response to my demand for the record of a prominent citizen, answer: "Well, you see, he began by keeping a saloon," etc. I prefer to believe that my informants are treating me as in the old sinful days in India I was used to treat the wondering globe-trotter. They declare that they speak the truth, and the news of dog politics lately vouchsafed to me in groggeries inclines me to believe, but I won't. The people are much too nice to slangander as recklessly as I have been doing.

Besides, I am hopelessly in love with about eight American maidens—all perfectly delightful till the next one comes into the room.

O-Toyo was a darling, but she lacked several things—conversation for one. You cannot live on giggles. She shall remain unmarried at Nagasaki, while I roast a battered heart before the shrine of a big Kentucky blonde, who had for a nurse when she was little a negro "mammy."

By consequence she has welded on California beauty, Paris dresses, Eastern culture, Europe trips, and wild Western originality, the queer, dreamy superstitions of the quarters, and the result is soul-shattering. And she is but one of many stars.

Item, a maiden, who believes in education and possesses it, with a few hundred thousand dollars to boot and a taste for slumming.

Item, the leader of a sort of informal salon where girls congregate, read papers, and daringly discuss metaphysical problems and candy —a sloe-eyed, black-browed, imperious maiden she.

Item, a very small maiden, absolutely without reverence, who can in one swift sentence trample upon and leave gasping half a dozen young men.

Item, a millionairess, burdened with her money, lonely, caustic, with a tongue keen as a sword, yearning for a sphere, but chained up to the rock of her vast possessions.

Item, a typewriter maiden earning her own bread in this big city, because she doesn't think a girl ought to be a burden on her parents, who quotes Théophile Gautier and moves through the world manfully, much respected for all her twenty inexperienced summers.

Item, a woman from cloud-land who has no history in the past or future, but is discreetly of the present, and strives for the confidences of male humanity on the grounds of "sympathy" (methinks this is not altogether a new type).

Item, a girl in a "dive," blessed with a Greek head and eyes, that seem to speak all that is best and sweetest in the world. But woe is me! She has no ideas in this world or the next beyond the consumption of beer (a commission on each bottle), and protests that she sings the songs allotted to her nightly without more than the vaguest notion of their meaning.

Sweet and comely are the maidens of Devonshire; delicate and of gracious seeming those who live in the pleasant places of London; fascinating for all their demureness the damsels of France, clinging closely to their mothers, with large eyes wondering at the wicked world; excellent in her own place and to those who understand her is the Anglo-Indian "spin" in her second season; but the girls of America are above and beyond them all. They are clever, they can talk—yea, it is said that they think. Certainly they have an appearance of so doing which is delightfully deceptive.

They are original, and regard you between the brows with unabashed eyes as a sister might look at her brother. They are instructed, too, in the folly and vanity of the male mind, for they have associated with "the boys" from babyhood, and can discerningly minister to both vices or pleasantly snub the possessor. They possess, moreover, a life among themselves, independent of any masculine associations. They have societies and clubs and unlimited tea-fights where all the guests are girls. They are self-possessed, without parting with any tenderness that is their sex-right; they understand; they can take care of themselves; they are superbly independent. When you ask them what makes them so charming, they say:

"It is because we are better educated than your girls, and—and we are more sensible in regard to men. We have good times all round, but we aren't taught to regard every man as a possible husband. Nor is he expected to marry the first girl he calls on regularly."

Yes, they have good times, their freedom is large, and they do not abuse it. They can go driving with young men and receive visits from young men to an extent that would make an English mother wink with horror, and neither driver nor drivee has a thought beyond the enjoyment of a good time. As certain, also, of their own poets have said:

> "Man is fire and woman is tow,
> And the devil he comes and begins to blow."

In America the tow is soaked in a solution that makes it fire-proof, in absolute liberty and large knowledge; consequently, accidents do not exceed the regular percentage arranged by the devil for each class and climate under the skies.

But the freedom of the young girl has its drawbacks. She is—I say it with all reluctance—irreverent, from her forty-dollar bonnet to the buckles in her eighteen-dollar shoes. She talks flippantly to her parents and men old enough to be her grandfather. She has a prescriptive right to the society of the man who arrives. The parents admit it.

This is sometimes embarrassing, especially when you call on a man and his wife for the sake of information—the one being a merchant of varied knowledge, the other a woman of the world. In five minutes your host has vanished. In another five his wife has followed him, and you are left alone with a very charming maiden, doubtless, but certainly not the person you came to see. She chatters, and you grin, but you leave with the very strong impression of a wasted morning. This has been my experience once or twice. I have even said as pointedly as I dared to a man:

"I came to see you."

"You'd better see me in my office, then. The house belongs to my women folk—to my daughter, that is to say."

He spoke the truth. The American of wealth is owned by his family. They exploit him for bullion. The women get the ha'pence, the kicks are all his own. Nothing is too good for an American's daughter (I speak here of the moneyed classes).

The girls take every gift as a matter of course, and yet they develop greatly when a catastrophe arrives and the man of many millions goes up or goes down, and his daughters take to stenography or typewriting. I have heard many tales of heroism from the lips of girls who counted the principals among their friends. The crash came, Mamie, or Hattie, or Sadie, gave up their maid, their carriages and candy, and with a No. 2 Remington and a stout heart set about earning their daily bread.

"And did I drop her from the list of my friends? No, sir," said a scarlet-lipped vision in white lace; "that might happen to us any day."

It may be this sense of possible disaster in the air that makes San Francisco society go with so captivating a rush and whirl. Recklessness is in the air. I can't explain where it comes from, but there it is. The roaring winds of the Pacific make you drunk to begin with. The aggressive luxury on all sides helps out the intoxication, and you spin forever "down the ringing grooves of change" (there is no small change, by the way, west of the Rockies) as long as money lasts. They make greatly and they spend lavishly; not only the rich, but the artisans, who pay nearly five pounds for a suit of clothes, and for other luxuries in proportion.

The young men rejoice in the days of their youth. They gamble, yacht, race, enjoy prize-fights and cock-fights, the one openly, the other in secret; they establish luxurious clubs; they break themselves over horse-flesh and other things, and they are instant in a quarrel. At twenty they are experienced in business, embark in vast enterprises, take partners as experienced as themselves, and go to pieces with as much splendor as their neighbors. Remember that the men who stocked California in the fifties were physically, and, as far as regards certain tough virtues, the pick of the earth. The inept and the weakly died *en route*, or went under in the days of construction. To this nucleus were added all the races of the

Continent—French, Italian, German, and, of course, the Jew.

The result you can see in the large-boned, deep-chested, delicate-handed women, and long, elastic, well-built boys. It needs no little golden badge swinging from the watch-chain to mark the native son of the golden West, the countrybred of California.

Him I loved because he is devoid of fear, carries himself like a man, and has a heart as big as his boots. I fancy, too, he knows how to enjoy the blessings of life that his province so abundantly bestows upon him. At least, I heard a little rat of a creature with hock-bottle shoulders explaining that a man from Chicago could pull the eyeteeth of a Californian in business.

Well, if I lived in fairyland, where cherries were as big as plums, plums as big as apples, and strawberries of no account, where the procession of the fruits of the seasons was like a pageant in a Drury Lane pantomime and the dry air was wine, I should let business slide once in a way and kick up my heels with my fellows. The tale of the resources of California—vegetable and mineral—is a fairy-tale. You can read it in books. You would never believe me.

All manner of nourishing food, from sea-fish to beef, may be bought at the lowest prices, and the people are consequently well-developed and of a high stomach. They demand ten shillings for tinkering a jammed lock of a trunk; they receive sixteen shillings a day for working as carpenters; they spend many sixpences on very bad cigars, which the poorest of them smoke, and they go mad over a prize-fight. When they disagree they do so fatally, with fire-arms in their hands, and on the public streets. I was just clear of Mission Street when the trouble began between two gentlemen, one of whom perforated the other.

When a policeman, whose name I do not recollect, "fatally shot Ed Hearney" for attempting to escape arrest, I was in the next street. For these things I am thankful. It is enough to travel with a policeman in a tram-car, and, while he arranges his coat-tails as he sits down, to catch sight of a loaded revolver. It is enough to know that fifty per cent. of the men in the public saloons carry pistols about them.

The Chinamen waylays his adversary, and methodically chops him to pieces with his hatchet. Then the press roars about the brutal ferocity of the pagan.

The Italian reconstructs his friend with a long knife. The press complains of the waywardness of the alien.

The Irishman and the native Californian in their hours of discontent use the revolver, not once, but six times. The press records the fact, and asks in the next column whether the world can parallel the progress of San Francisco. The American who loves his country will tell you that this sort of thing is confined to the lower classes. Just at present an ex-judge who was sent to jail by another judge (upon my word I cannot tell whether these titles mean anything) is breathing red-hot vengeance against his enemy. The papers have interviewed both parties, and confidently expect a fatal issue.

Now, let me draw breath and curse the negro waiter, and through him the negro in service generally. He has been made a citizen with a vote, consequently both political parties play with him. But that is neither here nor there. He will commit in one meal every *bêtise* that a *senllion* fresh from the plow-tail is capable of, and he will continue to repeat those faults. He is as complete a heavy-footed, uncomprehending, bungle-fisted fool as any *mem-sahib* in the East ever took into her establishment. But he is according to law a free and independent citizen—consequently above reproof or criticism. He, and he alone, in this insane city, will wait at table (the Chinaman doesn't count).

He is untrained, inept, but he will fill the place and draw the pay. Now, God and his father's fate made him intellectually inferior to the Oriental. He insists on pretending that he serves tables by accident—as a sort of amusement. He wishes you to understand this little fact. You wish to eat your meals, and, if possible, to have them properly served. He is a big, black, vain baby and a man rolled into one.

A colored gentleman who insisted on getting me pie when I wanted something else, demanded information about India. I gave him some facts about wages.

"Oh, hell!" said he, cheerfully, "that wouldn't keep me in cigars for a month."

Then he fawned on me for a ten-cent piece. Later he took it upon himself to pity the natives of India. "Heathens," he called them—this woolly one, whose race has been the butt of every comedy on the native stage since the beginning. And I turned and saw by the head upon his shoulders that he was a Yoruba man if there be any truth in ethnological castes. He did his thinking in English, but he was a Yoruba negro, and the race type had remained the same throughout his generations. And the room was full of other races—some that looked exactly like Gallas (but the trade was never recruited from that side of Africa), some duplicates of Cameroon heads, and some Kroomen, if ever Kroomen wore evening dress.

The American does not consider little matters of descent, though by this time he ought to know all about "damnable heredity." As a general rule he keeps himself very far from the negro, and says things about him that are not pretty. There are six million negroes, more or less, in the States, and they are increasing. The American, once having made them citizens, cannot unmake them. He says, in his newspapers, they ought to be elevated by education. He is trying this, but it is likely to be a long job, because black blood is much more adhesive than white, and throws back with annoying persistence.

When the negro gets religion he returns directly as a hiving bee to the first instincts of his people. Just now a wave of religion is sweeping over some of the Southern States.

Up to the present two Messiahs and a Daniel

have appeared, and several human sacrifices have been offered up to these incarnations. The Daniel managed to get three young men, who he insisted were Shadrach, Meshach, and Abednego, to walk into a blast furnace, guaranteeing non-combustion. They did not return. I have seen nothing of this kind, but I have attended a negro church. They pray, or are caused to pray by themselves in this country. The congregation were moved by the spirit to groans and tears, and one of them danced up the aisle to the mourners' bench. The motive may have been genuine. The movements of the shaken body were those of a Zanzibar stick dance, such as you see at Aden on the coal-boats, and even as I watched the people, the links that bound them to the white man snapped one by one, and I saw before me the *hubshi* (woolly hair) praying to a God he did not understand. Those neatly dressed folk on the benches, and the grey-headed elder by the window, were savages, neither more nor less.

What will the American do with the negro? The South will not consort with him. In some States miscegenation is a penal offence. The North is every year less and less in need of his services.

And he will not disappear. He will continue as a problem. His friends will urge that he is as good as the white man. His enemies —well, you can guess what his enemies will do from a little incident that followed on a recent appointment by the President. He made a negro an assistant in a post office where—think of it!—he had to work at the next desk to a white girl, the daughter of a Colonel, one of the first families of Georgia's modern chivalry, and all the weary, weary rest of it. The Southern chivalry howled, and hanged or burned some one in effigy. Perhaps it was the President, and perhaps it was the negro—but the principal remains the same. They said it was an insult. It is not good to be a negro in the land of the free and the home of the brave.

But this is nothing to do with San Francisco and her merry maidens, her strong, swaggering men, and her wealth of gold and pride. They bore me to a banquet in honor of a brave lieutenant—Carlin, of the "Vandalia" —who stuck by his ship in the great cyclone at Apia and comported himself as an officer should. On that occasion—'twas at the Bohemian Club—I heard oratory with the roundest of o's, and devoured a dinner the memory of which will descend wi me into the hungry grave.

There were about forty speeches delivered, and not one of them was average or ordinary. It was my first introduction to the American eagle screaming for all it was worth. The lieutenant's heroism served as a peg from which the silver-tongued ones turned themselves loose and kicked.

They ransacked the clouds of sunset, the thunderbolts of heaven, the deeps of hell, and the splendor of the resurrection for tropes and metaphors, and hurled the result at the head of the guest of the evening.

Never since the morning stars sung together for joy, I learned, had an amazed creation witnessed such superhuman bravery as that displayed by the American navy in the Samoa cyclone. Till earth rotted in the phosphorescent star-and-stripe slime of a decayed universe, that godlike gallantry would not be forgotten. I grieve that I cannot give the exact words. My attempt at reproducing their spirit is pale and inadequate. I sat bewildered on a coruscating Niagara of blatherumskite. It was magnificent—it was stupendous—and I was conscious of a wicked desire to hide my face in a napkin and grin. Then according to rule, they produced their dead, and across the snowy table-cloths dragged the corpse of every man slain in the Civil War, and hurled defiance at "our natural enemy" (England, so please you), "with her chain of fortresses across the world." Thereafter they glorified their nation afresh from the beginning, in case any detail should have been overlooked, and that made me uncomfortable for their sakes. How in the world can a white man, a sahib, of our blood, stand up and plaster praise on his own country? He can think as highly as he likes, but this open-mouthed vehemence of adoration struck me almost as indelicate. My hosts talked for rather more than three hours, and at the end seemed ready for three hours more.

But when the lieutenant—such a big, brave, gentle giant—rose to his feet, he delivered what seemed to me as the speech of the evening. I remember nearly the whole of it, and it ran something in this way:

"Gentlemen—It's very good of you to give me this dinner and tell me all these pretty things, but what I want you to understand—the fact is, what we want and what we ought to get at once, is a navy—more ships—lots of 'em"—

Then we howled the top of the roof off, and I for one fell in love with Carlin on the spot. Wallah! He was a man.

The prince among merchants bid me take no heed to the warlike sentiments of some of the old generals.

"The sky-rockets are thrown in for effect," quoth he, "and whenever we get on our hind legs we always express a desire to chaw up England. It's a sort of family affair."

And, indeed, when you come to think of it, there is no other country for the American public speaker to trample upon.

France has Germany; we have Russia; for Italy Austria is provided; and the humblest Pathan possesses an ancestral enemy.

Only America stands out of the racket, and therefore to be in fashion makes a sand-bag of the mother country, and hangs her when occasion requires.

"The chain of fortresses" man, a fascinating talker, explained to me after the affair that he was compelled to blow off steam. Everybody expected it.

When we had chanted "The Star Spangled Banner" not more than eight times, we adjourned. America is a very great country, but it is not yet heaven, with electric lights and plush fittings, as the speakers professed to believe. My listening mind went back to the politicians in the saloon, who wasted no time in talking about freedom, but quietly made arrangements to impose their will on the citizens. "The judge is a great man, but give thy presents to the clerk," as the proverb saith.

And what more remains to tell? I cannot write connectedly, because I am in love with all those girls aforesaid, and some others who do not appear in the invoice. The typewriter is an institution of which the comic papers make much capital, but she is vastly convenient. She and a companion rent a room in a business quarter, and, aided by a typewriting machine, copy MSS. at the rate of six annas a page. Only a woman can operate a typewriting machine, because she has served apprenticeship to the sewing machine. She can earn as much as one hundred dollars a month, and professes to regard this form of bread-winning as her natural destiny. But, oh! how she hates it in her heart of hearts! When I had got over the surprise of doing business with and trying to give orders to a young woman of coldly, clerkly aspect intrenched behind gold-rimmed spectacles, I made inquiries concerning the pleasures of this independence. They liked it —indeed they did. 'Twas the natural fate of almost all girls—the recognized custom in America—and I was a barbarian not to see it in that light.

"Well, and after?" said I. "What happens?"

"We work for our bread."

"And then what do you expect?"

"Then we shall work for our bread."

"Till you die?"

"Ye-es—unless"—

"Unless what? This is your business, you know. A man works until he dies."

"So shall we"—this without enthusiasm—"I suppose."

Said the partner in the firm audaciously:

"Sometimes we marry our employers—at least, that's what the newspapers say."

The hand banged on half a dozen of the keys of the machine at once. "Yet I don't care. I hate it—I hate it—I hate it—and you needn't look so!"

The senior partner was regarding the rebel with grave-eyed reproach.

"I thought you did," said I. "I don't suppose American girls are much different from English ones in instinct."

"Isn't it Théophile Gautier who says that the only differences between country and country lie in the slang and the uniform of the police?"

Now, in the name of all the gods at once,

what is one to say to a young lady (who in England would be a person) who earns her own bread, and very naturally hates the employ, and slings out-of-the-way quotations at your head? That one falls in love with her goes without saying, but that is not enough.

A mission should be established.

AMERICAN SALMON

III

AMERICAN SALMON

The race is neither to the swift nor the battle to the strong; but time and chance cometh to all.

I HAVE lived!

The American Continent may now sink under the sea, for I have taken the best that it yields, and the best was neither dollars, love, nor real estate.

Hear now, gentlemen of the Punjab Fishing Club, who whip the reaches of the Tavi, and you who painfully import trout to Octamund, and I will tell you how old man California and I went fishing, and you shall envy.

We returned from The Dalles to Portland by the way we had come, the steamer stopping *en route* to pick up a night's catch of one of the salmon wheels on the river, and to deliver it at a cannery down-stream.

When the proprietor of the wheel announced that his take was two thousand two hundred and thirty pounds weight of fish, "and not a heavy catch neither," I thought he lied. But he sent the boxes aboard, and I counted the salmon by the hundred—huge fifty-pounders hardly dead, scores of twenty and thirty pounders, and a host of smaller fish. They were all Chenook salmon, as distinguished from the "steel head" and the "silver side." That is to say, they were royal salmon, and California and I dropped a tear over them, as monarchs who deserved a better fate; but the lust of slaughter entered into our souls, and we talked fish and forgot the mountain scenery that had so moved us a day before.

The steamer halted at a rude wooden warehouse built on piles in a lonely reach of the river, and sent in the fish. I followed them up a scale-strewn, fishy incline that led to the cannery. The crazy building was quivering with the machinery on its floors, and a glittering bank of tin scraps twenty feet high showed where the waste was thrown after the cans had been punched.

Only Chinamen were employed on the work, and they looked like blood-besmeared yellow devils as they crossed the rifts of sunlight that lay upon the floor. When our consignment arrived, the rough wooden boxes broke of themselves as they were dumped down under a jet of water, and the salmon burst out in a stream of quicksilver. A Chinaman jerked up a twenty-pounder, beheaded and detailed it with two swift strokes of a knife, flicked out its internal arrangements with a third, and cast it into a blood-dyed tank. The headless fish leaped from under his hands as though they were facing a rapid. Other Chinamen pulled them from the vat and thrust them under a thing like a chaff-cutter, which, descending, hewed them into unseemly red gobbets fit for the can.

More Chinamen, with yellow, crooked fingers, jammed the stuff into the cans, which slid down some marvelous machine forthwith, soldering their own tops as they passed. Each can was hastily tested for flaws, and then sunk with a hundred companions into a vat of boiling water, there to be half cooked for a few minutes. The cans bulged slightly after the operation, and were therefore slidden along by the trolleyful to men with needles and soldering-irons who vented them and soldered the aperture. Except for the label, the "Finest Columbia Salmon" was ready for the market. I was impressed not so much with the speed of the manufacture as the character of the factory. Inside, on a floor ninety by forty, the most civilized and murderous of machinery. Outside, three footsteps, the thick-growing pines and the immense solitude of the hills. Our steamer only stayed twenty minutes at that place, but I counted two hundred and forty finished cans made from the catch of the previous night ere I left the slippery, blood-stained, scale-spangled, oily floors and the offal-smeared Chinamen.

We reached Portland, California and I crying for salmon, and a real-estate man, to whom we had been intrusted by an insurance man, met us in the street, saying that fifteen miles away, across country, we should come upon a place called Clackamas, where we might perchance find what we desired. And California, his coat-tails flying in the wind, ran to a livery-stable and chartered a wagon and team forthwith. I could push the wagon about with one hand, so light was its structure. The team was purely American—that is to say, almost human in its intelligence and docility. Some one said that the roads were not good on the way to Clackamas, and warned us against smashing the springs. "Portland," who had watched the preparations, finally reckoned "He'd come along, too;" and under heavenly skies we three companions of a day set forth, California carefully lashing our rods into the carriage, and the bystanders overwhelming us with directions as to the saw-mills we were to pass, the ferries we were to cross, and the sign-posts we were to seek signs from. Half a mile from this city of fifty thousand souls we struck (and this must be taken literally) a plank road that would have been a disgrace to an Irish village.

Then six miles of macadamized road showed us that the team could move. A railway ran between us and the banks of the Willamette, and another above us through the mountains All the land was dotted with small townships, and the roads were full of farmers in their town wagons, bunches of tow-haired, boggle-eyed urchins sitting in the hay behind. The men generally looked like loafers, but their women were all well dressed.

Brown braiding on a tailor-made jacket does not, however, consort with hay-wagons. Then we struck into the woods along what California called a *camina reale*—a good road—and Portland a "fair track." It wound in and out among fire-blackened stumps under pine-trees, along the corners of log fences, through hollows, which must be hopeless marsh in the winter, and up absurd gradients.

But nowhere throughout its length did I see any evidence of road-making. There was a track—you couldn't get off it, and it was all you could do to stay on it. The dust lay a foot thick in the blind ruts, and under the dust we found bits of planking and bundles of brushwood that sent the wagon bounding into the air. The journey in itself was a delight. Sometimes we crashed through bracken; anon, where the blackberries grew rankest, we found a lonely little cemetery, the wooden rails all awry and the pitiful, stumpy head-stones nodding drunkenly at the soft green mullions. Then, with oaths and the sound of rent underwood, a yoke of mighty bulls would swing down a "skid" road, hauling a forty-foot log along a rudely made slide.

A valley full of wheat and cherry-trees succeeded, and halting at a house, we bought ten-pound weight of lucious black cherries for something less than a rupee, and got a drink of icy-cold water for nothing, while the untended team browsed sagaciously by the roadside. Once we found a wayside camp of horse-dealers lounging by a pool, ready for a sale or a swap, and once two sun-tanned youngsters shot down a hill on Indian ponies, their full creels banging from the high-pommeled saddle.

They had been fishing, and were our brethren, therefore. We shouted aloud in chorus to scare a wild cat; we squabbled over the reasons that had led a snake to cross a road; we heaved bits of bark at a venturesome chipmunk, who was really the little grey squirrel of India, and had come to call on me; we lost our way, and got the wagon so beautifully fixed on a khud-bound road that we had to tie the two hind wheels to get it down.

Above all, California told tales of Nevada and Arizona, of lonely nights spent out prospecting, the slaughter of deer and the chase of men, of woman—lovely woman—who is a fire-brand in a Western city and leads to the popping of pistols, and of the sudden changes and chances of Fortune, who delights in making the miner or the lumberman a quadruplicate millionaire and in "busting" the railroad king.

That was a day to be remembered, and it had only begun when we drew rein at a tiny farmhouse on the banks of the Clackamas and sought horse feed and lodging, ere we hastened to the river that broke over a weir not a quarter of a mile away. Imagine a stream seventy yards broad divided by a pebbly island, running over seductive "riffles" and swirling into deep, quiet pools, where the good salmon goes to smoke his pipe after meals. Get such a stream amid fields of breast-high crops surrounded by hills of pines, throw in where you please quiet water, long-fenced meadows, and a hundred-foot bluff just to keep the scenery from growing too monotonous, and you will get some faint notion of the Clackamas. The weir had been erected to pen the Chenook salmon from going further upstream. We could see them, twenty or thirty pounds, by the score in the deep pools, or flying madly against the weir and foolishly skinning their noses. They were not our prey, for they would not rise at a fly, and we knew it. All the same, when one made his leap against the weir, and landed on the foot-plank with a jar that shook the board I was standing on, I would fain have claimed him for my own capture.

Portland had no rod. He held the gaff and the whiskey. California sniffed up-stream and down-stream, across the racing water, chose his ground, and let the gaudy fly drop in the tail of a riffle. I was getting my rod together when I heard the joyous shriek of the reel and the yells of California, and three feet of living silver leaped into the air far across the water. The forces were engaged.

The salmon tore up-stream, the tense line

cutting the water like a tide-rip behind him, and the light bamboo bowed to breaking. What happened thereafter I cannot tell. California swore and prayed, and Portland shouted advice, and I did all three for what appeared to be half a day, but was in reality a little over a quarter of an hour, and sullenly our fish came home with spurts of temper, dashes head on and sarabands in the air, but home to the bank came he, and the remorseless reel gathered up the thread of his life inch by inch. We landed him in a little bay, and the spring weight in his gorgeous gills checked at eleven and one half pounds. Eleven and one half pounds of fighting salmon! We danced a war-dance on the pebbles, and California caught me round the waist in a hug that went near to breaking my ribs, while he shouted:

"Partner! Partner! This is glory! Now you catch your fish! Twenty-four years I've waited for this!"

I went into that icy-cold river and made my cast just above the weir, and all but foul-hooked a blue-and-black water-snake with a coral mouth who coiled herself on a stone and hissed maledictions.

The next cast—ah, the pride of it, the regal splendor of it! the thrill that ran down from finger-tip to toe! Then the water boiled. He broke for the fly and got it. There remained enough sense in me to give him all he wanted when he jumped not once, but twenty times, before the up-stream flight that ran my line out to the last half-dozen turns, and I saw the nickeled reel-bar glitter under the thinning green coils. My thumb was burned deep when I strove to stopper the line.

I did not feel it till later, for my soul was out in the dancing weir, praying for him to turn ere he took my tackle away. And the prayer was heard. As I bowed back, the butt of the rod on my left hip-bone and the top joint dipping like unto a weeping willow, he turned and accepted each inch of slack that I could by any means get in as a favor from on high. There lie several sorts of success in this world that taste well in the moment of enjoyment, but I question whether the stealthy theft of line from an able-bodied salmon who knows exactly what you are doing and why you are doing it is not sweeter than any other victory within human scope. Like California's fish, he ran at me head on, and leaped against the line, but the Lord gave me two hundred and fifty pairs of fingers in that hour. The banks and the pine-trees danced dizzily round me, but I

"He ran at me, head on."

American Salmon, p. 298

only reeled—reeled as for life—reeled for hours, and at the end of the reeling continued to give him the butt while he sulked in a pool. California was further up the reach, and with the corner of my eye I could see him casting with long casts and much skill. Then he struck, and my fish broke for the weir in the same instant, and down the reach we came, California and I, reel answering reel even as the morning stars sing together.

The first wild enthusiasm of capture had died away. We were both at work now in deadly earnest to prevent the lines fouling, to stall off a down-stream rush for shaggy water just above the weir, and at the same time to get the fish into the shallow bay down-stream that gave the best practicable landing. Portland bid us both be of good heart, and volunteered to take the rod from my hands.

I would rather have died among the pebbles than surrender my right to play and land a salmon, weight unknown, with an eight-ounce rod. I heard California, at my ear, it seemed, gasping: "He's a fighter from Fightersville, sure!" as his fish made a fresh break across the stream. I saw Portland fall off a log fence, break the overhanging bank, and clatter down to the pebbles, all sand and landing-net, and

I dropped on a log to rest for a moment. As I drew breath the weary hands slackened their hold, and I forgot to give him the butt.

A wild scutter in the water, a plunge, and a break for the head-waters of the Clackamas was my reward, and the weary toil of reeling in with one eye under the water and the other on the top joint of the rod was renewed. Worst of all, I was blocking California's path to the little landing bay aforesaid, and he had to halt and tire his prize where he was.

"The father of all the salmon!" he shouted. "For the love of Heaven, get your trout to bank, Johnny Bull!"

But I could do no more. Even the insult failed to move me. The rest of the game was with the salmon. He suffered himself to be drawn, skipping with pretended delight at getting to the haven where I would fain bring him. Yet no sooner did he feel shoal water under his ponderous belly than he backed like a torpedo-boat, and the snarl of the reel told me that my labor was in vain. A dozen times, at least, this happened ere the line hinted he had given up the battle and would be towed in. He was towed. The landing-net was useless for one of his size, and I would not have him gaffed. I stepped into the shallows and heaved him out with respectful hand under the gill, for which kindness he battered me about the legs with his tail, and I felt the strength of him and was proud. California had taken my place in the shallows, his fish hard held. I was up the bank lying full length on the sweet-scented grass and gasping in company with my first salmon caught, played and landed on an eight-ounce rod. My hands were cut and bleeding, I was dripping with sweat, spangled like a harlequin with scales, water from my waist down, nose peeled by the sun, but utterly, supremely, and consummately happy.

The beauty, the darling, the daisy, my Salmon Bahadur, weighed twelve pounds, and I had been seven-and-thirty minutes bringing him to bank! He had been lightly hooked on the angle of the right jaw, and the hook had not wearied him. That hour I sat among princes and crowned heads greater than them all. Below the bank we heard California scuffling with his salmon and swearing Spanish oaths. Portland and I assisted at the capture, and the fish dragged the spring balance out by the roots. It was only constructed to weigh up to fifteen pounds. We stretched the three fish on the grass—the eleven and a half, the twelve and fifteen pounder—and we gave an oath that all who came after should merely be weighed and put back again.

How shall I tell the glories of that day so that you may be interested? Again and again did California and I prance down that reach to the little bay, each with a salmon in tow, and land him in the shallows. Then Portland took my rod and caught some ten-pounders, and my spoon was carried away by an unknown leviathan. Each fish, for the merits of the three that had died so gamely, was hastily hooked on the balance and flung back. Portland recorded the weight in a pocket-book, for he was a real-estate man. Each fish fought for all he was worth, and none more savagely than the smallest, a game little six-pounder. At the end of six hours we added up the list. Read it. Total: Sixteen fish; aggregate weight, one hundred and forty pounds. The score in detail runs something like this—it is only interesting to those concerned: fifteen, eleven and a half, twelve, ten, nine and three quarters, eight, and so forth; as I have said, nothing under six pounds, and three ten-pounders.

Very solemnly and thankfully we put up our rods—it was glory enough for all time—and returned weeping in each other's arms, weeping tears of pure joy, to that simple, bare-legged family in the packing-case house by the waterside.

The old farmer recollected days and nights of fierce warfare with the Indians "way back in the fifties," when every ripple of the Columbia River and her tributaries hid covert danger. God had dowered him with a queer, crooked gift of expression and a fierce anxiety for the welfare of his two little sons—tanned and reserved children, who attended school daily and spoke good English in a strange tongue.

His wife was an austere woman, who had once been kindly, and perhaps handsome.

Very many years of toil had taken the elasticity out of step and voice. She looked for nothing better than everlasting work—the chafing detail of housework—and then a grave somewhere up the hill among the blackberries and the pines. But in her grim way she sympathized with her eldest daughter, a small and silent maiden of eighteen, who had thoughts very far from the meals she tended and the pans she scoured.

We stumbled into the household at a crisis, and there was a deal of downright humanity in that same. A bad, wicked dressmaker had promised the maiden a dress in time for a to-morrow's railway journey, and though the barefooted Gregory, who stood in very whole-some awe of his sister, had scoured the woods on a pony in search, that dress never arrived. So, with sorrow in her heart and a hundred Sister-Anne glances up the road, she waited upon the strangers and, I doubt not, cursed them for the wants that stood between her and her need for tears. It was a genuine little tragedy. The mother, in a heavy, passionless voice, rebuked her impatience, yet sat up far into the night, bowed over a heap of sewing for the daughter's benefit.

These things I beheld in the long marigold-scented twilight and whispering night, loafing round the little house with California, who un-folded himself like a lotus to the moon, or in the little boarded bunk that was our bedroom, swapping tales with Portland and the old man.

Most of the yarns began in this way:

"Red Larry was a bull-puncher back of Lone County, Montana," or "There was a man rid-ing the trail met a jack-rabbit sitting in a cac-tus," or " 'Bout the time of the San Diego land boom, a woman from Monterey," etc.

You can try to piece out for yourselves what sort of stories they were.

THE YELLOWSTONE

IV.

THE YELLOWSTONE

ONCE upon a time there was a carter who brought his team and a friend into the Yellowstone Park without due thought. Presently they came upon a few of the natural beauties of the place, and that carter turned his team into his friend's team, howling:

"Get out o' this, Jim. All hell's alight under our noses!"

And they called the place Hell's Half-Acre to this day to witness if the carter lied.

We, too, the old lady from Chicago, her husband, Tom, and the good little mares, came to Hell's Half-Acre, which is about sixty acres in extent, and when Tow said:

"Would you like to drive over it?"

We said:

"Certainly not, and if you do we shall report you to the park authorities."

There was a plain, blistered, peeled, and abominable, and it was given over to the sportings and spoutings of devils who threw mud, and steam, and dirt at each other with whoops, and halloos, and bellowing curses.

The places smelled of the refuse of the pit, and that odor mixed with the clean, wholesome aroma of the pines in our nostrils throughout the day.

This Yellowstone Park is laid out like Ollendorf, in exercises of progressive difficulty. Hell's Half-Acre was a prelude to ten or twelve miles of geyser formation.

We passed hot streams boiling in the forest; saw whiffs of steam beyond these, and yet other whiffs breaking through the misty green hills in the far distance; we trampled on sulphur in crystals, and sniffed things much worse than any sulphur which is known to the upper world; and so journeying, bewildered with the novelty, came upon a really park-like place where Tom suggested we should get out and play with the geysers on foot.

Imagine mighty green fields splattered with lime-beds, all the flowers of the summer growing up to the very edge of the lime. That was our first glimpse of the geyser basins.

The buggy had pulled up close to a rough, broken, blistered cone of spelter stuff between ten and twenty feet high. There was trouble in that place—moaning, splashing, gurgling, and the clank of machinery. A spurt of boiling water jumped into the air, and a wash of water followed.

I removed swiftly. The old lady from Chicago shrieked. "What a wicked waste!" said her husband.

I think they call it the Riverside Geyser. Its spout was torn and ragged like the mouth of a gun when a shell has burst there. It grumbled madly for a moment or two, and then was still. I crept over the steaming lime—it was the burning marl on which Satan lay—and looked fearfully down its mouth. You should never look a gift geyser in the mouth.

I beheld a horrible, slippery, slimy funnel with water rising and falling ten feet at a time. Then the water rose to lip level with a rush, and an infernal bubbling troubled this Devil's Bethesda before the sullen heave of the crest of a wave lapped over the edge and made me run.

Mark the nature of the human soul! I had begun with awe, not to say terror, for this was my first experience of such things. I stepped back from the banks of the Riverside Geyser, saying:

"Pooh! Is that all it can do?"

Yet for aught I knew, the whole thing might have blown up at a minute's notice, she, he, or it being an arrangement of uncertain temper.

We drifted on, up that miraculous valley. On either side of us were hills from a thousand to fifteen hundred feet high, wooded from crest to heel. As far as the eye could range forward were the columns of steam in the air, misshapen lumps of lime, mist-like preadamite monsters, still pools of turquoise-blue, stretches of blue corn-flowers, a river that coiled on itself twenty times, pointed bowlders of strange colors, and ridges of glaring, staring white.

A moon-faced trooper of German extraction —never was park so carefully patrolled—came up to inform us that as yet we had not seen any of the real geysers; that they were all a mile or so up the valley, and tastefully scattered round the hotel in which we would rest for the night.

America is a free country, but the citizens look down on the soldier. I had to entertain that trooper. The old lady from Chicago would have none of him; so we loafed along together, now across half-rotten pine logs sunk in swampy ground, anon over the ringing geyser formation, then pounding through river-sand or brushing knee-deep through long grass.

"And why did you enlist?" said I.

The moon-faced one's face began to work. I thought he would have a fit, but he told me a story instead—such a nice tale of a naughty little girl who wrote pretty love letters to two men at once. She was a simple village wife, but a wicked "family novelette" countess couldn't have accomplished her ends better. She drove one man nearly wild with the pretty little treachery, and the other man abandoned her and came West to forget the trickery.

Moon-face was that man.

We rounded and limped over a low spur of hill, and came out upon a field of aching, snowy lime rolled in sheets, twisted into knots, riven with rents, and diamonds, and stars, stretching for more than half a mile in every direction.

On this place of despair lay most of the big, bad geysers who know when there is trouble in Krakatoa, who tell the pines when there is a cyclone on the Atlantic seaboard, and who are exhibited to visitors under pretty and fanciful names.

The first mound that I encountered belonged to a goblin who was splashing in his tub.

I heard him kick, pull a shower-bath on his shoulders, gasp, crack his joints, and rub himself down with a towel; then he let the water out of the bath, as a thoughtful man should, and it all sunk down out of sight till another goblin arrived.

So we looked and we wondered at the Beehive, whose mouth is built up exactly like a hive, at the Turban (which is not in the least like a turban), and at many, many other geysers, hot holes, and springs. Some of them rumbled, some hissed, some went off spasmodically, and others lay dead still in sheets of sapphire and beryl.

Would you believe that even these terrible creatures have to be guarded by the troopers to prevent the irreverent Americans from chipping the cones to pieces, or, worse still, making the geyser sick? If you take a small barrel full of soft soap and drop it down a geyser's mouth, that geyser will presently be forced to lay all before you, and for days afterward will be of an irritated and inconstant stomach.

When they told me the tale I was filled with sympathy. Now I wish that I had had soft-soap and tried the experiment on some lonely little beast far away in the woods. It sounds so probable and so human.

Yet he would be a bold man who would administer emetics to the Giantess. She is flat-lipped, having no mouth; she looks like a pool, fifty feet long and thirty wide, and there is no ornamentation about her. At irregular intervals she speaks and sends up a volume of water over two hundred feet high to begin with, then she is angry for a day and a half—sometimes for two days.

Owing to her peculiarity of going mad in the night, not many people have seen the Giantess at her finest; but the clamor of her unrest, men say, shakes the wooden hotel, and echoes like thunder among the hills.

The congregation returned to the hotel to put down their impressions in diaries and notebooks, which they wrote up ostentatiously in the verandas. It was a sweltering hot day, albeit we stood somewhat higher than the level of Simla, and I left that raw pine creaking caravansary for the cool shade of a clump of pines between whose trunks glimmered tents.

A batch of United States troopers came down the road and flung themselves across the country into their rough lines. The Melican cavalryman can ride, though he keeps his accoutrements pig-fashion and his horse cow-fashion.

I was free of that camp in five minutes—free to play with the heavy, lumpy carbines, have the saddles stripped, and punch the horses knowingly in the ribs. One of the men had been in the fight with "Wrap-up-his-Tail," and he told me how that great chief, his horse's tail tied up in red calico, swaggered in front of the United States Cavalry, challenging all to a single combat. But he was slain, and a few of his tribe with him.

"There's no use in an Indian, anyway," concluded my friend.

A couple of cowboys—real cowboys—jingled through the camp amid a shower of mild chaff. They were on their way to Cook City, I fancy, and I know that they never washed. But they were picturesque ruffians exceedingly, with long spurs, hooded stirrups, slouch hats, fur weather-cloth over their knees, and pistol-butts just easy to hand.

"The cowboy's goin' under before long," said my friend. "Soon as the country's settled up he'll have to go. But he's mighty useful now. What would we do without the cowboy?"

"As how?" said I, and the camp laughed.

"He has the money. We have the skill. He comes in winter to play poker at the military posts. We play poker—a few. When he's lost his money we make him drunk and let him go. Sometimes we get the wrong man."

And he told me a tale of an innocent cowboy who turned up, cleaned out, at an army post, and played poker for thirty-six hours. But it was the post that was cleaned out when that long-haired Caucasian removed himself, heavy with everybody's pay and declining the proffered liquor.

"Noaw," said the historian, "I don't play with no cowboy unless he's a little bit drunk first."

Ere I departed I gathered from more than one man the significant fact that up to one hundred yards he felt absolutely secure behind his revolver.

"In England, I understand," quoth the limber youth from the South,—"in England a man isn't allowed to play with no firearms. He's got to be taught all that when he enlists. I didn't want much teaching how to shoot straight 'fore I served Uncle Sam. And that's just where it is. But you was talking about your Horse Guards now?"

I explained briefly some peculiarities of equipment connected with our crackest crack cavalry. I grieve to say the camp roared.

"Take 'em over swampy ground. Let 'em run around a bit an' work the starch out of 'em, an' then, Almighty, if we wouldn't plug 'em at ease I'd eat their horses."

There was a maiden—a very little maiden—who had just stepped out of one of James's novels. She owned a delightful mother and an equally delightful father—a heavy-eyed, slow-voiced man of finance. The parents thought that their daughter wanted change.

She lived in New Hampshire. Accordingly, she had dragged them up to Alaska and to the Yosemite Valley, and was now returning leisurely, via the Yellowstone, just in time for the tail-end of the summer season at Saratoga.

We had met once or twice before in the park, and I had been amazed and amused at her critical commendation of the wonders that she saw. From that very resolute little mouth I received a lecture on American literature, the nature and inwardness of Washington society, the precise value of Cable's works as compared with Uncle Remus Harris, and a few other things that had nothing whatever to do with geysers, but were altogether pleasant.

Now, an English maiden who had stumbled on a dust-grimed, lime-washed, sun-peeled, collarless wanderer come from and going to goodness knows where, would, her mother inciting her and her father brandishing his umbrella, have regarded him as a dissolute adventurer—a person to be disregarded.

Not so those delightful people from New Hampshire. They were good enough to treat him—it sounds almost incredible—as a human being, possibly respectable, probably not in immediate need of financial assistance.

Papa talked pleasantly and to the point.

The little maiden strove valiantly with the accent of her birth and that of her rearing, and mamma smiled benignly in the background.

Balance this with a story of a young English idiot I met mooning about inside his high collar, attended by a valet. He condescended to tell me that "you can't be too careful who you talk to in these parts." And stalked on, fearing, I suppose, every minute for his social chastity.

That man was a barbarian (I took occasion to tell him so), for he comported himself after the manner of the head-hunters and hunted of Assam who are at perpetual feud one with another.

You will understand that these foolish stories are introduced in order to cover the fact that this pen cannot describe the glories of the Upper Geyser Basin. The evening I spent under the lee of the Castle Geyser, sitting on a log with some troopers and watching a baronial keep forty feet high spouting hot water. If the Castle went off first, they said the Giantess would be quiet, and *vice versâ,* and then they told tales till the moon got up and a party of campers in the woods gave us all something to eat.

Then came soft, turfy forest that deadened the wheels, and two troopers on detachment duty stole noiselessly behind us. One was the Wrap-up-his-Tail man, and they talked merrily while the half-broken horses bucked about among the trees. And so a cavalry escort was with us for a mile, till we got to a mighty hill all strewn with moss agates, and everybody had to jump out and pant in that thin air. But how intoxicating it was! The old lady from Chicago ducked like an emancipated hen as she scuttled about the road, cramming pieces of rock into her reticule. She sent me fifty yards down the hillside to pick up a piece of broken bottle which she insisted was moss agate.

"I've some o' that at home, an' they shine. Yes, you go get it, young man."

As we climbed the long path the road grew viler and viler till it became, without disguise, the bed of a torrent; and just when things were at their rockiest we nearly fell into a little sapphire lake—but never sapphire was so blue—called Mary's Lake; and that between eight and nine thousand feet above the sea.

Afterward, grass downs, all on a vehement slope, so that the buggy, following the new-made road, ran on the two off-wheels mostly till we dipped head-first into a ford, climbed up a cliff, raced along down, dipped again, and pulled up disheveled at "Larry's" for lunch and an hour's rest.

Then we lay on the grass and laughed with sheer bliss of being alive. This have I known once in Japan, once on the banks of the Columbia, what time the salmon came in and California howled, and once again in the Yellowstone by the light of the eyes of the maiden from New Hampshire. Four little pools lay at my elbow, one was of black water (tepid), one clear water (cold), one clear water (hot), one red water (boiling). My newly washed handkerchief covered them all, and we two marveled as children marvel.

"This evening we shall do the Grand Canyon of the Yellowstone," said the maiden.

"Together?" said I; and she said, "Yes."

The sun was beginning to sink when we heard the roar of falling waters and came to a broad river along whose banks we ran. And then—I might at a pinch describe the infernal regions, but not the other place. The Yellowstone River has occasion to run through a gorge about eight miles long. To get to the bottom of the gorge it makes two leaps, one of about one hundred and twenty and the other of three hundred feet. I investigated the upper or lesser fall, which is close to the hotel.

Up to that time nothing particular happens to the Yellowstone—its banks being only rocky, rather steep, and plentifully adorned with pines.

At the falls it comes round a corner, green, solid, ribbed with a little foam, and not more than thirty yards wide. Then it goes over, still green, and rather more solid than before. After a minute or two, you, sitting upon a rock directly above the drop, begin to understand that something has occurred; that the river has jumped between solid cliff walls, and that the gentle froth of water lapping the sides of the gorge below is really the outcome of great waves.

And the river yells aloud; but the cliffs do not allow the yells to escape.

That inspection began with curiosity and finished in terror, for it seemed that the whole world was sliding in chrysolite from under my feet. I followed with the others round the corner to arrive at the brink of the canyon. We had to climb up a nearly perpendicular ascent to begin with, for the ground rises more than the river drops. Stately pine woods fringe either lip of the gorge, which is the gorge of the Yellowstone. You'll find all about it in the guide books.

All that I can say is that without warning or preparation I looked into a gulf seventeen hundred feet deep, with eagles and fish-hawks circling far below. And the sides of that gulf were one wild welter of color—crimson, emerald, cobalt, ochre, amber, honey splashed with port wine, snow white, vermilion, lemon, and silver grey in wide washes. The sides did not fall sheer, but were graven by time, and water, and air into monstrous head of kings, dead chiefs—men and women of the old time. So far below that no sound of its strife could reach us, the Yellowstone River ran a finger-wide strip of jade green.

The sunlight took those wondrous walls and gave fresh hues to those that nature had already laid there.

Evening crept through the pines that shadowed us, but the full glory of the day flamed in that canyon as we went out very cautiously to a jutting piece of rock—blood-red or pink it was—that overhung the deepest deeps of all.

Now I know what it is to sit enthroned amid

the clouds of sunset as the spirits sit in Blake's pictures. Giddiness took away all sensation of touch or form, but the sense of blinding color remained.

When I reached the mainland again I had sworn that I had been floating.

The maid from New Hampshire said no word for a very long time. Then she quoted poetry, which was perhaps the best thing she could have done.

"And to think that this show-place has been going on all these days an' none of we ever saw it," said the old lady from Chicago, with an acid glance at her husband.

"No, only the Injians," said he, unmoved; and the maiden and I laughed.

Inspiration is fleeting, beauty is vain, and the power of the mind for wonder limited. Though the shining hosts themselves had risen choiring from the bottom of the gorge, they would not have prevented her papa and one baser than he from rolling stones down those stupendous rainbow-washed slides. Seventeen hundred feet of steepest pitch and rather more than seventeen hundred colors for log or bowlder to whirl through!

So we heaved things and saw them gather way and bound from white rock to red or yellow, dragging behind them torrents of color, till the noise of their descent ceased and they bounded a hundred yards clear at the last into the Yellowstone.

"I've been down there," said Tom, that evening. "It's easy to get down if your're careful —just sit an' slide; but getting up is worse. An' I found down below there two stones just marked with a picture of the canyon. I wouldn't sell these rocks not for fifteen dollars."

And papa and I crawled down to the Yellowstone—just above the first little fall—to wet a line for good luck. The round moon came up and turned the cliffs and pines into silver; and a two-pound trout came up also, and we slew him among the rocks, nearly tumbling into that wild river.

* * * * * *

Then out and away to Livingstone once more. The maiden from New Hampshire disappeared, papa and mamma with her. Disappeared, too, the old lady from Chicago, and the others.

CHICAGO

V

CHICAGO

> "I know thy cunning and thy greed,
> Thy hard high lust and wilful deed,
> And all thy glory loves to tell
> Of specious gifts material."

I HAVE struck a city—a real city—and they call it Chicago.

The other places do not count. San Francisco was a pleasure-resort as well as a city, and Salt Lake was a phenomenon.

This place is the first American city I have encountered. It holds rather more than a million of people with bodies, and stands on the same sort of soil as Calcutta. Having seen it, I urgently desire never to see it again. It is inhabited by savages. Its water is the water of the Hooghly, and its air is dirt. Also it says that it is the "boss" town of America.

I do not believe that it has anything to do with this country. They told me to go to the Palmer House, which is overmuch gilded and mirrored, and there I found a huge hall of tessellated marble crammed with people talking about money, and spitting about everywhere. Other barbarians charged in and out of this inferno with letters and telegrams in their hands, and yet others shouted at each other. A man who had drunk quite as much as was good for him told me that this was "the finest hotel in the finest city on God Almighty's earth." By the way, when an American wishes to indicate the next country or state, he says, "God A'mighty's earth." This prevents discussion and flatters his vanity.

Then I went out into the streets, which are long and flat and without end. And verily it is not a good thing to live in the East for any length of time. Your ideas grow to clash with those held by every right-thinking man. I looked down interminable vistas flanked with nine, ten, and fifteen-storied houses, and crowded with men and women, and the show impressed me with a great horror.

Except in London—and I have forgotten what London was like—I had never seen so many white people together, and never such a collection of miserables. There was no color in the street and no beauty—only a maze of wire ropes overhead and dirty stone flagging under foot.

A cab-driver volunteered to show me the

glory of the town for so much an hour, and with him I wandered far. He conceived that all this turmoil and squash was a thing to be reverently admired, that it was good to huddle men together in fifteen layers, one atop of the other, and to dig holes in the ground for offices.

He said that Chicago was a live town, and that all the creatures hurrying by me were engaged in business. That is to say they were trying to make some money that they might not die through lack of food to put into their bellies. He took me to canals as black as ink, and filled with untold abominations, and bid me watch the stream of traffic across the bridges.

He then took me into a saloon, and while I drank made me note that the floor was covered with coins sunk in cement. A Hottentot would not have been guilty of this sort of barbarism. The coins made an effect pretty enough, but the man who put them there had no thought of beauty, and, therefore, he was a savage.

Then my cab-driver showed me business blocks gay with signs and studded with fantastic and absurd advertisements of goods, and looking down the long street so adorned, it was as though each vender stood at his door, howling:

"For the sake of money, employ or buy of me, and me only!"

Have you ever seen a crowd at a famine-relief distribution? You know then how the men leap into the air, stretching out their arms above the crowd in the hope of being seen, while the women dolorously slap the stomachs of their children and whimper. I had sooner watch famine relief than the white man engaged in what he calls legitimate competition. The one I understand. The other makes me ill.

And the cabman said that these things were the proof of progress, and by that I knew he had been reading his newspaper, as every intelligent American should. The papers tell their *clientèle* in language fitted to their comprehension that the snarling together of telegraph-wires, the heaving up of houses, and the making of money is progress.

I spent ten hours in that huge wilderness, wandering through scores of miles of these terrible streets and jostling some few hundred thousand of these terrible people who talked *paisa bat* through their noses.

The cabman left me; but after awhile I

picked up another man, who was full of figures, and into my ears he poured them as occasion required or the big blank factories suggested. Here they turned out so many hundred thousand dollars' worth of such and such an article; there so many million other things; this house was worth so many million dollars; that one so many million, more or less. It was like listening to a child babbling of its hoard of shells. It was like watching a fool playing with buttons. But I was expected to do more than listen or watch. He demanded that I should admire; and the utmost that I could say was:

"Are these things so? Then I am very sorry for you."

That made him angry, and he said that insular envy made me unresponsive. So, you see, I could not make him understand.

About four-and-a-half hours after Adam was turned out of the Garden of Eden he felt hungry, and so, bidding Eve take care that her head was not broken by the descending fruit, shinned up a cocoanut-palm. That hurt his legs, cut his breast, and made him breathe heavily, and Eve was tormented with fear lest her lord should miss his footing, and so bring the tragedy of this world to an end ere the curtain had fairly risen. Had I met Adam then, I should have been sorry for him. To-day I find eleven hundred thousand of his sons just as far advanced as their father in the art of getting food, and immeasurably inferior to him in that they think that their palm-trees lead straight to the skies. Consequently, I am sorry in rather more than a million different ways.

In the East bread comes naturally, even to the poorest, by a little scratching or the gift of a friend not quite so poor. In less favored countries one is apt to forget. Then I went to bed. And that was on a Saturday night.

Sunday brought me the queerest experiences of all—a revelation of barbarism complete. I found a place that was officially described as a church. It was a circus really, but that the worshippers did not know. There were flowers all about the building, which was fitted up with plush and stained oak and much luxury, including twisted brass candlesticks of severest Gothic design.

To these things and a congregation of savages entered suddenly a wonderful man, completely in the confidence of their God, whom he treated colloquially and exploited very much as a newspaper reporter would exploit a foreign potentate. But, unlike the newspaper reporter, he never allowed his listeners to forget that he, and not He, was the centre of attraction. With a voice of silver and with imagery borrowed from the auction-room, he built up for his hearers a heaven on the lines of the Palmer House (but with all the gilding real gold, and all the plate-glass diamond), and set in the centre of it a loud-voiced, argumentative, very shrewd creation that he called God. One sentence at this point caught my delighted ear. It was apropos of some question of the Judgment, and ran:

"No! I tell you God doesn't do business that way."

He was giving them a deity whom they could comprehend, and a gold and jeweled heaven in which they could take a natural interest. He interlarded his performance with the slang of the streets, the counter, and the exchange, and he said that religion ought to enter into daily life. Consequently, I presume he introduced it as daily life—his own and the life of his friends.

Then I escaped before the blessing, desiring no benediction at such hands. But the persons who listened seemed to enjoy themselves, and I understood that I had met with a popular preacher.

Later on, when I had perused the sermons of a gentleman called Talmage and some others, I perceived that I had been listening to a very mild specimen. Yet that man, with his brutal gold and silver idols, his hands-in-pocket, cigar-in-mouth, and hat-on-the-back-of-the-head style of dealing with the sacred vessels, would count himself, spiritually, quite competent to send a mission to convert the Indians.

All that Sunday I listened to people who said that the mere fact of spiking down strips of iron to wood, and getting a steam and iron thing to run along them was progress, that the telephone was progress, and the net-work of wires overhead was progress. They repeated their statements again and again.

One of them took me to their City Hall and Board of Trade works, and pointed it out with pride. It was very ugly, but very big, and the streets in front of it were narrow and unclean. When I saw the faces of the men who did business in that building, I felt that there had been a mistake in their billeting.

By the way, 'tis a consolation to feel that I am not writing to an English audience. Then I should have to fall into feigned ecstasies over the marvelous progress of Chicago since the days of the great fire, to allude casually to the raising of the entire city so many feet above the level of the lake which it faces, and generally to grovel before the golden calf. But you, who are desperately poor, and therefore by these standards of no account, know things, will understand when I write that they have managed to get a million of men together on flat land, and that the bulk of these men together appear to be lower than Mahajans and not so companionable as a Punjabi Jat after harvest.

But I don't think it was the blind hurry of the people, their *argot,* and their grand ignorance of things beyond their immediate interests that displeased me so much as a study of the daily papers of Chicago.

Imprimis, there was some sort of a dispute between New York and Chicago as to which town should give an exhibition of products to be hereafter holden, and through the medium of their more dignified journals the two cities were yahooing and hi-yi-ing at each other like opposition newsboys. They called it humor, but it sounded like something quite different.

That was only the first trouble. The second lay in the tone of the productions. Leading articles which include gems such as "Back of such and such a place," or, "We noticed, Tuesday, such an event," or, "don't" for "does not," are things to be accepted with thankfulness. All that made me want to cry was that in these papers were faithfully reproduced all the war-cries and "back-talk" of the Palmer House bar, the slang of the barber-shops, the mental elevation and integrity of the Pullman car porter, the dignity of the dime museum, and the accuracy of the excited fish-wife. I am sternly forbidden to believe that the paper educates the public. Then I am compelled to believe that the public educate the paper; yet suicides on the press are rare.

Just when the sense of unreality and oppression was strongest upon me, and when I most wanted help, a man sat at my side and began to talk what he called politics.

I had chanced to pay about six shillings for a traveling-cap worth eighteen-pence, and he made of the fact a text for a sermon. He said that this was a rich country, and that the people liked to pay two hundred per cent. on the value of a thing. They could afford it. He said that the government imposed a protective duty of from ten to seventy per cent. on foreign-made articles, and that the American manufacturer consequently could sell his goods for a healthy sum. Thus an imported hat would, with duty, cost two guineas. The American manufacturer would make a hat for seventeen shillings, and sell it for one pound fifteen. In these things, he said, lay the greatness of America and the effeteness of England. Competition between factory and factory kept the prices down to decent limits, but I was never to forget that this people were a rich people, not like the pauper Continentals, and that they enjoyed paying duties.

To my weak intellect this seemed rather like juggling with counters. Everything that I have yet purchased costs about twice as much as it would in England, and when native made is of inferior quality.

Moreover, since these lines were first thought of, I have visited a gentleman who owned a factory which used to produce things. He owned the factory still. Not a man was in it, but he was drawing a handsome income from a syndicate of firms for keeping it closed in order that it might not produce things. This man said that if protection were abandoned, a tide of pauper labor would flood the country, and as I looked at his factory I thought how entirely better it was to have no labor of any kind whatever rather than face so horrible a future.

Meantime, do you remember that this peculiar country enjoys paying money for value not received? I am an alien, and for the life of me I cannot see why six shillings should be paid for eighteen-penny caps, or eight shillings for half-crown cigar-cases. When the country fills up to a decently populated level a few million people who are not aliens will be smitten with the same sort of blindness.

But my friend's assertion somehow thoroughly suited the grotesque ferocity of Chicago.

See now and judge! In the village of Isser Jang, on the road to Montgomery, there be four Changar women who winnow corn—some seventy bushels a year. Beyond their hut lives Purun Dass, the money-lender, who on good security lends as much as five thousand rupees in a year. Jowala Singh, the smith, mends the village plows—some thirty, broken at the share, in three hundred and sixty-five days; and Hukm Chund, who is letter-writer and head of the little club under the travelers' tree, generally keeps the village posted in such gossip as the barber and the midwife have not yet made public property.

Chicago husks and winnows her wheat by the million bushels, a hundred banks lend hundreds of millions of dollars in the year, and scores of factories turn out plow-gear and machinery by steam. Scores of daily papers do work which Hukm Chund and the barber and the midwife perform, with due regard for public opinion, in the village of Isser Jang. So far as manufactories go, the difference between Chicago on the lake, and Isser Jang on the Montgomery road, is one of degree only, and not of kind. As far as the understanding of the users of life goes, Isser Jang, for all its seasonal cholers, has the advantage over Chicago.

Jowala Singh knows and takes care to avoid the three or four ghoul-haunted fields on the outskirts of the village; but he is not urged by millions of devils to run about all day in the sun and swear that his plowshares are the best in the Punjab; nor does Purun Dass fly in an ekka more than once or twice a year, and he knows, on a pinch, how to use the railway and the telegraph as well as any son of Israel in Chicago. But this is absurd.

The East is not the West, and these men must continue to deal with the machinery of life, and to call it progress. Their very preachers dare not rebuke them. They gloss over the hunting for money and the thrice-sharpened bitterness of Adam's curse, by saying that such things dower a man with a larger range of thoughts and higher aspirations. They do not say, "Free yourselves from your own slavery," but rather, "If you can possibly manage it, do not set quite so much store on the things of this world."

And they do not know what the things of this world are!

I went off to see cattle killed, by way of clearing my head, which, as you will perceive was getting muddled. They say every Englishman goes to the Chicago stock-yards. You shall find them about six miles from the city; and once having seen them, you will never forget the sight.

As far as the eye can reach stretches a township of cattle-pens, cunningly divided into blocks, so that the animals of any pen can be speedily driven out close to an inclined timber path which leads to an elevated covered way straddling high above the pens. These viaducts are two-storied. On the upper story tramp the doomed cattle, stolidly for the most part. On the lower, with a scuffling of sharp hoofs and multitudinous yells, run the pigs, the same end being appointed for each. Thus you will see the gangs of cattle waiting their turn—as they wait sometimes for days; and they need not be distressed by the sight of their fellows running about in the fear of death. All they know is that a man on horseback causes their next-door neighbors to move by means of a whip. Certain bars and fences are unshipped and behold! that crowd have gone up the mouth of a sloping tunnel and return no more.

It is different with the pigs. They shriek back the news of the exodus to their friends, and a hundred pens skirl responsive.

It was to the pigs I first addressed myself. Selecting a viaduct which was full of them, as I could hear, though I could not see, I marked a sombre building whereto it ran. and went there, not unalarmed by stray cattle who had managed to escape from their proper quarters. A pleasant smell of brine warned me of what was coming. I entered the factory and found it full of pork in barrels, and on another story more pork unbarrelled, and in a huge room the halves of swine, for whose behoof great lumps of ice were being pitched in at the window. That room was the mortuary chamber where the pigs lay for a little while in state ere they began their progress through such passages as kings may sometimes travel.

Turning a corner, and not noting an overhead arrangement of greased rail, wheel, and pulley, I ran into the arms of four eviscerated carcasses, all pure white and of a human aspect, pushed by a man clad in vehement red. When I leaped aside, the floor was slippery under me. Also there was a flavor of farmyard in my nostrils and the shouting of a multitude in my ears. But there was no joy in that shouting. Twelve men stood in two lines, six a side. Between them and overhead ran the railway of death that had nearly shunted me through the window. Each man carried a knife, the sleeves of his shirt were cut off at the elbows, and from bosom to heel he was blood-red.

Beyond this perspective was a column of steam, and beyond that was where I worked my awe-struck way, unwilling to touch beam or wall. The atmosphere was stifling as a night in the rains by reason of the steam and the crowd. I climbed to the beginning of things and, perched upon a narrow beam, overlooked very nearly all the pigs ever bred in Wisconsin. They had just been shot out of the mouth of the viaduct and huddled together in a large pen. Thence they were flicked persuasively, a few at a time, into a smaller chamber, and there a man fixed tackle on their hinder legs, so that they rose in the air, suspended from the railway of death.

Oh! it was then they shrieked and called on their mothers, and made promises of amendment, till the tackle-man punted them in their backs and they slid head down into a brick-floored passage, very like a big kitchen sink, that was blood-red. There awaited them a red man with a knife, which he passed jauntily through their throats, and the full-voiced shriek became a splutter, and then a fall as of heavy tropical rain, and the red man, who was backed against the passage-wall, you will understand, stood clear of the wildly kicking hoofs and passed his hand over his eyes, not from any feeling of compassion, but because the spurted blood was in his eyes, and he had barely time to stick the next arrival. Then that first stuck swine dropped, still kicking, into a great vat of boiling water, and spoke no more words, but wallowed in obedience to some unseen machinery, and presently came forth at the lower end of the vat, and was heaved on the blades of a blunt paddle-wheel, things which said "Hough, hough, hough!" and skelped all the hair off him, except what little a couple of men with knives could remove.

Then he was again hitched by the heels to that said railway, and passed down the line of the twelve men, each man with a knife—losing with each man a certain amount of his individuality, which was taken away in a wheelbarrow, and when he reached the last man he was very beautiful to behold, but excessively unstuffed and limp. Preponderance of individuality was ever a bar to foreign travel. That pig could have been in case to visit you in India had he not parted with some of his most cherished notions.

The dissecting part impressed me not so much as the slaying. They were so excessively alive, these pigs. And then, they were so excessively dead, and the man in the dripping, clammy, hot passage did not seem to care, and ere the blood of such a one had ceased to foam on the floor, such another and four friends with him had shrieked and died. But a pig is only the unclean animal—the forbidden of the prophet.

THE AMERICAN ARMY

VI

THE AMERICAN ARMY

I SHOULD very much like to deliver a dissertation on the American army and the possibilities of its extension. You see, it is such a beautiful little army, and the dear people don't quite understand what to do with it. The theory is that it is an instructional nucleus round which the militia of the country will rally, and from which they will get a stiffening in time of danger. Yet other people consider that the army should be built, like a pair of lazy tongs—on the principle of elasticity and extension—so that in time of need it may fill up its skeleton battalions and empty saddle troops. This is real wisdom, because the American army, as at present constituted, is made up of:

Twenty-five regiments infantry, ten companies each.

Ten regiments cavalry, twelve companies each.

Five regiments artillery, twelve companies each.

Kip. 6—L

Now there is a notion in the air to reorganize the service on these lines:

Eighteen regiments infantry at four battalions, four companies each; third battalion, skeleton; fourth on paper.

Eight regiments cavalry at four battalions, four troops each; third battalion, skeleton; fourth on paper.

Five regiments artillery at four battalions, four companies each; third battalion, skeleton; fourth on paper.

Observe the beauty of this business. The third battalion will have its officers, but no men; the fourth will probably have a rendezvous and some equipment.

It is not contemplated to give it anything more definite at present. Assuming the regiments to be made up to full complement, we get an army of fifty thousand men, which after the need passes away must be cut down fifty per cent., to the huge delight of the officers.

The military needs of the States be three: (a) Frontier warfare, an employment well within the grip of the present army of twenty-five thousand, and in the nature of things growing less arduous year by year; (b) internal riots and commotions which rise up like a dust devil, whirl furiously, and die out long before the authorities at Washington could begin to fill up even the third skeleton battalions, much less hunt about for material for the fourth; (c) civil war, in which, as the case in the affair of the North and South, the regular army would be swamped in the mass of militia and armed volunteers that would turn the land into a hell.

Yet the authorities persist in regarding an external war as a thing to be seriously considered.

The Power that would disembark troops on American soil would be capable of heaving a shovelful of mud into the Atlantic in the hope of filling it up. Consequently, the authorities are fascinated with the idea of the sliding scale or concertina army. This is an hereditary instinct, for you know that when we English have got together two companies, one machine gun, a sick bullock, forty generals, and a mass of W. O. forms, we say we possess "an army corps capable of indefinite extension."

The American army is a beautiful little army. Some day, when all the Indians are happily dead or drunk, it ought to make the finest scientific and survey corps that the world has ever seen; it does excellent work now, but there is this defect in its nature: It is officered, as you know, from West Point.

The mischief of it is that West Point seems to be created for the purpose of spreading a general knowledge of military matters among the people. A boy goes up to that institution, gets his pass, and returns to civil life, so they tell me, with a dangerous knowledge that he is a suckling Von Moltke, and may apply his learning when occasion offers. Given trouble, that man will be a nuisance, because he is a hideously versatile American, to begin with, as cock-sure of himself as a man can be, and with all the racial disregard for human life to back him through any demi-semi-professional generalship.

In a country where, as the records of the daily papers show, men engaged in a conflict with police or jails are all too ready to adopt a military formation and get heavily shot in a sort of cheap, half-constructed warfare, instead of being decently scared by the appearance of the military, this sort of arrangement does not seem wise.

The bond between the States is of an amazing tenuity. So long as they do not absolutely march into the District of Columbia, sit on the Washington statues, and invent a flag of their own, they can legislate, lynch, hunt negroes through swamps, divorce, railroad, and rampage as much as ever they choose. They do not need knowledge of their own military strength to back their genial lawlessness.

That regular army, which is a dear little army, should be kept to itself, blooded on detachment duty, turned into the paths of science, and now and again assembled at feasts of Free Masons, and so forth.

It is too tiny to be a political power. The immortal wreck of the Grand Army of the Republic is a political power of the largest and most unblushing description. It ought not to help to lay the foundations of an amateur military power that is blind and irresponsible.

By great good luck the evil-minded train, already delayed twelve hours by a burned bridge, brought me to the city on a Saturday by way of that valley which the Mormons, over their efforts, had caused to blossom like the rose. Twelve hours previously I had entered into a new world where, in conversation, every one was either a Mormon or a Gentile. It is not seemly for a free and independent citizen to dub himself a Gentile, but the Mayor of Ogden—which is the Gentile city of the valley—told me that there must be some distinction between the two flocks.

Long before the fruit orchards of Logan or

the shining levels of the Salt Lake had been reached, that mayor—himself a Gentile, and one renowned for his dealings with the Mormons—told me that the great question of the existence of the power within the power was being gradually solved by the ballot and by education.

All the beauty of the valley could not make me forget it. And the valley is very fair. Bench after bench of land, flat as a table against the flanks of the ringing hills, marks where the Salt Lake rested for awhile in its collapse from an inland sea to a lake fifty miles long and thirty broad.

There are the makings of a very fine creed about Mormonism. To begin with, the Church is rather more absolute than that of Rome. Drop the polygamy plank in the platform, but on the other hand deal lightly with certain forms of excess; keep the quality of the recruit down to the low mental level, and see that the best of all the agricultural science available is in the hands of the elders, and there you have a first-class engine for pioneer work. The tawdry mysticism and the borrowing from Freemasonry serve the low caste Swede and Dane, the Welshman and the Cornish cotter, just as well as a highly organized heaven.

Then I went about the streets and peeped into people's front windows, and the decorations upon the tables were after the manner of the year 1850. Main Street was full of country folk from the desert, come in to trade with the Zion Mercantile Coöperative Institute. The Church, I fancy, looks after the finances of this thing, and it consequently pays good dividends.

The faces of the women were not lovely. Indeed, but for the certainty that ugly persons are just as irrational in the matter of undivided love as the beautiful, it seems that polygamy was a blessed institution for the women, and that only the dread threats of the spiritual power could drive the hulking, board-faced men into it. The women wore hideous garments, and the men appeared to be tied up with strings.

They would market all that afternoon, and on Sunday go to the praying-place. I tried to talk to a few of them, but they spoke strange tongues, and stared and behaved like cows. Yet one woman, and not an altogether ugly one, confided to me that she hated the idea of Salt Lake City being turned into a show-place for the amusement of the Gentiles.

"If we 'ave our own institutions, that ain't no reason why people should come 'ere and stare at us, his it?"

The dropped "h" betrayed her.

"And when did you leave England?" I said.

"Summer of '84. I am Dorset," she said. "The Mormon agent was very good to us, and we was very poor. Now we're better off—my father, an' mother, an' me."

"Then you like the State?"

She misunderstood at first.

"Oh, I ain't livin' in the state of polygamy. Not me, yet. I ain't married. I like where I am. I've got things o' my own—and some land."

"But I suppose you will"—

"Not me. I ain't like them Swedes an' Danes. I ain't got nothin' to say for or against polygamy. It's the elders' business, an' between you an' me, I don't think it's going on much longer. You'll 'ear them in the 'ouse to-morrer talkin' as if it was spreadin' all over America. The Swedes, they think it his. I know it hisn't."

"But you've got your land all right?"

"Oh, yes; we've got our land, an' we never say aught against polygamy, o' course—father, an' mother, an' me."

On a table-land overlooking all the city stands the United States garrison of infantry and artillery. The State of Utah can do nearly anything it pleases until that much-to-be-desired hour when the Gentile vote shall quietly swamp out Mormonism; but the garrison is kept there in case of accidents. The big, shark-mouthed, pig-eared, heavy-boned farmers sometimes take to their creed with wildest fanaticism, and in past years have made life excessively unpleasant for the Gentile when he was few in the land. But today, so far from killing openly or secretly, or burning Gentile farms, it is all the Mormon dare do to feebly try to boycott the interloper. His journals preach defiance to the United States Government, and in the Tabernacle on a Sunday the preachers follow suit.

When I went there, the place was full of people who would have been much better for a washing. A man rose up and told them that they were the chosen of God, the elect of Israel; that they were to obey their priests, and that there was a good time coming. I fancy that they had heard all this before so many times it produced no impression whatever, even as the sublimest mysteries of another faith lose salt through constant iteration. They breathed heavily through their noses, and stared straight in front of them—impassive as flat fish.

AMERICA'S DEFENCELESS COASTS

VII

AMERICA'S DEFENCELESS COASTS

JUST suppose that America were twenty days distant from England. Then a man could study its customs with undivided soul; but being so very near next door, he goes about the land with one eye on the smoke of the flesh-pots of the old country across the seas, while with the other he squints biliously and prejudicially at the alien.

I can lay my hand upon my sacred heart and affirm that up to to-day I have never taken three consecutive trips by rail without being delayed by an accident. That it was an accident to another train makes no difference. My own turn may come next.

A few miles from peaceful, pleasure-loving Lakewood they had managed to upset an express goods train to the detriment of the flimsy permanent way; and thus the train which should have left at three departed at seven in the evening. I was not angry. I was scarcely even interested. When an American train starts on time I begin to anticipate disaster—a visitation for such good luck, you understand.

Buffalo is a large village of a quarter of a million inhabitants, situated on the seashore, which is falsely called Lake Erie. It is a peaceful place, and more like an English county town than most of its friends.

Once clear of the main business streets, you launch upon miles and miles of asphalted roads running between cottages and cut-stone residences of those who have money and peace. All the Eastern cities own this fringe of elegance, but except in Chicago nowhere is the fringe deeper or more heavily widened than in Buffalo.

The American will go to a bad place because he cannot speak English, and is proud of it; but he knows how to make a home for himself and his mate, knows how to keep the grass green in front of his veranda, and how to fullest use the mechanism of life—hot water, gas, good bell-ropes, telephones, etc. His shops sell him delightful household fitments at very moderate rates, and he is encompassed with all manner of labor-saving appliances. This does not prevent his wife and his daughter working themselves to death over household drudgery; but the intention is good.

When you have seen the outside of a few hundred thousand of these homes and the insides of a few score, you begin to understand why the American (the respectable one) does not take a deep interest in what they call "politics," and why he is so vaguely and generally proud of the country that enables him to be so comfortable. How can the owner of a dainty châlet, with smoked-oak furniture, imitation Venetian tapestry curtains, hot and cold water laid on, a bed of geraniums and hollyhocks, a baby crawling down the veranda, and a self-acting twirly-whirly hose gently hissing over the grass in the balmy dusk of an August evening—how can such a man despair of the Republic, or descend into the streets on voting days and mix cheerfully with "the boys"?

No, it is the stranger—the homeless jackal of a stranger—whose interest in the country is limited to his hotel-bill and a railway-ticket, that can run from Dan to Beersheba, crying: "All is barren!"

Every good American wants a home—a pretty house and a little piece of land of his very own; and every other good American seems to get it.

It was when my gigantic intellect was grappling with this question that I confirmed a discovery half made in the West. The natives of most classes marry young—absurdly young. One of my informants—not the twenty-two-year-old husband I met on Lake Chautauqua—said that from twenty to twenty-four was about the usual time for this folly. And when I asked whether the practice was confined to the constitutionally improvident classes, he said "No" very quickly. He said it was a general custom, and nobody saw anything wrong with it.

"I guess, perhaps, very early marriage may account for a good deal of the divorce," said he, reflectively.

Whereat I was silent. Their marriages and their divorces only concern these people; and neither I traveling, nor you, who may come after, have any right to make rude remarks about them. Only—only coming from a land where a man begins to lightly turn to thoughts of love not before he is thirty, I own that playing at house-keeping before that age rather surprised me. Out in the West, though, they marry, boys and girls, from sixteen upward, and I have met more than one bride of fifteen—husband aged twenty.

"When man and woman are agreed, what can the Kazi do?"

From those peaceful homes, and the envy they inspire (two trunks and a walking-stick and a bit of pine forest in British Columbia are not satisfactory, any way you look at them), I turned me to the lake front of Buffalo, where the steamers bellow to the grain elevators, and the locomotives yell to the coal-shutes, and the canal barges jostle the lumber-raft half a mile long as it snakes across the water in tow of a launch, and earth, and sky, and sea alike are thick with smoke.

In the old days, before the railway ran into the city, all the business quarters fringed the lake-shore where the traffic was largest. To-day the business quarters have gone up-town to meet the railroad; the lake traffic still exists, but you shall find a narrow belt of red-brick desolation, broken windows, gap-toothed doors, and streets where the grass grows between the crowded wharves and the bustling city. To the lake front comes wheat from Chicago, lumber, coal, and ore, and a large trade in cheap excursionists.

It was my felicity to catch a grain steamer and an elevator emptying that same steamer. The steamer might have been two thousand tons burden. She was laden with wheat in bulk; from stem to stern, thirteen feet deep, lay the clean, red wheat. There was no twenty-five per cent. dirt admixture about it at all. It was wheat, fit for the grindstones as it lay. They manœuvred the fore-hatch of that steamer directly under an elevator—a house of red tin a hundred and fifty feet high. Then they let down into that fore-hatch a trunk as if it had been the trunk of an elephant, but stiff, because it was a pipe of iron-champed wood. And the trunk had a steel-shod nose to it, and contained an endless chain of steel buckets.

Then the captain swore, raising his eyes to heaven, and a gruff voice answered him from the place he swore at, and certain machinery, also in the firmament, began to clack, and the glittering, steel-shod nose of that trunk burrowed into the wheat, and the wheat quivered and sunk upon the instant as water sinks when the siphon sucks, because the steel buckets within the trunk were flying upon their endless round, carrying away each its appointed morsel of wheat.

The elevator was a Persian well wheel—a wheel squashed out thin and cased in a pipe, a wheel driven not by bullocks, but by much horse-power, licking up the grain at the rate of thousands of bushels the hour. And the wheat sunk in the fore-hatch while a man looked—sunk till the brown timbers of the bulkheads showed bare, and men leaped down through clouds of golden dust and shoveled the wheat furiously round the nose of the trunk, and got a steam-shovel of glittering steel and made that shovel also, till there remained of the grain not more than a horse leaves in the fold of his nose-bag.

In this manner do they handle wheat at Buffalo. On one side of the elevator is the steamer, on the other the railway track; and the wheat is loaded into the cars in bulk. Wah! wah! God is great, and I do not think He ever intended Gar Sahai or Luckman Narain to supply England with her wheat. India can cut in not without profit to herself when her harvest is good and the American yield poor; but this very big country can, upon the average, supply the earth with all the beef and bread that is required.

A man in the train said to me:

"We kin feed all the earth, jest as easily as we kin whip all the earth."

Now the second statement is as false as the first is true. One of these days the respectable Republic will find this out.

Unfortunately we, the English, will never be the people to teach her; because she is a chartered libertine allowed to say and do anything she likes, from demanding the head of the empress in an editorial waste-basket, to chevying Canadian schooners up and down the Alaska Seas. It is perfectly impossible to go to war with these people, whatever they may do.

They are much too nice, in the first place, and in the second, it would throw out all the passenger traffic of the Atlantic, and upset the financial arrangements of the English syndicates who have invested their money in breweries, railways, and the like, and in the third, it's not to be done. Everybody knows that, no one better than the American.

Yet there are other powers who are not "ohai band" (of the brotherhood)—China, for instance. Try to believe an irresponsible writer when he assures you that China's fleet to-day, if properly manned, could waft the entire American navy out of the water and into the blue. The big, fat Republic that is afraid of nothing, because nothing up to the present date has happened to make her afraid, is as unprotected as a jelly-fish. Not internally, of course —it would be madness for any Power to throw men into America; they would die—but as far as regards coast defence.

From five miles out at sea (I have seen a test of her "fortified" ports) a ship of the power of H. M. S. "Collingwood" (they haven't run her on a rock yet) would wipe out any or every town from San Francisco to Long Branch; and three first-class ironclads would account for New York, Bartholdi's Statue and all.

Reflect on this. 'Twould be "Pay up or go up" round the entire coast of the United States. To this furiously answers the patriotic American:

"We should not pay. We should invent a Columbiad in Pittsburg or—or anywhere else, and blow any outsider into h—l."

They might invent. They might lay waste their cities and retire inland, for they can subsist entirely on their own produce. Meantime, in a war waged the only way it could be waged by an unscrupulous Power, their coast cities and their dock-yards would be ashes. They could construct their navy inland if they liked, but you could never bring a ship down to the water-ways, as they stand now.

They could not, with an ordinary water patrol, despatch one regiment of men six miles across the seas. There would be about five million excessively angry, armed men pent up within American limits. These men would require ships to get themselves afloat. The country has no such ships, and until the ships were built New York need not be allowed a single-wheeled carriage within her limits.

Behold now the glorious condition of this Republic which has no fear. There is ransom and loot past the counting of man on her seaboard alone—plunder that would enrich a nation—and she has neither a navy nor half a dozen first-class ports to guard the whole. No man catches a snake by the tail, because the creature will sting; but you can build a fire around a snake that will make it squirm.

The country is supposed to be building a navy now. When the ships are completed her alliance will be worth having—if the alliance of any republic can be relied upon. For the next three years she can be hurt, and badly hurt. Pity it is that she is of our own blood, looking at the matter from a Pindarris point of view. Dog cannot eat dog.

These sinful reflections were prompted by the sight of the beautifully unprotected condition of Buffalo—a city that could be made to pay up five million dollars without feeling it. There are her companies of infantry in a sort of port there. A gun-boat brought over in pieces from Niagara could get the money and get away before she could be caught, while an unarmored gun-boat guarding Toronto could ravage the towns on the lakes. When one hears so much of the nation that can whip the earth, it is, to say the least of it, surprising to find her so temptingly spankable.

The average American citizen seems to have a notion that any Power engaged in strife with the Star Spangled Banner will disembark men from flat-bottomed boats on a convenient beach for the purpose of being shot down by local militia. In his own simple phraseology:

"Not by a darned sight. No, sir."

Ransom at long range will be about the size of it—cash or crash.

Let us revisit calmer scenes.

In the heart of Buffalo there stands a magnificent building which the population do innocently style a music-hall. Everybody comes here of evenings to sit around little tables and listen to a first-class orchestra. The place is something like the Gaiety Theatre at Simla, enlarged twenty times. The "Light Brigade" of Buffalo occupy the boxes and the stage, "as it was at Simla in the days of old," and the others sit in the parquet. Here I went with a friend—poor or boor is the man who cannot pick up a friend for a season in America—and here was shown the really smart folk of the city. I grieve to say I laughed, because when an American wishes to be correct he sets himself to imitate the Englishman. This he does vilely, and earns not only the contempt of his brethren, but the amused scorn of the Briton.

I saw one man who was pointed out to me as being the glass of fashion hereabouts. He was aggressively English in his get-up. From eye-glass to trouser-hem the illusion was perfect, but—he wore with evening-dress buttoned boots with brown cloth tops! Not till I wandered about this land did I understand why the comic papers belabor the Anglomaniac.

Certain young men of the more idiotic sort launch into dog-carts and raiment of English cut, and here in Buffalo they play polo at four in the afternoon. I saw three youths come down to the polo-ground faultlessly attired for the game and mounted on their best ponies. Expecting a game, I lingered; but I was mistaken. These three shining ones with the very new yellow hide boots and the red silk sashes had assembled themselves for the purpose of knocking the ball about. They smote with great solemnity up and down the grounds, while the little boys looked on. When they trotted, which was not seldom, they rose and sunk in their stirrups with a conscientiousness that cried out "Riding-school!" from afar.

Other young men in the park were riding after the English manner, in neatly cut riding-trousers and light saddles. Fate in derision had made each youth bedizen his animal with a checkered enameled leather brow-band visible half a mile away—a black-and-white checkered brow-band! They can't do it, any more than an Englishman, by taking cold, can add that indescribable nasal twang to his orchestra.

The other sight of the evening was a horror. The little tragedy played itself out at a neighboring table where two very young men and two very young women were sitting. It did not strike me till far into the evening that the pimply young reprobates were making the girls drunk. They gave them red wine and then white, and the voices rose slightly with the maidens' cheek flushes. I watched, wishing to stay, and the youths drank till their speech thickened and their eye-balls grew watery. It was sickening to see, because I knew what was going to happen. My friend eyed the group, and said:

"Maybe they're children of respectable people. I hardly think, though, they'd be allowed out without any better escort than these boys. And yet the place is a place where every one comes, as you see. They may be Little Immoralities—in which case they wouldn't be so hopelessly overcome with two glasses of wine. They may be"—

Whatever they were they got indubitably drunk—there in that lovely hall, surrounded by the best of Buffalo society. One could do nothing except invoke the judgment of Heaven on the two boys, themselves half sick with liquor. At the close of the performance the quieter maiden laughed vacantly and protested she couldn't keep her feet. The four linked arms, and staggering, flickered out into the street—drunk, gentlemen and ladies, as Davy's swine, drunk as lords! They disappeared down a side avenue, but I could hear their laughter long after they were out of sight.

And they were all four children of sixteen and seventeen. Then, recanting previous opinions, I became a prohibitionist. Better it is that a man should go without his beer in public places, and content himself with swearing at the narrow-mindedness of the majority; better it is to poison the inside with very vile temperance drinks, and to buy lager furtively at back-doors, than to bring temptation to the lips of young fools such as the four I had seen. I understand now why the preachers rage against drink. I have said: "There is no harm in it, taken moderately;" and yet my own demand for beer helped directly to send those two girls reeling down the dark street to —God alone knows what end.

If liquor is worth drinking, it is worth taking a little trouble to come at—such trouble as a man will undergo to compass his own desires. It is not good that we should let it lie before the eyes of children, and I have been a fool in writing to the contrary. Very sorry for myself, I sought a hotel, and found in the hall a reporter who wished to know what I thought of the country. Him I lured into conversation about his own profession, and from him gained much that confirmed me in my views of the grinding tyranny of that thing which they call the Press here. Thus:

I—But you talk about interviewing people whether they like it or not. Have you no bounds beyond which even your indecent curiosity must not go?

HE—I haven't struck 'em yet. What do you think of interviewing a widow two hours after her husband's death, to get her version of his life?

I—I think that is the work of a ghoul. Must the people have no privacy?

HE—There is no domestic privacy in America. If there was, what the deuce would the papers do? See here. Some time ago I had an assignment to write up the floral tributes when a prominent citizen had died.

I—Translate, please; I do not understand your pagan rites and ceremonies.

HE—I was ordered by the office to describe the flowers, and wreaths, and so on, that had been sent to a dead man's funeral. Well, I went to the house. There was no one there to stop me, so I yanked the tinkler—pulled the bell—and drifted into the room where the corpse lay all among the roses and smilax. I whipped out my notebook and pawed around among the floral tributes, turning up the tickets on the wreaths and seeing who had sent them. In the middle of this I heard some one saying: "Please, oh, please!" behind me, and there stood the daughter of the house, just bathed in tears—

I—You unmitigated brute!

He—Pretty much what I felt myself. "I'm very sorry, miss," I said, "to intrude on the privacy of your grief. Trust me, I shall make it as little painful as possible."

I—But by what conceivable right did you outrage—

He—Hold your horses. I'm telling you. Well, she didn't want me in the house at all, and between her sobs fairly waved me away. I had half the tributes described, though, and the balance I did partly on the steps when the stiff 'un came out, and partly in the church. The preacher gave the sermon. That wasn't my assignment. I skipped about among the floral tributes while he was talking. I could have made no excuse if I had gone back to the office and said that a pretty girl's sobs had stopped me obeying orders. I had to do it. What do you think of it all?

I (slowly)—Do you want to know?

He (with his notebook ready)—Of course. How do you regard it?

I—It makes me regard your interesting nation with the same shuddering curiosity that I should bestow on a Pappan cannibal chewing the scalp off his mother's skull. Does that convey any idea to your mind? It makes me regard the whole pack of you as heathens—

real heathens—not the sort you send missions to—creatures of another flesh and blood. You ought to have been shot, not dead, but through the stomach, for your share in the scandalous business, and the thing you call your newspaper ought to have been sacked by the mob, and the managing proprietor hanged.

HE—From which, I suppose you have nothing of that kind in your country?

Oh! *Pioneer,* venerable *Pioneer,* and you, not less honest press of India, who are occasionally dull but never blackguardly, what could I say? A mere "No," shouted never so loudly, would not have met the needs of the case. I said no word.

The reporter went away, and I took a train for Niagara Falls, which are twenty-two miles distant from this bad town, where girls get drunk of nights and reporters trample on corpses in the drawing-rooms of the brave and the free!